Santa Finds His Way

Island of Misfits, Book 2

J.L. Hendricks

Other Books by J.L. Hendricks

<u>Worlds Away Series</u>

Book 0: Worlds Revealed (join my Newsletter to get this exclusive freebie)

Book 1: Worlds Away

Book 2: Worlds Collide

Book 2.5: Worlds Explode

Book 3: Worlds Entwined

<u>A Miss Claus Shifter Christmas Romance Series</u>

Book 0: Santa Meets Mrs. Claus

Book 1: Miss Claus and the Secret Santa

Book 2: Miss Claus under the Mistletoe

Book 3: Miss Claus and the Christmas Wedding

Book 4: Miss Claus and Her Polar Opposite

J.L. HENDRICKS

<u>The FBI Dragon Chronicles</u>

Book 1: A Ritual of Fire

Book 2: A Ritual of Death

Book 3: A Ritual of Conquest

<u>New Orleans Magic Series</u>

Book 1: New Orleans Magic

Book 2: Hurricane of Magic

Book 3: Council of Magic

<u>Island of Misfits</u>

Book 0: Island of Misfits

Book 1: The Vampire Gets His Mate

Book 2: Santa Finds His Way

<u>Chronicles of the Fae Princess</u> –

Trilogy Published by LMBPN Publishing

See these titles and get their links at <u>https://www.jlhendrick-sauthor.com/</u>

Acknowlegements

Thank you so much to all of my Beta readers and ARC readers! I wouldn't have been able to get this book out without your help.

You all rock!

Contents

Prologue

6 months earlier – North Pole

"Chris, take a seat." The current Santa Claus, previously known as Palo, motioned for his oldest son to take the seat in front of his ancient, oak desk.

"Father?" Chris, or Christian Kringle as he had been named at birth, sat in the chair and furrowed a brow as he waited for his dad to explain why he summoned him in the middle of fight practice.

Santa cleared his throat. "It seems something is happening in the shifter community, as a whole." He wiped his face with his hand. "I thought it was only limited to one rogue Arctic Wolf Shifter pack, but Rock has found evidence that it is a much wider problem."

Chris shook his head. "I don't follow. What problem are you referring to?"

Santa thought for a moment, then proceeded to explain, "there's a pack in Siberia who have never been fans of mine, even before I became Santa." He shook his head thinking back to before he met Chris' mother. "I should have taken out this pack long ago, but I kept hoping they would turn around and do better. When my informants failed to call in, I should have stepped in then and there." He sat back in his plush chair and sighed.

"Father, just tell me what's going on." Christian leaned forward and rested his elbows on his thighs.

"Remember studying the Winter of Rebellion?"

Christian nodded.

"Your mom was expecting another pup, and one of her sister's had been abducted." On Santa's face was an uncharacteristically stoney expression. "There were other packs around the world who took advantage of that time and began participating in things they shouldn't have. Once we recovered your aunt, I sought out undercover agents in packs I suspected of turning away from the Way of the Wolf."

"Were there a lot of packs that needed to be stopped?" Christian knew that his father had destroyed several packs over the years, but it only happened to those who killed innocent wolves, or humans, and didn't repent of their ways. Basically, the worst of the worst.

"No, not many. Most just got up to mischief and quickly got themselves back under control. But there were several I had to visit. One of those packs worried me and I recruited a few agents." Santa shook his head. "It seems I wasn't as covert as I had hoped. They were murdered but I had no way of proving it."

"Father!" Chris stood up and fisted his hands at his side. "Why haven't we taken care of this pack? Your Beta, Rock, should have already destroyed them."

While Santa is the Alpha of the top wolf pack, he relies heavily upon his second in command, a Beta. Rock has been Palo's right-hand man, or wolf, since the very beginning of his reign as Santa Claus.

"Because, my overeager son," he waved for Chris to sit back down, "I had no proof. Even Santa can't just go in and destroy a pack without evidence. That pack seemed to toe the line after that, and I let family life distract me. The deaths appeared to be an accident, but I never believed the story the pack's Alpha spewed." A hollow chuckle escaped the lips of Santa.

"I take it this means they took advantage of your distraction?" Chris sat back in his chair and tilted his head to the side.

Santa nodded. "Yes. I didn't know it at the time, but I know now. While I still can't prove it all, I just know that something evil is coming. And I need your help to find the proof."

"I'll do it." Chris stood up. "Where do I start?"

Santa grinned. "Not so fast. I need to tell you more. But suffice it to say, there is a rather large underground black market that has thrived for years. They sell anything from drugs, to supes, to dragon eggs."

Christian sucked in a breath. "Not dragon eggs." He shook his head.

"Sadly, yes. But no fears, none of your aunts' dragonlings have been abducted. The royal family is very well protected."

With a deep sigh of relief, Christian waited for the rest of the background.

Once his father had briefed him on everything he knew, Christian packed lightly and dressed down to make himself appear as a normal human young man before taking off for the journey of his life.

Chapter 1

Present Day

"Alright, listen up you mangy mutts!" Sofka had always wanted to say that.

But KeeKee cringed when she noticed how the gathered wolves bristled at her comment. It wasn't that KeeKee thought she was too good to be considered mangy, it was how Sofka said it. Ever since everyone on the island had defended against the invading forces of her former Alpha, Sofka had been a bit over the top.

"Sofka, I think it's time to take a chill-pill." Ree pleaded with her enigmatic leader and best friend.

At first, Sofka's steely ice blue eyes narrowed on Ree. Anyone else would have backed away from the intensity of her gaze, but not Ree. "What?"

Ree took her life into her own hands when she tried to get Sofka to lighten up. Instead of backing down, she put her hands on her hips and returned Sofka's glare.

KeeKee, the one who always wanted peace amongst the group, was close to backing down, but she straightened her shoulders and looked at her best friend. "Sofka, I know you're only trying to help us all get into fighting shape, but don't you think you've gone a little battle-crazed?"

Before anyone could respond, a tall, handsome male growled and showed his pointy fangs and red eyes for all to see. "I don't think you know what battle-crazed is, not yet little wolf."

"Max, please." KeeKee waved a hand in front of her face. While the vampire standing next to Sofka was intimidating, she knew that Maxim Volkov would never harm a hair on her wolfy body. The vamp was mated to KeeKee's best friend, Sofka. They were all practically family now.

When the new guy, Christian Icingberry, sauntered in and stood next to Maxim, he smirked. "Come on, isn't anyone going to cower down in front the big-bad vampire?" He pointed to Maxim, who didn't look amused.

Sofka put her hands on her hips and ignored the joking atmosphere trying to take over the serious vibes she was putting out for all to feel. "Hey, we barely made it out alive the last time our island was attacked. I don't want to take any chances the next time Kirill attacks. And you all know he's not going to back down."

KeeKee sighed. "I know, he's never backed-down a day in his life." She rubbed a hand over her face. "Maybe you were right, Sofka."

"Of course, I was." Sofka wiggled her brows, then frowned. "Wait, what was I right about?"

"When you said we should have just let Kirill sell us on the supernatural black market. We brought all of this death and destruction to Misfit Island."

The newcomer, Christian Icingberry, frowned. "KeeKee, No, you didn't bring this to the island. That is all on Kirill. You know as well as I do that no shifter pack is allowed to sell their members, or any shifter for that matter. If Santa ever found out, Kirill would be wiped out, and you know it."

KeeKee licked her lips and looked from Christian to the throng of supernatural creatures who had been practicing a variety of combat moves Sofka was attempting to teach them all. Moves that had been taught to her by none other than the male supe who sent an invading force to the island for no real reason. He had stated it was to take back what was his, but no one owned supernatural creatures.

And certainly no one was allowed to lay claim to Arctic Wolf Shifters. Santa Claus himself was an Arctic Wolf Shifter and he had destroyed other packs for doing things like what Kirill was doing. If it wasn't so close to Christmas Eve, KeeKee figured Santa would already be taking Kirill down.

Maybe that was why Christian was on the island? He was a purebred Arctic Wolf Shifter. And he was trying to mask his true identity to everyone on the island. The only problem with that was the fact that any Arctic Wolf Shifter would recognize a member of the Claus family. And Christian was most definitely a Claus in disguise. Christian Icingberry? Please. KeeKee saw through that made up name in less than two seconds.

"Is no one going to say it?" Marcus Whitehead, the fae prince in exile on the island, looked between his mate Ree and Christian. When no one said anything, he sighed. "Where is Santa Claus and his pack of enforcers? If trying to sell Arctic Wolf Shifters on the Supernatural Black Market is outlawed, where is Santa?" Marcus arched a perfectly shaped brow.

Maxim looked around at the males and females who had stopped their training to watch and listen in on the conversation. "Ah, maybe we should take this discussion elsewhere?" He nodded to the group closest to them. One of the members was part of the newest island residents.

Aelita, who hadn't shown her true form to anyone yet was watching intently. Consensus was that she was some sort of shifter, probably feline since she was so tall and lithe. She stood almost six feet tall, and her long auburn hair glistened whenever a stray beam of sunlight shone on her. The female's sparkling green eyes seemed to pull the males into her orbit, and they all practically drooled at her feet.

One of the males who always seemed to find his way near her, took two steps closer to her and whispered in her ear loud enough for those nearby to hear, "we should probably get back to training." Horatio Hackensack, a polar bear shifter and the island's unofficial mayor, nodded at Maxim. He was also quite tall and with his light looks, he was a handsome contrast to Aelita's darker complexion. They made a very striking couple. Not that they were dating, but if Horatio got his way, they would be.

"Horatio," Aelita put a hand on his arm and smiled. "Maybe we should stick around? Just in case Sofka needs our help?"

"Maybe you should all get back to practicing your hand-to-hand combat?" Sofka, taking it down a few notches, arched a brow.

Christian stood there, looking at everyone, but not saying a thing. He had always played it cool when supes spoke about Santa around him. He never wanted anyone to figure out who he was because he went off on a tirade about respecting Santa. Although, no one hadn't really shown any disrespect here, just a valid question regarding Santa's whereabouts and why he hadn't stepped in yet to put a stop to Kirill.

What no one seemed to realize was that Kirill wasn't working alone. He had help. Lots of help. Santa wasn't all knowing. Well, he was in one sense. He did know who was on the naughty or nice list, but as far as details went, it was usually just the children that he had a clear picture of. When an adult committed a crime, all Santa knew was that person had moved over to the naughty list. He didn't receive updates on criminals and the crimes they committed, just that a name still hadn't made its way back to the nice list.

And when any of the male members of the Clause family met someone, they could tell immediately if that person was naughty, or nice. And not in the fun t-shirt or ugly Christmas sweater wearing sort of naughty. They could tell if someone had an evil heart.

The one thing that surprised Christian the most since arriving on Misfit Island was the amount of supes who were in the gray area. Not all supes were either good or bad, some were somewhere in the middle. Take Maxim for example, he was a vampire, so one would expect that he'd be on the naughty list for the rest of his long existence. Killing humans in order to feed on them wasn't a nice list sort of activity.

Instead, Christian sensed that Maxim had been on the nice list for quite some time, although he did sense that there was a time when he wasn't. If Christian was so inclined, he could look the vampire up and see when he moved to the nice list since the North Pole kept good records, but he wasn't too worried. Everyone on the island seemed to respect the supe. And he was mated to Sofka, who was the island's Deputy Sheriff. He doubted the deputy would have mated with the vampire if he was bad.

Sofka was an Arctic Wolf Shifter. She might not be purebred, but she was still part of the shifter society that was governed by Santa. While Christian wasn't Santa, yet, he was in the line of succession. In fact, he was the next in line to the so-called throne. Which meant that he was a fantastic judge of character.

Sofka and her mate were alright.

Christian had decided to befriend them when they discovered who he was, and still kept the secret to themselves.

Christian couldn't help but grin when the beautiful Aelita smiled at him and then pulled Horatio aside. She was smart. But she was also in the group he had followed to the island only a few short weeks ago. Something was up with her and her friends, but he couldn't put his finger on it. Aelita was still on the nice list. Three of her traveling partners were on the naughty list and had been for some time. That had Christian wondering what she was really up to.

"Horatio, do you think we should move on? Looks to me as though Sofka is busy and will most likely be so for a while." Aelita nodded in the direction of the Arctic Wolf Shifter who had been leading the class on fighting off invaders.

The unofficial mayor of Misfit Island turned his gaze from the stunning Aelita to the deputy sheriff. "I think Sofka is trying to get back to leading our group." Horatio's eyes narrowed and his ears perked up. "However, she does seem to be trying to get everyone to leave her alone." He chuckled and shook his head.

Aelita put her perfectly manicured long fingers on Horatio's arm and leaned in closer. "You know we could sneak away and have some fun instead of hanging out here fighting each other while Sofka calls us all silly names."

Horatio's head pulled back, and small lines formed across his forehead. "I thought you and Sofka were becoming friends?"

Realizing that she wasn't going to get Horatio to ditch fight school with her, Aelita sighed and dropped her arms to her side. With a puff of air, she said drily, "really? You want to stand around here and wait to be tortured some more?"

With a shake of his head, Horatio gave in. "Fine, but for the record Sofka wasn't torturing us. She's just..." He struggled to find the right words and stopped and started a few times before giving up and shrugging his shoulders. "It's not torture, but it's not a stroll in the park, either."

Thinking no one would notice, Aelita led Horatio away from the class and back toward the center of town.

Christian noticed. He smirked as he watched Aelita take Horatio's hand in hers and head toward her restaurant.

Aelita operated a barbecue restaurant that was only open for dinner. It was the sort that would cost a lot of money if it were in Seattle or New York. Here on the island, money wasn't something that was used very often. For the most part, the residents all worked jobs on the island to earn their keep, so to speak. But there were times when they needed to head to the mainland for something that couldn't be picked up here, so there was some money.

Christian hadn't worked enough to earn any money while on the island. However, he wasn't exactly on Misfit Island to live out the rest of his days. Although, the place did seem like the perfect spot for a supernatural creature to live. He just had other plans. Or, to be precise, his father had other plans for him.

All of a sudden, Christian was jerked out of his thoughts when he heard a loud yell.

"Where did everyone go?" Sofka threw her hands in the air and turned around in circles looking out to the mostly empty training field. "If we don't practice and get in better shape, we might not be able to defend against the next attack."

"Sofka, my darling, it's alright. That last attack by Kirill had to have depleted his resources and followers. It's going to take him a lot of time to rebuild." Maxim patted Sofka's shoulder and dipped his head for a quick kiss.

While Christian was very happy for the newly mated couple, he also felt a little bit jealous. It wasn't that he was into Sofka, no, he just wanted what Sofka and Maxim had found – love.

All of the residents of Misfit Island left their packs, families, groups, etc. to come to Misfit Island and find a new family or pack. This island had been a safe haven for those who did not fit in with the ones they were born with. Or with those who had created them, like Maxim. The island reminded him of one of those old-timey Christmas cartoons about Santa finding an island full of toys that had been forgotten.

For the first time in his life, Christian believed that family meant more than blood, it meant acceptance. He looked around at the small groups of supes and realized that vampires found family with shifters. And shifters found themselves including fae in their families. So many

more on the island seemed to choose to be a family with other creatures that had made no sense to him when he first arrived. But now?
Now, it all made so much sense.

And he liked it.

Chapter 2

Christian Icingberry sat on the covered porch just outside the best coffee shop on the island. The sign above the Frozen Bean Coffee Shop said it was the only coffee shop in all of Antarctica, not just on Misfit Island. He actually hadn't had a cup of coffee this good since he left home. His family employed some of the best coffee roasters on the planet, and he missed those beans. They also had a corner on the hot cocoa market.

However, The Frozen Bean Coffee Shop was giving the North Pole coffee roasters a run for their candy canes.

The group sitting at the table next to him were discussing something that caught his attention and wrested his thoughts away from his family coffee and cocoa to what they were saying.

"This morning, when I got up, there was a pretty package on my front step." The woman moved her hands to show the small package. "It was wrapped in craft paper with a red and black buffalo check ribbon, very pretty. Did one of you leave it for me?"

A man, who wore a gray ski cap, black puffy jacket, and hair covering most of his face, shook his head. "No, it wasn't me. But I've heard similar stories. I think there is a Secret Santa on the island."

Christian bowed his head and turned slightly so he could see them. Hoping that they didn't notice him eavesdropping on their conversation, he looked at the woman who was talking about the gift. He didn't recognize any of them. She had deep red hair, a nose ring, and black lipstick. She kinda reminded him of a goth chick he'd seen once in a mall when helping his dad with Santa duty. But that woman was a human, and this one was not. The biggest sign of her unhuman status were the horns that came out of the side of her head. She must be some sort of goat shifter who didn't revert back to her full human look.

Since arriving on the island, Christian had noticed that some of the shifters liked to keep their wilder side showing. He didn't mind it as long as they were on the island. Since no human could make it there without help from either the island itself, or one of the residents, it didn't matter that vampires walked around with fangs out proud, or shifters shifted right in the middle of Main Street.

It was all a bit freeing. Even back home in the North Pole they weren't so obvious about their shifter status. Although, he did have a few friends who liked to shift out in public.

"Do you think Santa is here?" When the man asked that question, Christian sat up straight and looked forward before taking a long sip of his hot coffee. The last thing he needed was for the entire island to know who he was.

The redheaded female shook her head. "Nah, I think this is just another little gift of the island. After that battle a lot of us had...well...difficulty. I still don't sleep well." She shifted her in seat and looked down at her hands.

The third person at their table nodded. "I hear ya. I think I've lost a stone since that day." The light British accent had Christian wondering if the male was a sprite, or some other supe that preferred the British Isles. Some supernatural creatures weren't easy to identify when in their full human form.

Not that he cared one way or the other, it was just really cool to see so much diversity and everyone getting along, for the most part. It caused him to miss home and all of the creatures who called the North Pole region their home.

Sometimes, he even missed his family.

But lately, he'd discovered that a certain shifter could take all thoughts of home away with just her sweet smile.

Speaking of the angel...

"Hi, Christian. Is this seat taken?" Standing next to his table, a beautiful young woman with long blonde hair and a smile that was brighter than the North Star stood with a hot beverage in her hand.

KeeKee Sidorov had noticed the newcomer sitting all alone and hoped he was making friends. She'd seen him speaking with Aelita, but she spoke to all of the handsome males on the island. KeeKee also knew that her family were working hard to ensure that Christian felt welcomed and part of the island family. Only, she hadn't tried too hard to be his friend.

He was too handsome, and most obviously a pureblood. Her status of being only a half-blood was always at the top of her mind. But when she compared her looks to Christian's, she felt as though she wasn't even a blond. His hair was white as snow, not the gray sort of white that the elderly sported, but shocking white that most humans her age got from a dye job. Even though KeeKee had blond hair, it wasn't the same. Hers was more like the humans' version – super light brown stripes mixed with almost yellow hair. It looked good and KeeKee always had compliments from male supes, and human men, but she knew her looks made her stand out as a half-blood in the shifter community.

Not to mention the little secret that probably wasn't much of a secret on this island. Christian was a Claus. There was no doubt about it. As an Arctic Wolf Shifter, she could see through his disguise. Although, to be fair, the only thing he had disguised was his name. Which KeeKee thought strange, since he didn't want anyone to recognize him. It wouldn't have been difficult for him to alter his looks just enough to ensure no one seriously considered him a Claus.

And his reindeer with the sled was hiding in an outbuilding far from town. Thankfully, no one had found that yet. Once they did, it would be all over the island. Even those in the Dark Hills would know a Claus was on the island.

"Please join me." Christian stood and held a seat out for KeeKee.

She grinned and looked down at the drink in her hands. "Thank you." KeeKee took the offered seat and cleared her throat. "So, what do you think about the training that Sofka has instituted?"

Christian blinked a few times and opened his mouth, then shut it. Then he opened it again. "What? No comment about the weather or the roads?" He grinned.

Under KeeKee's arm was a copy of Pride and Prejudice. She felt her cheeks grow warm and took the book and turned it face down before setting it on the table. "Back then, society dictated what unmarried men and women were allowed to discuss. But today?" She shrugged her shoulders and held her hands palm side up. "We aren't human, so we don't have to follow the dictates of society. I say, we should speak our minds, when we can."

KeeKee wasn't normally so outspoken to those she didn't know well. But there was something about Christian that just brought out her braver side. Once the words were out of her mouth, she didn't even try to take them back, not that she could. It would take a spell from a witch to make someone forget the past few minutes of conversation. And she would never use a witch's spell.

A chuckle escaped Christian's lips and he nodded. "I think I must agree with you." He leaned in and in a whispered voice asked, "what's going on with Sofka? Is she normally so militaristic?" He sat back and took a sip of coffee while he watched the expressions on KeeKee's face change from curiosity to anger and then indifference.

"Sofka only has our best interests at heart." KeeKee looked around and then leaned in herself before whispering, "if Santa had any interest in our welfare, he would have rid the planet of Kirill long ago." Then she sat back and crossed her arms over her chest and raised a brow in expectation of what the son of Santa might say.

"Touché." Christian didn't say more for a few moments. Instead, he took a sip of his hot coffee, which wasn't too bad. It wasn't the same as what the elves back home made, but it was so much better than those coffee shops that loved to take up every street corner they could get. "Have you ever thought about *how* Kirill was able to do what he did? I mean, could it be he was working with someone even more powerful? Or perhaps he was working with a cabal?"

KeeKee froze in her seat. Even her facial expression froze in place. Her brows were drawn together, and her lips pursed. Christian wasn't sure if she was having an episode or if she'd frozen in fear. "Are you alright?" He outstretched his hand to touch hers, but she pulled it back.

When KeeKee took in a breath, she blinked. "A cabal? You mean like those political groups who are secretly running the human world without anyone else knowing about them? Except everyone does and has decided to conveniently forget about it?" KeeKee wasn't normally so gullible, neither did she fall for crazy and outlandish rumors and conspiracy theories. But her time out in the real world had changed her thinking. It was too crazy for elected politicians to actually be running things. Maybe not all political spots were controlled by Cabal members, but some had to be. Those human governments were nuts. And it wasn't just one, they were all run by irrational humans.

She cleared her throat and looked Christian directly in the eyes. "I think that we need to find at least one member of this cabal and find out who else is working with Kirill. Sitting around on our laurels isn't going to help things."

Christian looked around and ensured no one was listening in on their conversation, then he leaned in and put his hands up around his mouth. "What do you think I'm doing here?"

KeeKee sat back hard in her chair. So hard, it made a loud scratching sound on the floor and all heads turned her way. Once again, she felt the signs of a blush creeping up her cheeks. "Sorry." She meant her apology for the entire coffee shop, as well as for Christian.

"Maybe we should take this conversation elsewhere." Christian finished his drink in one long gulp, then stood up and motioned with his head for KeeKee to follow him.

Thankfully, KeeKee had gotten her drink to go so it was in an insulated cup that would keep her coffee warm for a few more minutes outside. She really needed to get one of those Snowman insulated mugs that was rated for thirty-two below so her coffee would stay hot for hours. Not that she ever took that long to drink her coffee, but it would be nice to know her cup of java would last as long as she needed it to.

"You know, I've been saying that a lot lately." Christian held open the door to allow KeeKee to walk out in front of him.

"Hm? Saying what?" KeeKee stepped down and then turned to watch the handsome pureblood practically glide down the steps. Her heart palpitated just a bit before she got a handle on her girly emotions.

Christian looked around. "It's just that there aren't very many places one can have a private conversation around here, is there? I want to talk about what I'm doing here, but I don't feel anywhere is safe from prying ears."

It was KeeKee's turn to look around and ensure no one was watching them. "Are you saying that Santa sent you here to investigate Kirill?"

Christian had his hands in his jacket pockets and was looking down at the ground as he walked. He didn't always wear his gloves, but today was one of those days when he should have. The temperature was more than just chilly, it was downright cold. Even though he was an Arctic shifter, and could withstand quite a bit of cold, today was colder than he usually liked. His nose felt as though icicles were hanging off of it. He swiped at his nose, but nothing was there. He sniffed and was grateful he wore the down jacket with the fleece lining. "In a way. I was actually on a different assignment, but I think the two might be related."

KeeKee continued to walk by Christian's side and wondered if he was going to say more. When he didn't, she looked over at him. "And?"

When Christian turned his ice-blue eyes on her, she felt a zing go up and down her spine. It reminded her of when they first met, and she had to cough to hide her moan.

"This has to stay between us." He shook his head. "I shouldn't even be telling you this much." He ran a hand down his face and sighed before straightening and looking around once more. "A few weeks ago, I tracked a group of supes who have been trading on the supernatural black market."

"Oh!" KeeKee's breath left her body so suddenly, she thought she might faint. She bent over trying to breathe.

Christian came to her side quickly and put his arms around her. "It's better if you stand up straight. You'll get more air in your lungs." He helped her to stand tall and then supported her with his arms when he realized she couldn't keep herself upright. "Will you be alright?"

KeeKee shook her head. A whispered, "no" was all she could say.

Chapter 3

"Kee Kee!" Sofka screamed and ran to her and Christian as they walked up to the Sheriff's office. "What happened? Are we under attack again?" She looked with pleading eyes from KeeKee to Christian and then back to KeeKee.

"No, nothing like that." Christian winced. "I might have said something that threw her for a loop."

"Supernatural traffickers are on the island." For the first time since Christian had told her what he was doing, KeeKee spoke. She also let go of his assistance and stood on her own before she walked inside the station and slumped down in the first chair. "We have spies on the island."

"Well, we knew that already." Sofka put her hands on her hips and narrowed her eyes. Then she turned to Christian. "Spill it."

"Ah." He put a hand behind his neck and rubbed it. "Are you going to almost pass out when I tell you?"

Sofka spluttered. "Me? No. Now stop delaying and tell me what's going on."

"This can't get out. I'm on a secret mission. You shouldn't even know who I am," Christian pleaded with his hands outstretched.

"Dude, you know that we know who you are. You can't hide your identity from Arctic Wolves. I don't know why you even tried to." Sofka scoffed and shook her head.

"I wasn't necessarily trying to hide from you, but from those I've been tracking." He arched a brow.

A snuffle then a loud snore sounded from the corner of the room. While the Sheriff had been much more active and awake for the first two weeks after the big battle, he had begun taking mid-day naps. But at least it was only for an hour or two. The rest of the day he was alert and went on his patrols.

"Don't worry about him. The sheriff still has at least an hour before he wakes up from his nap." Sofka chuckled. Then she turned serious eyes on Christian. "Now tell me who you tracked here and why."

KeeKee worked hard to bite back a laugh. She loved her fearless leader, but sometimes Sofka was a little over the top, but she and Ree loved her anyway. That's what family did, right?

While she did want to tell Sofka to calm down, she also wanted the entire story. A story she might have already had if she hadn't been such a baby and almost passed out while Christian was telling it the first time.

With his hands held high, Christian resigned himself to coming clean. "Fine, but you can't share this with anyone, not even your mates."

Sofka scoffed. "Yeah, right."

Christian crossed his arms over his chest and glared at Sofka. She glared right back and added an arched eyebrow.

"Okay, okay, but no one else. If it gets out then my time away from home has been for nothing." Christian sat down, or more accurately, plopped down, in the nearest chair. He began his story when Sofka agreed to his terms.

"Last year Santa began hearing grumblings about a supernatural black market starting up. Normally, he didn't mess with them, but when he heard that Arctic Wolves were being sold there, he started looking into it."

"Really? Santa is involved in this?" Sofka shook her head, not able to believe what Christian was saying was the truth.

"I know what you're thinking, Santa usually moves right in and stops bad wolves, but there's a lot more going on here than a few bad Arctic Wolf shifters, or even a whole pack. This issue encompasses all of the supernatural community, not just wolves." Christian sat up and rubbed his hands together before putting them between his knees, for added warmth.

"I've been tracking one small group. It's a mixed group of out-siders who aren't happy with the way things work in the supernatural world..." Christian was cut off before he could finish his thoughts.

"You mean to say that a variety of supernatural beings are working together? Really?" KeeKee didn't understand how that might work on the outside. Here on the island, it was easy. There were a lot of supes who didn't have a regular job, or even a skill for one, so they were assigned menial tasks by the island. Here everyone pulled their own weight together, even if they didn't have a special talent. But out in the world the supes stayed clear of each other...usually

"Yup." He nodded.

Hesitantly, Sofka asked, "So, who did you track here?"

Christian scrunched his nose and then looked down at the laces on his boots. "You know them. They arrived only a few days after you did."

The color drained from Sofka's face. "Aelita?"

"Yes, I know she is part of the group that helped you to defend against the evil forces who invaded the island." Christian noted the sadness and pain that crossed KeeKee's and Sofka's faces. "I'm sorry."

KeeKee took in a deep breath. "Me too. But if she's part of the group who's operating the supernatural black market, we have to stop her."

"Are you sure she's part of the supernatural black-market group?" Sofka couldn't believe it was true. Even though she had questioned Aelita's part in the whole battle, since then, Sofka knew that Aelita was a good supe. She wanted to get involved on the island and they were becoming friends.

"Sadly, I'm not sure about Aelita, yet. But I do know that some of those in her group are working with the supernatural black market." Christian snarled the last few words. The idea of anyone working with the supernatural black market turned his stomach.

"If that's true, it also means she, and her group, are the ones who were helping Kirill before the battle." Sofka bit her lip and looked out the window. "But that doesn't make sense. I can't say much about the rest of her group, but Aelita fought hard during the battle. I saw her a few times taking down enemy troops."

"Were they troops from the Dark Hills? Or from off-island?" Christian asked.

"Good question." KeeKee wracked her brain. "I know I saw Aelita fighting Sigurd at one point, but then some redcaps came and tried to rip her to shreds. Sigurd left her to them, and she was able to fend them off. But I don't know if they were from the island or from the invading army."

Sofka shook her head. "I can't say I remember seeing her fight against anyone from the Dark Hills, except Sigurd."

"That's what I was afraid of. I arrived too late to join the fight and I didn't see her fighting anywhere near where I was. But I did see two of her friends fighting against two other supes who I know are from the Dark Hills. So, either the Dark Hills supes are against the island, or two of Aelita's friends are. While I'm betting on the latter, we'll have to find out the truth." Christian didn't relish the idea of having to search out the truth. Christmas was getting close, and his family needed him back at the North Pole. This quest was taking much longer than he expected.

The background sounds of snoring and snuffling stopped, and it caused Christian to stop what he was saying and look back to see if the Sheriff had heard them or not. The sheriff turned in his chair and almost fell out, but stopped moving before his butt came off the chair.

Sofka snickered. "It would serve him right if he fell off. That bear really needs to go home and hibernate the rest of the winter."

Christian shook his head. "We need him. If the island is attacked again, he'll be very helpful. Keep in mind that he is a large black bear, and the Sheriff."

"I know." A sigh escaped Sofka and she turned her focus back on their conversation. "But what about Sienna? She was attacked by the Bully Boys and left tied up to a dead body in the island dump. Was she in on it? Or is she just caught up in the middle of what's going on with Aelita's group?"

KeeKee put a finger on her chin and thought for a moment. "You know, I don't think she's involved with the bad guys. And remember, that group just happened to all come in at the same time. Some of them didn't know each other until they met in Chile."

"Maybe that's what they want us to think." Sofka raised a brow and looked thoughtful. "Actually, I haven't seen them all hanging out together. Aelita, Sienna, and a couple of others from that group seem to separate themselves from the rest. But, they all do share a very large house."

"I think they share a house because the island assigned them all to it when they arrived. That's pretty common. Whoever you arrive with on the boat becomes your roommate. It's one way the island has created a small, tight-knit community." The Sheriff's answer had them all jumping and turning at the same time.

KeeKee put a hand over her chest. "I thought you were sleeping?" Her voice was ragged and low, as though she really was scared by the Sheriff waking up.

Sheriff Roscoe Coldtrain chuckled and stood up. He grabbed ahold of the belt holding his pants around his hips and pulled it up high around his waist. "You know, I've been losing weight since you three little wolves arrived. You all are really trying to keep me on my toes. I thought when the island assigned me a deputy that I'd have less work, not more."

Sofka eyed the sheriff and pursed her lips. "Were you eavesdropping on our conversation?"

"It's not eavesdropping if I'm in the same room in plain sight while you are speaking." He winked and put a finger to the side of his nose. "But, I did hear some things." He turned his gaze to Christian and eyed him up and down. "So, you're him are you?"

Christian crossed his arms over his chest and arched a brow. "Him who?"

"Santa's right-hand man. I can't imagine the big guy would send anyone else on such an errand." Roscoe rubbed his chin with his index finger. "I thought you'd be older somehow."

Christian relaxed his shoulders and chuckled. "Nope, not the Big-Man's Beta. But I am here on an assignment directly from my f...fearless leader." He coughed in an effort to cover up his almost mistake. "I hope you can keep this to yourself."

KeeKee chuckled.

Christian eyed her with distrust.

"The good sheriff spends too much time sleeping and eating to gossip. Well," she shook her head. "I guess we don't have that situation to worry about."

"What situation would that be?" A deep angry growl emanated from Christian. One neither of the girls had heard from him before.

Sofka raised a placating hand. "Let's all calm down. KeeKee was just being facetious. Roscoe doesn't gossip. Sweet jingle bells, even I can't get him to share town gossip with me when we're alone." She shook her head.

"Yeah, what she said." KeeKee pointed to Sofka and nodded. "I was just joking. Probably too soon for that, huh?"

Christian's nostrils flared. "Look, I get that you all are friends and some sort of family unit, but this is serious. I thought of all people, you two would understand."

All joking fled the building. Sofka and KeeKee completely understood. They had almost been victims themselves of supernatural black market slave traders. The entire reason they ran away from their pack was because their alpha was going to sell them to those who trafficked in supes on the black market. Who knows what would have happened to them if they had been sold.

KeeKee shivered and shook her head. "You're right, and I'm sorry." She winced. "It's just so terrible I can't think about it."

Sofka put an arm around KeeKee's shoulder. "We're safe here. Even though Kirill knows where we are and he tried to get us back, the island isn't going to let him take us."

KeeKee sniffed and ran a finger under her nose. "You're right. I'll be stronger. And I'll take island defense classes more seriously, too."

With a sigh, Sofka shook her head. "No, I'm sorry. I know I've been a bit over the top lately, I just don't want to lose any more of our new friends and family to Kirill. He's gonna try again and I want us all to be ready."

KeeKee patted her friend's back. "I know. We all know. It's just." She shrugged. "Maybe dial it down just a bit and enjoy the Christmas season. Before you know it, Christmas will be over and then we'll all have tons of time to work out and train more."

Christian slapped his hands together. "Great. So, you'll all keep my secret and help me to discover which ones in Aelita's group are spies?" He tilted his head while he waited for a response.

KeeKee couldn't help but smile. She knew that Christian was off-limits, but no one ever said she couldn't enjoy looking at him. He was like a life-sized candy cane, great to look at and dream about, but too much to have.

Chapter 4

KeeKee noticed how Sofka had calmed down in her efforts to get everyone into fighting shape. She had to give it to her friend, she was talented when it came to training. "Sofka, what's the plan for today?"

The sheriff's deputy put her hands on her hips and looked around. Most of the trainees had shown up today. The past two days the class had been almost empty. Somehow word got around that she'd chilled out and was actually working with them on their level, instead of her robocop level. "I think that today we should pair off and practice hand-to-hand combat. I don't want anyone throwing hard punches, or trying to hurt their opponent, just get used to blocking punches and learning how to find an opening in your opponent's defenses."

Sofka paired off with KeeKee and demonstrated what she meant. While Sofka was a better fighter, KeeKee had had the same training as her friend so they both worked quite well together. Sofka got in one good kidney punch, while KeeKee got in an upper cut to Sofka's chin. Other than that, all of their punches were blocked.

KeeKee turned to the crowd that had showed up as they were sparring. "Did you see how Sofka blocked my left hook?"

When the crowd nodded, KeeKee went on, "she was watching my shoulders and noticed that even though I'm a righty, I was about to hit with my left and her arm was up in a defensive position before I could get my left fist in her face."

The gathered crowd chuckled. One person yelled out, "I thought we weren't supposed to try and hurt each other?"

Sofka grinned. "When you've sparred together as much as KeeKee and I have, you'll be able to throw punches like we did and know that the other won't get hurt. We both pulled back with the intensity of our hits, too. So even though I got in a good punch to her kidney, it wasn't hard."

"And my punch to Sofka's chin wasn't hard enough to leave a bruise." KeeKee grinned and winked. She did get in the better punch, but like she said, it wasn't a hard punch.

Sofka rubbed her chin and grimaced. When the audience laughed, she winked and clapped her hands. "Alright, pair up and see what you can do, just don't try to hurt each other."

When practice was over and the almost one hundred participants all walked away smiling, Sofka realized that her friends had been right. "KeeKee, do you have time to help me with a project?"

"Sure, what's up? Need some help creating an actual gym?" She laughed. Then she quieted down when Sofka didn't say anything. "Oh, please tell me you don't want me to help you build a gym."

Sofka bit her lower lip, then a huge smile spread over her face. "Well..."

"No, absolutely not." KeeKee put her hands in the air. "You promised you weren't going to go overboard. If you believe you need a gym, ask the island to make one."

Sofka stopped walking and tapped her chin with her gloved finger. "You know, that's not a bad idea. But no, I was just messing with you. I have something a lot more fun in mind. Something that Arctic Wolves are known for." She grinned.

At first, KeeKee furrowed her brow and tilted her head in confusion. Then it dawned on her and she shared Sofka's grin. "I think I might like that kind of project."

"Good, let's go."

"Wow, that was fun!" KeeKee exclaimed after a full afternoon of secret work. "Can we stop in for a coffee? I think I could use it."

"Sure, just don't say anything about the hangar and what we were doing over there." Sofka had shown KeeKee the place where she first met Christian. At the end of the battle a few weeks ago, Sofka had gone looking for Ree, who was injured. Christian had seen her on the field of battle and pulled her to safety before a lion shifter could end her young life.

Since then, no one but Christian had been back to what looked like a rickety old shack on the outside. But on the inside was a large airplane hangar, thanks to the Island's magic. Christian's sleigh and reindeer were housed inside that building. While he did go back to feed the animals every day, no one else had really noticed. Or at least, no one cared enough to talk about it.

When they entered the Frozen Bean Coffee Shop, the place was packed, per usual. The residents liked to hang out there and chat over hot drinks in the morning and afternoon. While most did have jobs, not too many worked eight hours a day, five days a week. Except for those in the food business. But even they didn't have to, they chose to work longer hours. The island pretty much ran itself.

The supernatural residents of Misfit Island worked to help keep things going on the island. The residents enjoyed eating out or grabbing a cup of hot java, so there were restaurants and the coffee shop. There were also a few stores on Main Street where one could purchase items such as clothing or other necessities. Most items came with the house, but there was the odd pot or pan, or a need for bandages. So, stores popped up as needs arose over the years.

Plus, by having jobs, it helped the residents to be more active and engaged in their tiny community. No one lived to work, they all worked to live. It was a simpler life than back in the human world. They had all left the rat race behind them.

"How about barbecue at Aelita's place tonight?" KeeKee raised her brows to indicate to Sofka she wanted more than just to have the best barbecue in town.

"Maxim is helping Bart tonight. I'll see if they want to join us when they're done." Sofka looked out the window and waved.

KeeKee turned to see who she was waving at and couldn't help but grin. "Do you think they are safe to be around now?"

Sofka almost choked on her coffee. "What?"

"You know, since they mated a few months ago, they've been...well...very handsy when out in public." KeeKee turned around and eyed Sofka. "I thought all newly mated couples were that way. Why aren't you and Maxim all over each other all the time?"

Sofka's cheeks flamed red. She cleared her throat. "How do you know we aren't?"

KeeKee tilted her head and thought about it for a moment. Then it was as though a lightbulb went off and she scrunched her nose. "Eww. You mean you and he...all over town? Gross!"

"Shh, keep it quiet." Sofka looked down at the table they sat at and tried hiding her grin, but to no avail. "I didn't think you wanted to know the details."

"Oh, I don't." KeeKee raised her hands in front of her. "No more on this topic. When do you think we'll be able to make our midnight run?"

"Shh, not here. We can talk more about this back at your place." Sofka took a sip of her coffee, then set it down. "Which reminds me. How do you like your new apartment?"

KeeKee thought about Sofka's question, but when she caught sight of someone out of her peripheral vision, she jerked around and gaped.

Christian just walked inside the coffee shop with Aelita. Which wouldn't have been distracting except for one thing, she had her arms wrapped around one of his arms, and they were both smiling. They were so close to each other, KeeKee doubted air could even get between them. Aelita even let out a cute little tinkle of a laugh.

KeeKee pursed her lips and scooted around in her seat.

Sofka raised a brow when she noticed what caught KeeKee's attention. "So, do you think those two are a couple?"

"What?" KeeKee practically yelled.

People at the tables around the two Arctic Wolf Shifters stopped talking and looked at them.

"Nothing to see here folks." KeeKee made a shooing motion with her hands to try and get the people to stop looking at them. With all of the eyes and ears on their table, she decided they needed to leave if they were going to keep discussing anything important.

The only bad part of living on a tiny island full of supernatural creatures was the lack of privacy. Everyone had such good hearing, even whispers could be heard ten feet away.

But in someone's own home, it was an entirely different matter.

Once Sofka and Maxim had mated, KeeKee moved out of their house. She had zero desire to live with a newly mated couple who were so in love with one another. The island must have anticipated her need to move elsewhere so it had added a top floor to the Welcome Center before Sofka and Maxim had officially mated. The little apartment was perfect for her.

"Why don't we head back to my place?" KeeKee was starting to get tired of always having to leave a place when she wanted to have a serious conversation. Either they needed to find some tech to help disguise their private conversations while out of the house, or they just needed to stop getting in the middle of secret things.

"Sounds good." Sofka looked around. "How do you like living in town?"

"I love living in town. I mean, right above town." KeeKee giggled. "It wasn't as though it was a long walk into town when I lived with you, but now I can look out my window and see a friend walking down the street and then head down to say hi. I've had dinner out almost every night since the move with different supes. I've met so many of our new neighbors. I've even started a book club!"

"Really? Why didn't you invite me? You know how much I love to read." Sofka frowned and looked closer at her best friend as she stood up to leave. Then she realized why she hadn't been invited. "Never mind, I know. I am going to have some more time in the evenings now that Maxim is back on duty. Can I join the book club?"

KeeKee stood up holding her mug of coffee. "Sure, that would be awesome! We just started a book. It's a fun alien romance." She giggled.

Sofka raised her brows. "Really? Alien romance? I didn't think you were into those saucy romances."

"Oh, I'm not. This one is a bit different. It's full of all of the action and adventure one would expect from an alien romance, but nothing behind the bedroom door." KeeKee took a long sip of her peppermint mocha and sighed. "Another benefit to living in town is that I can come over here and get all of the peppermint mocha's I want."

Sofka laughed. "True. It is easier, and tastier, to get Micky's coffee drinks. She's really good at this." She closed her eyes when she inhaled the spicy aroma of her gingerbread latte.

"Hi ladies, whatcha doing?" The voice they both knew, but had barely heard over the past months, called out before joining them before they left the coffee shop.

KeeKee looked around. "What? No Marcus today?"

Ree pursed her lips. "No, we both had to get back to work today. And it looks like I'm going to have a new job." She looked up as Micky joined them.

Micky was the new manager of the Frozen Bean Coffee Shop, and a beautiful Polar Bear shifter. KeeKee admired her long white hair that had red and green streaks in it this month in honor of Christmas.

"Have you met my newest employee?" Micky grinned and motioned to Ree. "Ready to get started?"

Ree took in a deep breath. "As ready as I'll ever be." She followed Micky to the counter where they were talking all things coffee.

"You know, I never would have thought of this place for Ree, but it makes perfect sense." KeeKee watched as her friend donned the apron and nodded at what Micky was saying.

"She does love coffee. And now that she's working here, she'll get all the coffee she can drink." Sofka grinned. "I wonder, do we get the family discount now?"

Both girls laughed and changed their direction. Instead of heading to KeeKee's they decided to see what Ree was up to.

"So, you think Micky will let her make our drinks for free?" KeeKee grinned and took Sofka by her elbow and steered them both to where Micky was training Ree. It was a running joke as coffee was free on the island. When someone ordered they tipped, but didn't have to. And they only tipped what they could afford.

It only took three tries, but Ree was able to get KeeKee's peppermint mocha made just the way she liked it, hot and full of chocolate and pepperminty goodness.

"Ready to try mine?" Sofka asked. "The gingerbread latte shouldn't be too hard, right Micky?" She looked to Micky for confirmation.

"Exactly. A latte is more steamed milk than anything else. Sure, there's coffee and flavored syrup, but steamed milk is the important ingredient. What do you think? Wanna try it?" Micky held out the stainless-steel measuring cup they used to steam the milk. She'd steamed the milk for the mocha, so this would be Ree's first time using the steamer.

Ree nodded but didn't smile. "Sure. I can do it. It shouldn't be too difficult."

Ree took the jug and turned back to the espresso machine. Next to it was a gallon of milk on the counter. She poured the milk into the container and put it under the steamer. Before Micky could warn her, she turned it on and then was covered in cold milk.

KeeKee didn't laugh, but she did grin. "I wondered if that might happen. Next time try filling the jug up to the half-way mark. That should work better."

Ree closed her eyes and took a deep breath. "How did you know that?"

"Because I pay attention when they make my drinks. The baristas never fill the steel mug up more than halfway." KeeKee shrugged. "I thought everyone paid attention when their drinks were made."

Sofka bit her lip and shook her head. "Actually, I probably would have done the same thing as Ree. I never pay much attention when they make my drink. But I think I will moving forward."

"I could always train you two as well as Ree on the art of drink making." Micky's serious expression had KeeKee wondering if she was joking, or really did want to train them all on coffee making.

"I'm good, but thanks." KeeKee took a sip of her hot peppermint mocha and moaned as she enjoyed the goodness of the caffeine mixed with the sweetness of the rest of the ingredients. "This really is good. Ree, I think that once you get the mechanics down, you're doing to rival Micky with the drink making."

Once Sofka had her gingerbread latte, she and KeeKee left Ree behind to work on the basics of being a barista.

"I think we should come by every day this week and give Ree our support," KeeKee announced before they made it back to KeeKee's apartment.

Sofka drank the last of her beverage and sighed. "I agree. After we do our secret agent stuff, then we can reward our efforts with a sweet and hot beverage."

Once they were both upstairs and the door closed, Sofka turned to KeeKee. "Spill. What's going on with you and Christian?"

KeeKee shrugged. "Nothing. You saw him, he was with Aelita."

Sofka scrunched her nose. "What I saw was a female who was draped all over Christian as though she was his new winter coat. A bit much, if you ask me. And I don't think Christian was too happy about her."

The snort that came out of KeeKee's mouth and nose was far from lady-like. "Are you kidding me? Did we see the same thing? He was loving the attention she gave him. He was laughing, for Frosty's sake." She threw her hands in the air and plopped down on the sofa in her living room.

The view from the living room, when she had her curtains open, was of downtown and featured The Frozen Bean right in the middle of the picture window, almost as though the coffee shop had been built just so that someone from the apartment could see it perfectly.

If one was the sort to spy...

Which KeeKee was not.

The next few days were spent working on their extra-secret project and getting hot drinks when Ree was working.

"You know, you're really getting good at this, Ree." At first, KeeKee felt like she needed to help Ree feel good about what she was doing, but now, the compliments were totally the truth. Ree had found her stride.

"Thanks, now that I understand what I'm doing, I actually like it." Ree shook her head. "I never would have thought I'd enjoy being a barista."

Sofka chuckled. "I think this is perfect. It's much more difficult to get away and have a make-out session with your mate when you're working in the busiest place in town."

"Hey, we only did that once." Ree pouted.

"Ah, only once where you were walked in on. After you were caught in the coat closest, no one ever opened another room in the clothing shop again." KeeKee laughed and shook her head. Not long after Ree and Marcus were mated, they went back to work, together. And any chance they got they hid in the coat closest making out. It wasn't long before they were sent home to get the lust out of their systems.

"Not to change the subject, but what have you two been up to all week? I've seen you walk by in the morning out of town. Then you come back and come here before going anywhere else. I also heard that fight club has been moved to later in the day." Ree arched a brow and waited for their response.

KeeKee and Sofka looked at each other and shrugged. "Nothing much. Just checking on the island and doing my rounds." Sofka, as the deputy, should be doing exactly that. But KeeKee should have been working in the welcome center.

"And I've been helping. Horatio wanted me to work the late afternoon and evening shifts, and this is the only time I have to spend with Sofka." KeeKee shrugged. She tried to play off the project they were working on. The two of them had already decided that no one else, not even Maxim, would know what they were doing. It was to be a surprise for the entire island.

"I see. And coming in here is your way of spending time with me?" Ree asked as she began making a drink for a new customer.

"Exactly," KeeKee responded.

"Okay. I see how it is. Just let me know when you're ready to spill the beans." Ree grinned and moved away to add three shots of peppermint to a peppermint latte she was crafting.

"Well, I must be off. Time to get to work. But we really should find some time to have dinner together, just the three of us. I miss it." KeeKee's lower lip stuck out before she turned and exited the door.

Chapter 5

"Tonight, Maxim and I are heading over to Aelita's for dinner. Wanna join us?" Sofka grinned. "I promise, no kissy-kissy at the dinner table."

KeeKee's lips turned up at the corners. "Sure, why not. Maybe this time we'll actually get a chance to talk to Aelita. I was bummed that she wasn't there the other night when just you and I had dinner there."

"Me, too." Sofka agreed. After making plans for when to meet up, they parted ways and Sofka headed off to the Sheriff's office.

But KeeKee had a detour to make before she headed to the Welcome Center to begin her shift. After she arrived at her destination, she looked around and frowned. "Bart? Are you here?"

A short and squat statue spit water and grumbled. "Can't a man get a nap around here?"

KeeKee put her hands on her hips and turned a corner. "Why must you always spit water at me?"

"You know I don't do it on purpose, it's a side effect from being a gargoyle statue for so long before being animated, against my will mind you." The little gray gargoyle spit again, but this time, he turned his head ninety degrees and spit to the side.

"If you could, would you choose to go back to being a statue on the top of a building in Poland?" KeeKee asked.

"Concrete whiskey, no!" Bart waved a hand and began walking to the little office he kept on the boat dock. Bart was the only ship captain they had on the island. It was his job to pilot the ship that went to Chile to pick up new residents...or drop them off.

Since arriving, KeeKee and her friends had only been back to Chile once on a shopping trip. None of them enjoyed leaving the island, especially since they learned that Kirill was trying to get them back.

"So, then why complain that you were animated against your will?" KeeKee knew the answer, but she wanted him to think about it. The little guy was cool in her books, but sometimes he complained too much. Sure, it wasn't fair what the witches did to all of the gargoyles over a hundred years ago, but the time to complain had passed.

"I can't go back, so it doesn't matter now. I just want a nap every once in a while, that's all." He led the way into his little office. "Care for a cup of coffee?"

"No thanks." KeeKee took a seat near the front window as it afforded her a nice view of the water in front of the dock. "I had coffee before coming here."

"Ah, yes." Bart chuckled. "How's Ree doing with her new job?"

"Good, actually. She's really getting the hang of it. Haven't you been in to see her yet?" KeeKee tilted her head and waited for Bart's answer.

"Who needs a coffee shop coffee when I have my own coffee?" Bart nodded toward the tiny cabinet in the back of the room.

On top was an old Mr. Coffee that had definitely seen better days, but still worked. Next to it were several mugs, sugar, powdered cream, and a large canister of beans that had been roasted and ground from the Frozen Bean. The only reason KeeKee knew it was from the frozen bean was because the day before when she'd been in the coffee shop, she noticed Ree was grinding the beans. And when KeeKee asked her about it, she told her that it was an order for Bart.

"Makes sense. So, anyone new to the island lately?" KeeKee didn't trust anyone new. While they still hadn't sussed out who the spies were, she figured that Kirill would try to send in more spies since they had either arrested, or killed, most of the residents that had been on Kirill's payroll.

"As a matter of fact, we are going to get several newbies in tonight. Maxim will be here to greet them when I get back. Which was why I needed my nap. It's going to be a late night." He eyed her warily. "Will you be working at the welcome center tonight?"

"I wasn't planning on it. In fact, I was going to have dinner at Aelita's tonight with Sofka and Maxim, looks like that won't be happening now." KeeKee hoped that Maxim knew the plans had changed and was telling Sofka at that very moment. She hated to think that Maxim might forget to tell his new mate about the change in plans.

Bart grunted. "I think if they have an early dinner, it'll be fine. I should be back here by nine with them."

"Do you know how many there are coming tonight?" KeeKee didn't always hear about new arrivals to the island until they walked into the welcome center. It was kinda nice knowing ahead of time that newbies were due to arrive.

Normally, when someone shook their head, it wasn't so uniform. It might be a bit erratic. But when Bart shook his head, it looked more like a toy soldier moving its head from side to side. The image left KeeKee feeling a bit odd. Especially since Bart's eyes never left her face when he shook his head. "Nope. I only get a message from the island that newbies are due to arrive and when I should go to pick them up."

Bart looked up to the sky. "It would be nice if I knew how many were due to arrive and if they were evil or nice." He scoffed, then turned his head to spit out the water that had developed inside his squat, concrete body.

KeeKee watched the gargoyle and wondered if they felt love. Then a disturbing thought entered her mind, one that had her shaking her head and thinking about baby reindeer. "Sooo, what can you tell me about the supes who arrived with Aelita?"

"Aelita? Aren't you friends with her?" Bart's mouth moved in a side-to-side motion before he turned his head and spit clear water to the side.

KeeKee was beginning to see a pattern with the gargoyle. Speaking caused him to need to spit more. And he moved his mouth in an odd fashion just before hawking a water loogie. Then she focused back on Bart and his question. "Aelita? Yes, we are sort of friends, but I'm more curious about those who came over with her, but still keep to themselves. I've met Carmin and Sienna, and they both seem nice, but the rest of the group are, well..." she wasn't really sure how to describe the rest, other than to say rude.

"Offensive. Is that what you wanted to say?" Bart didn't have a lot of facial expressions, but he did have the raised eyebrow action down quite well.

She felt her cheeks turn warm and shook her head, her ponytail swooshing behind her as she did so. "No, not offensive. Maybe just a bit standoffish? They don't like to talk to anyone very much. But I have seen them getting coffee with a few who live in the Dark Hills, so I just wondered about them."

"Exactly, it's not easy to meet the residents of the Dark Hills, unless you live there. And even then, it's still not easy. The fact that they seem to already know some of the less savory of the island residents has my back tingling." Bart downed his cup of coffee and went to the coffee maker to pour another cup.

KeeKee chuckled. "I didn't realize gargoyles had Spidey senses."

"Well, we don't have hackles to rise like wolves do." Bart shuffled and grunted.

If KeeKee wasn't mistaken, this gargoyle did have hackles to rise, and they were standing up tall in that moment. Metaphorically speaking, that is. "Sorry, I didn't mean to offend, it's just that I don't know much about you or any gargoyle." She shrugged. "All I know is what I've read in books, and even that wasn't much. Plus, I highly doubt what I read was very accurate."

He grunted in return. It seemed that was the only response KeeKee was to receive.

In that very moment she wished she had a cup of coffee, if only to have something to do with her hands. "Well, this has been...interesting. Do you know anything else about the others in Aelita's group?"

While gargoyles didn't have a super expressive face, they could put some emotion in their facial features, and if KeeKee was reading Bart correctly, he was seriously ticked off.

"All I can say is that I don't trust any of them, including Aelita." Bart set his coffee mug down and then ushered KeeKee outside. "I've got work to do."

"Work? You don't have a pickup for several hours yet. How do you have work?" KeeKee backed out of the office with a frown on her face.

Bart didn't give her anything else, just practically shoved her out of his office.

"Well, that was rude." She knew she shouldn't have expected open arms or a tickertape parade, Bart wasn't exactly the loveable marshmallow kinda supe. He was usually brusque and bordered on rude, when he wasn't outright rude. But still, she had hoped he would have given her something to go on.

KeeKee walked outside and stood at the edge of the dock staring at the sky above. Even with the cold weather, it was a beautiful day. The island kept a bubble over them, and it usually mirrored the outside world's weather, but today they had wisps of white clouds overhead mixed with small patches of light blue sky. The breeze was chilly but not freezing cold as she imagined it would be outside of the protective bubble. Thanks to her other persona – Arctic Wolf Shifter – she was able to withstand some pretty cold temperatures.

Even though most of the Arctic Wolf Shifters enjoyed hanging out in the freezing cold winter weather, sometimes it was nice to be outside in the cold and clean air, no matter the temperature. It was also pleasantly quiet. While the little town they all lived in wasn't nearly as loud as a human town, the supes could be boisterous when they wanted. And after the battle there were quite a few parties in the streets to celebrate their victory. Or as some had said, "To celebrate living."

Things had calmed down, which KeeKee was grateful for. She preferred a hot cup of chocolate, or hot apple cider, and a fireplace to sit in front of. Her original island house had an outside sitting area that was perfect for sitting outside and enjoying a hot beverage while reading a good book, or even watching some TV. The firepit they had was perfect. But since she'd moved over the shop, she didn't have anything like that anymore.

KeeKee knew that she could go back to the house anytime she wanted and enjoy the back yard, but since Sofka and Maxim were so newly mated, she preferred to stay away, for now. When they got past the initial honeymoon phase, she'd go back to using that perfect back yard.

But for now, she'd just enjoy quiet moments like this one looking out over the bay and watching the clouds slowly pass by. The magical clouds had her in a trance. Somehow, she had completely tuned out all sounds, and people, from around her.

"Hi, is this spot taken?" A deep voice said from behind KeeKee.

She jumped and turned at the same time as she put a hand to her chest. "What is with supes trying to startle me lately?"

Christian Icingberry, AKA Christian Claus, took a step back. "I'm sorry, I didn't mean to interrupt your private moment. I'll head down to the other end."

"No, no. I'm the one who's sorry." KeeKee pushed a lock of hair that had fallen out of her ponytail behind her ear. "Ever since the attack on the island I think I've just been a bit jumpy."

Christian hesitated for just a moment before joining her at the railing. "I'm truly sorry we couldn't have prevented that attack. But also grateful that there weren't more lives lost in the battle. Was this the first time you'd seen real battle?"

KeeKee nodded. She didn't want to discuss her lack of experience, but she was curious about Christian's. She knew he was the son of Santa Claus. And that pack was known for taking down the really bad packs, when needed. "Have you seen battle before?"

After letting out a long sigh, Christian nodded. "I have but it wasn't on the same scale as that battle. I don't think our supernatural community has seen anything that large in quite some time. Definitely not in my lifetime."

"What does your father say about it?" No one had said anything about Santa coming to the island, or about his pack of enforcers going out and putting an end to Kirill and his pack of supernatural black marketeers. But KeeKee knew from the stories everyone told back in her old pack that Santa didn't let the bad guys get away with anything for long. She was really surprised that the Big Man himself hadn't come down to the island to get more answers. However, his son was there, so maybe that was his way of looking into it?

Christian's eyes widened. "I think he's rather angry and not just with Kirill, but also with himself for not stopping Kirill when he had the chance to do so."

"Why doesn't he just do it now?" KeeKee leaned her arms on the railing and focused on Christian.

"Kirill has gone into hiding. I spoke to my father earlier and almost the entire pack disappeared. I think there might be a total of six supes left behind to guard the den." Christian moved close to KeeKee and put his arms on the top of the railing, like KeeKee.

"Oh, wow." Unsure what to say after that revelation, KeeKee stared off into the distance not really seeing the beauty before her, or next to her.

Christian tried to be inconspicuous as he stared at KeeKee, but when little red circles showed up on her cheeks, he knew she had noticed. "Sorry, I can't seem to help myself."

KeeKee looked down and tried to hide her grin. While it wasn't the first time Christian had looked closely at her, it was the first time he'd done so while standing so close they could touch. Her left arm began to tingle, and she felt a warmth infuse her entire body. The kind a good cup of coffee, a large fire, and a good book could bring on. Only, Christian wasn't any of those things, he was a male that was totally off limits for her.

One rule was very plain, no member of Santa's pack ever mated with a mixed-blood supe. Sure, a few had mated with someone outside of their race, but those supes were royal dragons. Then she remembered one of Christian's aunts mated with a polar shifter, but if she wasn't mistaken, that supe was from a very long line of polar shifters who were of a class that she and her family could never belong to.

The entire situation reminded her of the romance novels she loved to read when no one was looking. The human regency romance novels were KeeKee's guilty pleasure. The one she did her best to keep secret. Although, no one could keep anything secret from Sofka. She should have been born a blood-hound shifter.

A tiny smile turned up the edges of KeeKee's lips as she thought about the book she was currently reading. It was about the son of a

Duke who falls for the governess next door. The situation was somewhat similar to hers, except Christian was more of a supernatural prince than a duke. And KeeKee wasn't even a daughter of the gentry who had fallen on hard times - she was an orphan from what those regency era books would call a poor family. And not just any orphan, but an orphan from a pack of wolf shifters that were now on Santa's most wanted list. Christian would never be able to even consider liking her.

However, he seemed to always be around her, and when they were alone, she had this feeling that there was a spark. Not all the time, but sometimes, like now. It was most likely just her imagination since both of her roommates had mated since coming to the island. For about two seconds she thought there might be something with her and Horatio, but she quickly realized that he was more like the big brother she never had.

"I thought I'd find you both here." A cackle from behind them startled KeeKee and she almost swore under her breath. Instead, she sighed and turned around.

Chapter 6

"Marcus, what a surprise." KeeKee crossed her arms over her chest and glared at the intruder.

It wasn't that KeeKee disliked Ree's mate, it was that he hadn't really tried to befriend Sofka and KeeKee. Sure, he looked out for them, but Ree was all he really seemed to care about. However, when KeeKee thought about it, she realized that was a huge start for the Fae Prince. The fae never cared for anyone but themselves, they didn't even care for their closest family members.

Marcus had begun to show he was different from his family. Since he was the second son of Mab, the Queen of the Unseelie Court, everyone just expected him to be evil. However, KeeKee had begun to see a new side to him, one that Ree must have seen before anyone else.

When Marcus smiled, his pearly whites and the glint of mischief that was always present in his eyes, could turn almost anyone's head. At first, she'd almost fallen for his charms, but now she just sighs when he looks at her this way.

"KeeKee, we're practically brother and sister now, can't we get along better?" In the beginning, Marcus didn't seem to care that the three little wolf shifters had claimed each other as packmates and sisters. They were a found family, or pack, as they liked to call themselves. But now that two of the three were mated, KeeKee didn't really know where she fit in anymore.

"Uh," KeeKee raised a finger, "how many times has your brother tried to kill you? Being siblings doesn't seem to mean anything for a fae." She arched a brow.

Marcus sighed and shook his head. "True, but I've been away from faerie for quite some time now. And besides," his killer smile returned, "I think I kinda like having sisters."

Knowing he was right, KeeKee put a real smile on her face and chuckled, the fae prince could be charming when he wanted. "You're right. We should get along. How can I help you today?"

Marcus eyed Christian. "First, you can get rid of this riff raff. We don't have need of anyone who stands by and lets an entire island be attacked." He sniffed and turned his shoulder on Christian. "You are better than him."

KeeKee's eyes shot up to her hairline and she felt her face turn hotter than a chestnut over an open fire. "Marcus, that's. Wow, rude much?" She knew he was. He'd never kept his thoughts to himself. And most of his thoughts were along this line, that no one was as good as he was. But still. This was taking it too far.

Christian chuckled and put a hand on KeeKee's arm. "Don't worry about me. I never pay attention to Mab's offspring. They aren't worth my attention." He smiled warmly at KeeKee before walking away.

She wondered at his reaction. Was he kinda flirting with her just to get Marcus' ire up? It was never smart to mess with the fae, especially a fae prince. Even if he was only a second son. KeeKee had seen Marcus go off the rails when he thought something bad had happened to Ree. Thankfully, she wasn't seriously injured. And it was Christian who pulled her from a rough situation in the big battle, not Marcus. So KeeKee thought Marcus should be grateful and thankful, not malicious. But as Christian said, the fae weren't worth Christian's attention.

It wasn't as though Marcus would do anything to Christian anyway. The ruling family members of the Unseelie Court would never dare to attack Santa's family. Santa and his pack were too formidable. Or they were at one time not too long ago. KeeKee wasn't sure anymore if Santa still had it in him.

But, Kirill was still out there. That had KeeKee wondering if something wasn't amiss in all of this. Was Santa losing his strength? Should Christian take over now that he was of age? Actually, he was older than the standard age. Usually, the new Santa took over at the ripe old age of eighteen. He also mated that same year.

If KeeKee wasn't mistaken, Christian was around twenty-two. And he hadn't taken a mate yet, either. Maybe something was wrong with the Claus pack and that was why Kirill had been able to amass so much power and soldiers.

While the human world thought Santa should be old, the supernatural world understood the importance of a young and strong Santa to keep the shifter community in line.

She turned her attention back to Marcus, who had raised a brow. "Stop it. You know as well as I do that there is nothing between me and Christian. What did you want?"

A deep chuckle escaped Marcus' lips before he turned his full attention back on KeeKee. "Ree wanted me to invite you to dinner tonight."

KeeKee bit her lower lip. "I was supposed to have dinner with Sofka and Maxim, but there's going to be a group of newbies coming in tonight. Maxim is going to have to meet them, so..." She shrugged.

"How about we all meet up? Where were you going to eat? Aelita's?" It seemed Marcus and Ree hadn't completely shut themselves away from everyone else. They knew about the latest restaurant, and the fact that most enjoyed dining at the best barbecue joint in town. Never mind the fact that it was the only one.

"Yes, we were. I need to find Sofka and see what the plan is. I'll let her know that you'd like to join us." KeeKee smiled half-heartedly and turned to head toward town and the Sheriff's office where Sofka should be. Well, if she wasn't off working on her super-secret project.

Ever since the battle, Sofka had been working on something. KeeKee was the only one who knew as she helped when she could. It was a lot of fun, too. She hoped she could keep helping while keeping it a secret from the rest of the island.

As it turned out, Sofka was also looking for KeeKee.

"KeeKee!" Sofka yelled out and waved her hands above her head before she ran toward her friend. "I'm so glad I found you."

"Funny, I was looking for you, too." KeeKee headed toward Sofka and hugged her best friend when they met.

KeeKee looked around expecting to see Maxim. A vampire could be out in the day on this island without too much trouble. The dome that covered the island protected the vampire's skin from solar rays, but it wasn't like a vampire was going to spend much time out in the sun. Even if the sun was mostly fabricated by the magic of the island.

During the winter, or was it summer? KeeKee was having a tough time adjusting to having the seasons flip-flop on her. When it clicked that it was technically summer in this part of the world, she shook her head. She supposed the Antarctic region didn't get much in the way of sunlight at any time of the year, which meant it probably didn't matter much what the actual season was. But the island did like to see its residents happy and outside as much as possible, so it gave them several hours a day of unnatural sunlight to help keep them outside and socializing.

"He's not here. I sent Maxim to Aelita's to see if we could reserve a large table for an early dinner. Have you heard?" Sofka nodded in the direction of the dock. "We're getting some new residents tonight."

KeeKee nodded and her nostrils flared. "Yes, and I'm rather worried about them. Are you?"

"Yes." Sofka breathed out. "I'm glad to know that I'm not alone in this worry. Maxim said it was nothing to worry about. He and Bart would check them out. And I'm sure Horatio will be working the Welcome Center tonight so he can give them a once over as well."

"He must be as I haven't been asked to work tonight. Even though it is my turn to work a late shift." Since it was usually just Horatio and KeeKee who checked in newcomers, they took turns working late or being on call should the welcome center services be needed.

"Well, I think we should help Horatio. Or at the very least, bring him dinner when we are done." The brows above Sofka's eyes raised conspiratorially.

KeeKee agreed and looked around. "Will Maxim be upset with you for checking out the newbies tonight?"

Sofka put her hands on her hips. "Hey, I'm still the Sheriff's Deputy here. So, if I feel the need to meet newcomers, then I will. No matter what my mate says."

"Which means he didn't want you anywhere near the Welcome Center tonight, right?" KeeKee grinned. She felt that Sofka had gone too soft when it came to Maxim and let him run roughshod over her. But it seems that Sofka still had some backbone in her.

The newly mated Arctic Wolf Shifter returned KeeKee's grin and then chuckled. "So, what's this I've heard about you spending time with Christian?" She arched a brow.

After letting out a long sigh, KeeKee ran a hand down her face. "There is nothing going on. I don't know why people even think it's possible. He's the next Santa, there's no way I'm going to be the next Mrs. Claus. And you know it." She pointed her index finger so closely to Sofka's nose, that she almost touched it.

Sofka batted away the finger. "Don't think that way. You'd make the perfect Mrs. Claus. You love kids, and you always want to help everyone else. What more could anyone ask for in a mate?"

"I'm not a pureblood. If Christian and I mated, it would dilute the Santa line. And you know it." KeeKee turned her head to see if anyone was listening in on their conversation.

When she felt no one was close enough to use their supernatural hearing to listen in, she relaxed just a bit. "This really isn't the place to discuss this."

"I know, I know." Sofka waved a hand in front of her face. "But, you're wrong. Lizzie's sisters mated with whomever they wanted, and none of them mated wolf shifters of any kind."

"I think you forget that none of them were slated to be the next Mrs. Claus. And as for those males they mated, two were practically royalty. One was. And remember, he kidnapped his future mate." That story had always given KeeKee the heebie jeebies. She'd never be able to mate with anyone if it was forced on her.

Sofka shook her head. "You've got it wrong. She mated the supe who saved her from her kidnapper. Plus, she was fated to mate with a dragon. It was agreed upon many years before they were born."

The memories of the stories they were told as kids about the Claus family were mostly embellished as a means to ensure they never felt they could trust Santa. KeeKee knew this, but she still thought most of the stories were true. Maybe the Claus girl who mated a dragon was embellished, but only a bit. "Still, none of them were to be the next Mrs. Claus, so it really didn't matter, did it?"

"We're getting off topic here." Sofka raised a hand to stop KeeKee from arguing her point any further. "We need to see if we can do dinner early. And I spoke with Ree before finding you. She wants us all to have dinner together."

KeeKee almost stuck her tongue out. She loved Ree and missed her greatly since she had mated with the fae prince. But the two of them were too much. Marcus couldn't seem to keep his hands, or his lips, off of his mate. And Ree loved the attention from him. "Yeah, Marcus just asked me to join them for dinner tonight. Looks like it will be the five of us." And she mentally added, *I'll be the fifth wheel, as usual*.

"Don't worry, we will all be on our best behavior tonight." Sofka's mouth quirked to the side. "Well, during dinner at least. I promise we won't make you lose your meal." She giggled.

KeeKee shook her head and laughed. "Thanks. I think."

"I have an idea that might help. Let me see if I can make it happen. If I can then you won't need to worry too much about Marcus and Ree being so over the top." When Sofka turned to head in the direction of the barbecue joint, KeeKee followed.

"What's your idea?" While KeeKee trusted her friend, she also knew that sometimes Sofka had strange ideas. It would probably be best if KeeKee understood what Sofka was up to.

"Don't worry. It's nothing too outrageous. Just enough to keep the guys in check." And with that she picked up her speed and almost ran to Aelita's restaurant.

Chapter 7

When KeeKee arrived, she almost turned around. At the large dinner table sat the four she expected, plus one. "Christian, so nice to see you." Her smile might not have reached her eyes, but Christian wouldn't have been able to notice as her eyes turned to Sofka and Ree with a question, and a glare, in them.

Christian stood up and pulled back the chair next to him, seeing that it was the only empty chair. "Maxim invited me and said he had something that we all needed to discuss." His smile for KeeKee was genuine and crinkles formed around his eyes.

KeeKee turned her gaze to the vampire and raised a brow.

"Why don't we first order and then later we can discuss business. For now, I want to just enjoy the time we all have together. This is a rarity for us." Maxim motioned to the hors d'oeuvres on the table.

Just as KeeKee was about to object, the scents of the grilled vegetables hit her olfactory receptors, and her stomach growled. She hadn't eaten since breakfast, other than a small snack, and she was ravenous.

She giggled. "I could eat a whole pack of squirrels right now." Warmth suffused her cheeks when she noticed how Christian was looking at her.

"Is there a good squirrel population on this island?" As a wolf shifter, Christian enjoyed the hunt but hadn't had a chance to let his wolf loose since arriving on the island.

The other five looked at him.

Marcus smirked. "Sure, but you'd have to shift in order to give chase, wouldn't you?"

Christian nodded.

Maxim picked up what Marcus left behind. "If you shifted, wouldn't others know who you are?"

The table next to theirs began laughing and one person pulled out a wooden puzzle.

Christian stiffened, praying they didn't know who he was.

"I found this on my doorstep this afternoon wrapped like a Christmas gift. Did any of you send it?" A tall, dark haired supe asked his dinner companions.

The others at the table looked at the intricately carved piece of wood. A woman with long, dark hair took the oddly shaped hexagon from the man and examined it. "Isn't this one of those logic puzzles the humans love so much?"

KeeKee had to bite her lip to keep from saying anything, or smiling. She knew exactly who put it on the supe's doorstep. And she wasn't going to say a word.

The man who received it nodded. "It is. And I've heard that a lot of supes on this island have received similar gifts. I just hope they aren't Trojan Horses."

The rest of his party all nodded solemnly. "It might be like that movie, where they release a bunch of fun gifts, only to see that they are full of explosives." He shivered.

The recipient of the gift waved a hand in front of his face. "Nah, it's nothing like that. If it was, I'd have already blown up."

His friends all laughed.

Marcus eyed Christian. "I take it you've been up to something here for your father?" He titled his head toward the table with the gift.

Christians eyes widened. "Who? Me?" He pointed to his chest and shook his head. "No, way. I'm trying to stay under the radar. It's like you said, when I shift, other wolf shifters will know who I am. I don't want that."

Maxim's eyes began to redden, and his fangs cracked through his lips. "Then why are you here? Exactly?"

Christian took in a deep breath and slowly released it. "You know. And you also know this isn't the place to have this discussion, again."

"Alright, alright. Enough." KeeKee rolled her eyes. She was beginning to feel as though she was the only adult at the table. "Let's not argue, or discuss anything that could be overheard. After dinner, we can go back to my place and discuss business." While she wasn't too keen on hanging out with Christian, she also didn't want her family to mistreat him, or accuse him of being an evil pawn, or was it spawn? Either way, Christian had already shown his loyalty when he rescued Ree during the big battle.

Ree's countenance darkened, and she leaned forward. "I am only going to say this once, Christian is a trusted friend." She lifted her pointer finger just above the plate on her table and pointed it at each of the troublesome males. "If any of you give him garbage, I'll personally come after you." She narrowed her eyes and turned to her mate. "And if you do anything to him, I'll move out."

"What?" Marcus held up a hand and shook his head. "Wait just a minute, my little Wolfie. I'm grateful for Christian and how he saved you. I'm not going to mess with him."

Sofka grinned, then turned to her mate. "The same goes with you. Leave Christian alone or you'll be living alone." She arched a brow and crossed her arms over her chest.

The vampire pulled his fangs back in and his eyes cleared up. "I think I hate being mated."

Marcus chuffed. "It's a Catch 22. We will never win, might as well follow the old adage."

Christian's head whipped back and forth as his dinner companions kept discussing him and he rubbed his neck. "I think I'm getting whiplash. What's the old adage?"

The grin that took over Marcus' sour face showed off his pearly white teeth, and their sharp canines stood out, almost as though he was a vampire. "Wait until you're mated, you'll see."

Maxim chuffed. "What my brother-in-law is trying to say is, "Happy Wife, Happy Life.""

Christian nodded. "Yes, my dad says the same thing."

The two mated women at the table grinned like the Chesire Cat who caught the canary.

"That's right, and don't you forget it." Ree stated.

"Right there," Sofka pointed to her friend. "She knows the score."

KeeKee chuckled and shook her head. "Can't we just put the animosity behind us and move forward? I know San..." She cut herself off when she noticed that the table next to them had quieted down and were watching her table.

Sofka put her hands in the air. "Alright, so you each have your favorite football teams, I get it. You don't need to fight over who is better than the other."

Marcus shook his head. "I don't understand why there is any debate, Manchester United is the best. And that's all there is to it." He shrugged.

Then the table of males next to them erupted and all conversation turned into which soccer club, or football to most of the world, has the best players.

Ree leaned over to Sofka who sat next to her. "At least no one will remember what we were talking about."

Sofka put a finger to her lips. "Let's keep it that way."

Three hours later the five of them crammed into KeeKee's apartment over the welcome center.

Maxim put his arm on the sofa behind Sofka's shoulders. "Alright, Christian. If you aren't here to play Santa, how is your mission coming along?"

Christian scratched his neck and winced. "Not too good. I've tracked a group of supes here who I believe to be a part of a supernatural trafficking team..."

Sofka jumped up and pointed a finger at him. "It's the traitors who are working with Kirill, right? Who are they?"

With a placating gesture, Christian moved his hands up and down in front of him. "Look, we've talked about this before. I don't know if they are a part of Kirill's team, that is one of my objectives on this trip."

Ice dripped from Marcus's next words, "If you don't know who you are tracking, how can you track them?"

"Look, I know who I'm tracking, and I know they are part of a group of supernatural traffickers. What I was looking into was dragon eggs."

A collective gasp encompassed the room.

KeeKee squeaked out, "no, not baby dragons."

Christian ran a hand down his face.

"You never told me about this." Sofka glared at him as her nostrils flared.

"I know, I know. I tried to keep this on the down low. Can you imagine what the supernatural world would do if they learned that dragon eggs were on the black market?"

Maxim stood up in one fluid motion. "You were right to keep this quiet. This changes things."

Marcus tilted his head and looked Christian up and down. "Are you saying that one of your Aunt's hybrid eggs have been stolen?"

"No, not my family, directly. But the stolen eggs are related distantly to my Aunt's husband." Christian didn't like the gleam he saw in Marcus' eyes. He knew that the fae had their own set of rules. And he also knew the kind of power a hybrid dragon egg could bestow upon the fae. Santa had already ruled out either of the Fae courts. The only problem here was that Marcus was operating outside of Mab's control.

When Christian first arrived and discovered that a second son of Mab, Queen of the Unseelie Court was on this island, and the supes he had tracked across the world were also here, he thought Marcus might be the one he was searching for. However, it didn't take long to determine that Marcus wasn't involved.

The Fae Prince might be a jerk, but he wasn't the sort to be involved in the supernatural black market. Others on this island would be, and that was what kept him there.

"Do you think the dragon eggs are here? On Misfit Island?" Ree asked.

"No." Christian shook his head. "I know they aren't. But I do know that at least one person here stole one egg and already sold it. My uncle is tailing the egg, to see where it goes and who is the final buyer. I'm here to see if the thief can lead me to the ringleader."

"Is there more than one supernatural black market?" KeeKee asked. Since she had led such a sheltered life, she'd not known much about these sorts of dealings.

"Sadly, yes. My targets could very easily be working for someone other than Kirill. They could be staying here in order to keep away from the heat they created when they stole an egg from the dragon court." Christian sat down on a chair next to the sofa where KeeKee took a seat.

"That would be one large coincidence, and I don't think I believe in coincidences." Sofka relaxed back into the cushions of the couch she sat on.

Christian sat forward with his forearms resting on the top of his thighs and his hands balled up between his knees. "I think I agree with you, but I don't have any proof that Kirill is behind this theft, just a hunch that he could be."

A long, deep sigh escaped Marcus and then everyone in the room looked at him. "It is most likely Kirill, and not because it's too much of a coincidence, but because of the power that the egg might give him. If he employs a witch, she could turn that power on this island and possibly bring down the shields for hours, maybe even days."

"What?" Sofka jumped up and stood directly in front of Marcus. "What are you saying? That Kirill has the power to destroy the island's defenses? And that power is from a dragonling who hasn't even been born yet?"

Marcus nodded.

"Will he kill the baby to harness the magic?" Ree's voice was so low, only a supernatural could have heard her.

"Possibly, probably." Christian hung his head as a tear trailed down his sculpted face.

Chapter 8

"This changes everything." The next morning Sofka was in the Sheriff's station discussing with her boss everything she had learned the night before.

Just then KeeKee walked in and joined their conversation. "I think there's still a lot we don't know."

Sheriff Coldtrain shook his head and put his hands on his service belt. "Agreed. But I think this new information might help clarify a few points. And if Kirill does have the dragon egg, then he'll be coming back sooner, rather than later. Which means we have to double our efforts to get this island prepared."

KeeKee stayed quiet, praying that Sofka wouldn't pull out her militant persona and grill all of the volunteers like they were new recruits for the Army.

Sofka scratched her head. "I don't get it. The cost to do everything he's done so far, and still has to do, is so much more than what he would have made on selling the three of us to the black market. Why not just pay the buyers back and move on? Why does he have to go so far to get us back?"

The sheriff rubbed the tip of his nose. "I don't know. But I think this is personal for him. And maybe it's more than just the three of you little wolf shifters. We know you were guided here for something. Maybe Kirill was already moving against the island when you left, and he just finagled it so that you were part of his plans."

"Well, melting Frosty." Sofka plopped down in her desk chair and released a deep sigh. "So, this new information doesn't really help much, does it."

"I wouldn't go that far. I do think there is a chunk or two of good intelligence here. We just need to know a bit more in order to understand it all." The sheriff leaned his large backside against the edge of the desk and crossed his left leg over his right.

After thinking for a moment, KeeKee said, "I told Christian that we'd coordinate with him. He has several supes he's been keeping an eye on. But it's not easy to be the only one to watch a group of supernatural beings. I thought we could put together some volunteers to help us watch the four or five supes in the circle that could be bad eggs." She wasn't sure, but felt in her bones that Aelita wasn't one of the traffickers. Christian had said he would tend to agree with her if she hadn't been traveling with the others.

Sheriff Coldtrain stood up and paced in front of the table that held their small coffee maker. "Who does Christian suspect to be a part of the group of traffickers? Maybe we should all work together and pool our information." He rubbed the stubble on his chin and poured himself another cup of coffee.

Ree scrunched her nose and decided next time she came to the Sheriff's office, she was going to stop by The Frozen Bean and get drinks for everyone. The scent of the burnt coffee was giving her a headache, and she'd only been in that office for a few minutes. "Why don't I go get Christian and see if the others want to discuss how we can set up some type of surveillance?"

She'd also go get a *real* cup of coffee while she was at it.

Christian was easy to find, as he was only next door to the coffee shop talking to one of the supes that shared the large house with Aelita and the other eight new residents.

"KeeKee, have you met Carmin yet?" Christian motioned to the short female he was speaking to. She couldn't have been taller than four feet. But she was striking with her dirty blonde hair and bright purple eyes.

She stood there mesmerized by the beautiful creature who seemed as though she wanted to fly away the moment KeeKee set eyes on her.

"KeeKee?" Christian put a hand on her arm. "Are you alright?"

With a shake of her head, KeeKee smiled. "I'm sorry, I know it's wrong to stare, but your eyes are so unique. Are purple eyes common for your..." She bit her lip, unsure how to ask what type of supernatural creature she was. It was rude to outright ask, but the aura of the young woman was something KeeKee hadn't come into contact with before.

Carmin smiled and put her hand out. "It's nice to meet you, KeeKee. Most of those in my Durante have purple eyes, it's a tribal trait." Her strong Latino accent told KeeKee that she was most likely from South America, but she wasn't sure where. Maybe this was one of those rare Amazonian shifters?

Durante. KeeKee wracked her brain for what that meant. She'd heard it before, but couldn't remember. She pursed her lips and narrowed her eyes. Then it hit her. "Oh." She put a hand over her mouth. "Forgive me." When she removed her hand, a genuine smile emerged. "I've not had much interaction with bird shifters. Are you a Toucan?"

The young woman lowered her head, but KeeKee caught sight of a tiny smile playing at the edges of her lips. "Si, I am."

Since KeeKee had been so brazen in asking what race Carmin was she decided to even the playing field. "I'm an Arctic Wolf Shifter and led a very sheltered life before my journey here. Please forgive me for being so rude. Before arriving here, I'd not met many other supes, it's been very eye opening meeting so many from all walks of life."

"Isn't it amazing how many different species of supes live here on this island in harmony?" Carmen chuckled.

KeeKee noticed the young woman's shoulders relax and she stood taller, not so closed in on herself. "I'm still amazed at how well most get along here." Since she didn't know anything about Carmen, she wondered if this supe was on Christian's suspect list. Hoping to see how well Carmen was getting along with the variety of supernatural creatures on this island, she asked, "Have you met anyone from the Dark Hills?"

If Carmen was buddy-buddy with supes from the Dark Hills, it could mean she was part of the Supernatural Black Market.

Immediately, Carmen pulled back into herself and hunched over. "Noooo, I've heard about that place." She shook her head. "I was here for the battle and saw some of them, too." Her body shook violently, as though she was freezing.

"I'm sorry, I didn't mean to bring up a sore subject." KeeKee wondered how Sofka always asked the right questions to get answers from her suspects. No one would ever ask KeeKee to work as a detective, or cop.

Carmen put a hand up. "Don't worry, I'm fine. I'm not much for fighting." She winced. "During the battle I was one of those who stayed here and hid out in the coffee shop. A lot of fighting went down before all of the invaders left."

KeeKee twisted her lips and her eyes hooded. "I remember what the coffee shop looked like after. I'm sorry you experienced that."

Christian had stood by and observed the interaction between the two female supes. But he had his own questions. "Carmen, have any of the residents from the Dark Hills been by your house to see your roommates?"

The short Toucan shifter tilted her head and moved it around in a jerky motion, like a bird trying to figure out who was in front of her. "I think that Nixie, Sigurd, had been by the house once or twice. I worried about him, but Chodrak said he was a pacifist. Guess Chodrak was wrong." Carmin pursed her lips and her eyes turned black, for just a moment.

Sigurd was one of the Dark Hills residents that had worked with Kirill's team in the attack on the island and was killed during the battle for his efforts.

KeeKee leaned back and wondered if there wasn't more to Carmin than the shifter wanted anyone to know. The black eyes gave her the heebie jeebies. It made her think of several different supes from the dark hills. However, the Toucans weren't known to be fighters, they were more laid back than other shifters from the Amazon region.

"Carmen, didn't you say you were from Suriname? What was that like? And why did you leave such a beautiful country?" Christian leaned against the edge of the building where they stood – right between the coffee shop and the bookstore.

Carmen's eyes turned back to their vibrant purple once more and a small smile crossed her lips. "Suriname is wonderful, but I didn't fit in with my Durante."

"I hear ya, three of us came to this island after problems with our pack back in Siberia. I don't know why some supes have to be so mean to their packmates." KeeKee's eyes welled up, but she kept the tears at bay. It wouldn't do to cry in front of a supe she had just met.

Carmen's head bobbed up and down. "Exactly. Which is why I think I've found my new home." She smiled.

"Does that mean your roommates are your new Durante?" There, thought KeeKee, that should be a good way of asking how close she was to her roommates without being so straightforward.

Carmen's mouth opened to respond, but before a sound escaped her lips, another sound captured KeeKee's attention.

A loud, piercing cry disrupted the peaceful scene and had both Christian and KeeKee turning everywhere to see what had happened.

The wailing got louder and louder when KeeKee noticed a group of children pulling a sled with a young boy on it writhing and screaming out in pain. He held his arm close to his body.

KeeKee put a hand on Christian's arm. "Oh, no. Can you go and get Sofka? I'll see if I can do something to help him."

"I'll go, you stay here." Carmen said as she took off toward the sheriff's office.

KeeKee nodded and felt drawn to the child in pain. The boy couldn't be older than eight or nine years old. Her heart began to break for the poor thing. He was wearing yellow snow pants with a brown snow jacket. His sandy blond hair was sticking up all over the place, as though he had been wearing a beanie but it fell off somewhere along the way. Before she even knew what she was doing, she had pushed aside the supes who'd crowded around the boy. "Make way. Give the poor boy some room."

When KeeKee had made her way to the sled, she knelt down and put a comforting hand on the boy's shoulder. "What happened?"

Instead of the injured boy speaking, one of his friends did, "we were sledding through the small hills outside of town when Abner's sled just took off. Almost like magic pulled it away. It zipped by me so fast, that I fell off of mine. And when I caught up to Abner, he was on his side screaming." The kid scratched his messed up dark brown hair. "I think he broke it."

The scream coming from Abner sounded as though he agreed with the other kid's assessment.

"Alright, everyone back up. Give us some space." KeeKee scowled at all of the looky-loos. Then she turned back to Abner and smiled at him. "I'm going to put some snow on your arm, it will help keep down the swelling, and might even lessen some of your pain. Hopefully, a medic will be here shortly."

Abner opened one eye and glanced at KeeKee before closing it again and whimpering.

"Okay, this is going to be cold." KeeKee scooped up two handfuls of snow on the ground next to her knees and then began to make a snow compress on the boy's arm.

Abner howled again and his canines popped out. KeeKee didn't think he was a vampire or an Arctic Wolf Shifter, but he was some sort of shifter. That much she felt in her being to be accurate. Instead of trying to think about what type of shifter the boy was, KeeKee focused on the ice pack she was in the process of making. She prayed the boy would be healed and his pain would abate.

As she added more and more snow, the boy calmed down and stopped screeching in pain. He also stopped moving around on the sled. For just one second, she feared he might have passed out, or worse. But one look at his face told her it was something else.

The boy's face had a golden glow around it, almost as though he was an angel. The lines on his face from all of the pain, and howling, had softened. The kid looked peaceful and KeeKee couldn't see any signs of pain on his face. She was at a loss for how the boy was able to withstand the pain so well.

"Abner?" She asked.

The boy smiled. "Thank you. It doesn't hurt anymore."

KeeKee blinked and opened her mouth but thought better of it and closed it. She looked up when Christian put a hand on her shoulder. "What happened? Did you do this?"

He shook his head. "No, I don't have the gift of healing. Only certain females in my family do." Christian knew his family wasn't missing anyone. There was no way this wolf shifter should have the gift of healing.

KeeKee furrowed her brows, then relaxed her face. She looked down at the ground and then back to Abner. "Looks like you're special. The island decided to heal you with its snow."

"But, that's impossible." Micky, the polar bear shifter who managed the Frozen Bean stated when she knelt down on the other side of Abner.

"I thought anything was possible on this island?" KeeKee grinned, confident that the island had just chosen to help the boy's pain, at the very least. "It may not be healed, it's possible the island used its own snow to remove the pain in the kid's arm."

To prove her wrong, Abner moved his arm around. "Hey, look." He grinned and flexed his hand and moved it in all directions. "I'm healed. Thanks, lady." He jumped up off of his sled and ran to his friends grinning from ear to ear.

"Huh, what do you know?" Christian looked back and forth between Abner and KeeKee.

"I think you just performed a miracle. Are you sure you don't have any sort of useable magic?" Micky asked.

Chapter 9

It had been two days since the snow healed Abner's arm and KeeKee was still trying to explain to everyone how the island chose to heal the boy, not her.

"I'm telling you, it wasn't me. I don't have any magic, other than what I need to shift." KeeKee crossed her arms over her chest and pursed her lips.

Christian chuckled. "I think you have more magic than you realize." He held his hands up when KeeKee threw her arms up and opened her mouth to respond. "Hold up. I'm not saying you used magic knowingly, I understand that magic use is abhorrent to most, if not all, Arctic Wolf Shifters. And I agree. But there is something strange going on here. Mickey said the island doesn't heal supes like that."

With a shrug, KeeKee thought about the possibilities. "Maybe the boy has some inherent magic? Or someone in the crowd healed him? I don't really know, but can we move on from this? We have much bigger fish to fry." KeeKee wasn't comfortable with the looks everyone was giving her, especially Christian.

She knew the lore about the future Mrs. Claus having the ability to heal. The only problem with that was she wasn't a pureblood. Only a pure blood can become Mrs. Claus and have the ability to heal. Besides, she didn't want to be the next Mrs. Claus. That would mean leaving the island and her sisters. She would never leave Sofka or Ree.

And while Santa's pack had welcomed in some different supes over the years, she highly doubted that they would welcome a vampire. Sofka would never leave her mate, and KeeKee wouldn't want her to. Which meant they wouldn't be moving to the North Pole.

Then there was the Unseelie Prince. He might be banned from Faerie, but Santa would never take him in. That would put too much stress on the very fragile peace accords between the Shifter Nations and those from Faerie. Not to mention Queen Mab herself. She doesn't care for Earth, or its inhabitants. Which is probably why Marcus came to Earth to begin with. Earth's inhabitants are beneath her. But KeeKee knew from all that Marcus had said that Mab had a special "hate" for Santa. No matter who wore the suit.

Which would mean that Santa couldn't take in Marcus because it would mean angering Mab. And that means that Ree would never move to the North Pole, either.

"Christian, why don't we focus on what we know for sure, there are spies here on our island and we must identify them before Kirill can attack again." KeeKee felt her shoulders relax when she'd decided that Christian would be impossible to mate with. And she knew that she didn't have the power anyway. The island always did strange things.

Maybe Abner has some special skill the island needs for down the road? She still didn't know what sort of supe Abner was.

He nodded. "You're right. That's what is most important."

"But…" KeeKee raised her index finger and frowned. "Could Abner's race have something to do with his healing ability? Or if it was the island, was it done because Abner is special?"

With a shake of his head and chuckle, Christian put a hand on KeeKee's shoulder. "What do you want? To talk more about Abner? Or to find the rogue supes working with your old alpha?"

KeeKee's shoulders slumped, and she took in a deep breath. "You're right. Of course. We need to figure out who the spies are - like yesterday."

Christian stepped closer and leaned down to whisper in KeeKee's ear, "are you sure you don't want to explore this more?" He motioned between the two of them.

KeeKee felt her cheeks heat up and she stared wide-eyed at Christian's overt flirting. "What? I mean," she cleared her throat and rubbed her hands down the side of her sweater. She looked around at her surroundings and realized that all of her friends had moved away from her. Almost as though they were trying to give Christian and KeeKee some privacy.

They were all in the sheriff's station, but only KeeKee and Christian were standing next to the coffee pot and discussing their next steps.

Christian put a hand on the table next to him and leaned closer. "How about we take a walk, just the two of us?"

KeeKee stepped back and narrowed her eyes. "What game are you playing?" There was no way on Frosty's white plains that Christian, the next Santa Claus, could seriously be interested in KeeKee. And she wasn't just being negative toward herself. She'd seen Christian and Aelita together. They made a striking couple, one that would have the entire Arctic Wolf Shifter Community jumping for candy canes when Christian dawned the big red suit.

"No game." He stood back and tilted his head. "I just want to get to know you better. That's it."

KeeKee arched a brow. She may have been known as the naïve one of the group when they lived back in Siberia, but since coming to the island she'd learned a thing or two about the "real world" and she wasn't going to be taken in by a smooth-talking and handsome male that made her insides tumble all around as though she was inside of a dryer, or on the tallest roller coaster in the world.

KeeKee thanked her lucky snowballs when Sofka and Maxim interrupted them. "I think we need to have a talk with Aelita. None of us are convinced she's part of the Supernatural Black Market, but we won't know until she's questioned." Sofka said.

"You mean interrogated?" Maxim crossed his arms over his chest and let just a bit of his inner vampire come through.

KeeKee always thanked her lucky nutcracker that Maxim was on their side from day one. She never wanted to have to fight him. Although, now that she really thought about it, she didn't like to fight anyone. KeeKee was more of a lover than a fighter. And she was very happy about that.

Except for when she needed to fend off an attack from Kirill's supes.

Then she wished she was better at fighting. At least she had Sofka, who was a total nutcracker when it came to battles.

KeeKee jumped when a loud bang interrupted their plans. She turned to see who had shoved the doors so hard they banged against the wall and sent ripples through the floor of the Sheriff's station.

"Quick, KeeKee you're needed in the city center," Micky yelled out before turning hastily and running back toward the center of town.

"What?" KeeKee frowned and looked at Christian.

"Come on, we can ask questions when we get there." Christian took KeeKee's hand and led her out of the office and down the small road toward a large crowd that surrounded something just outside of the Frozen Bean Coffee Shop.

"If they think I can heal, they're going to be very disappointed." KeeKee slowed her almost jog to a normal walking pace as she made her way inside the circle of supes. She stopped so quickly when she got into the center of the circle, Christian walked into her back.

"What's going on?" Christian asked.

"Surprise!" The entire group yelled at once. Then Abner and his parents walked toward KeeKee with smiles a mile wide.

Abner's mother took KeeKee's hand in hers. "Thank you so much for healing our son. I don't know what you did to heal his broken arm, but we are all so thankful to you."

"Ahhh." KeeKee didn't know what to say. "I don't think it was me. I am confident the island is the one you need to thank. I don't have the sort of magic needed to heal a broken arm, or even a papercut."

Abner's mother looked between Christian and KeeKee then smiled. "Oh, I think you might."

Before KeeKee could protest any further, Micky walked up to her and handed her a plate with a large slice of chocolate cake. "Here, for the supe of the hour. You may not believe, but we all do." She waved at the crowd around them. "Cake is on the table outside of the Frozen Bean, help yourselves." Micky motioned toward where the other baristas stood ready to hand out plates of cake to anyone who wanted a slice.

"Micky, I really don't think it was me. It's not possible for an Arctic Wolf Shifter to do that."

Micky only smiled and moved on.

Stunned, KeeKee stood there taking in the sights and sounds around her. While the town center had been decorated for Christmas for a while, they had obviously added more decorations. A sound system was set up playing traditional Christmas music over outdoor speakers.

Outside of the coffee shop was another Christmas tree, this one purple and decorated with silver and while ornaments. KeeKee focused her eyes on a few and grinned. Micky had decorated the tree with a coffee theme. There were miniature coffee mugs, bags of coffee, rectangular ornaments with the logo of the coffee shop, and a variety of tools used in making the different coffee drinks. A lot of effort had gone into that tree.

Plus, more twinkle lights had been added around the square. The lighting felt as though it was something from a Christmas movie the humans loved so much. The lights were on now and it was brighter than it had been yesterday when she was here.

There were other touches of Christmas added all over town. And if she wasn't mistaken, there was even a bough of mistletoe hanging from an evergreen garland in the very center of the square. She'd have to keep that in mind and steer clear of it whenever males were around.

A handsome male sauntered up next to KeeKee, a plate of cake in one hand, and a coffee in the other. "If I was you, I'd take the kudos for healing the boy." He saluted KeeKee with his mug before taking a sip. Then he put his cup down on one of the folding chairs that had been brought out just for this occasion.

KeeKee stared at the male supe, trying to remember his name. While she'd never formally met the guy, she knew who he was. It came to her, and she grinned. Nikolai Temuulen was probably one of the most handsome males on the island. He may even be more handsome than Marcus, but she'd never say that to Marcus.

From what KeeKee had witnessed, Nikolai was just as vain as Marcus was, too. "Um, thanks?" She shrugged. "Do you know Abner?"

He grinned, then licked a bit of icing from the edge of his lips. "Of course, he's my nephew."

KeeKee blinked a few times when he flipped his head and watched as his long sandy brown hair moved in a perfect arc to frame his face. When he smiled, two dimples showcased against his high cheekbones making him look as though he was a movie star who had perfected the head flip for the cameras. She even heard a few sighs behind her.

While KeeKee didn't know this supe, she knew of his reputation. Most of her friends who did know him, tended to steer clear of the prima donna. He loved the attention of any female and tended to ignore the males, unless they fawned all over him, which was rare. Usually, the males tended to resent Nikolai taking all of the female attention.

He leaned in close. "How about we have dinner tonight? You know, to celebrate your new celebrity status."

To say KeeKee was shocked would be an understatement. He had never even looked her way before today. "No, thanks. I have other plans."

His eyebrows raised and he stood taller. "Then, tomorrow we will have coffee together." He began to walk away, but KeeKee grabbed his arm.

"I don't think so. I'm really busy right now. And while most of the island might believe I healed Abner, I'm telling you, it wasn't me." KeeKee tilted her head and looked him up and down.

Nikolai gave her a sly smile. "Like what you see?"

"Hm? Oh, no. I'm trying to figure out what type of Supe you and Abner are. I was wondering if Abner had the ability to heal himself, or if the Island needed him to be healed for some reason." Again, KeeKee found herself asking rude questions, but if everyone was going to keep assuming she had done the healing, she really needed to find out the truth.

Nikolai smirked. "Of course you weren't checking me out. But since you asked so nicely, I'm an Altai Argali Shifter."

KeeKee had a bite of cake in her mouth, and she almost choked when Nikolai confessed to being a very rare Mountain Sheep shifter. No wonder he was so full of himself. She couldn't help it, her eyes moved to his biceps. He wore a thick, white winter coat that hid his muscles, but she'd heard about his kind. They were generally strong as oxen and every single one of them were extremely handsome. It was no wonder he attracted so much attention. "I've never met a Mountain Sheep Shifter. How many of you are on this island?"

"I'm not a mountain sheep, I'm a Mongolian Altai Argali Shifter." Nikolai bristled and walked away leaving behind his half-eaten cake and empty coffee mug.

"Well, okay then." KeeKee finished her cake and picked up the trash Nikolai left behind. She took it all and put in the trash can Micky had set up outside of the coffee shop.

"Micky, thank you for setting this up. The cake is fantastic." KeeKee hugged her friend and then turned to head back to the Sheriff's office.

Chapter 10

KeeKee felt the pressure of the expectations weighing heavily on her. Surrounded by all these festive decorations, the glittering snow, the twinkling lights, it felt all the more suffocating, when she couldn't shake the nagging sense that something was amiss. Misfit Island was filled with joy and perseverance, qualities that she herself had managed to nurture since she arrived. Yet now, standing amidst the suspicion and the talk of a supernatural black market, her heart clenched with the realization that trust, something which had come to her so tentatively before, was once again slipping out of her grasp.

As Abner's mother moved away, cooing at the still-smiling boy running to his friends, KeeKee looked to Christian, who was watching her with a contemplative furrow in his brow.

"Was it really the island?" Christian murmured, more to himself than to anyone else, although KeeKee heard every word. Her throat tightened as she wondered, for what felt like the hundredth time since the event of Abner's healing, if some latent power within her had decided to manifest all of a sudden. But no, that couldn't be true.

She inhaled deeply, letting the cold air sting her lungs before saying, "It has to be. I wouldn't even know where to begin with something like that." Her voice was firm, but somewhere deep down, uncertainty lingered.

Christian regarded her with those piercing ice-blue eyes of his, the ones that spoke of ancient wisdom far beyond his years. "KeeKee, you are an Arctic Wolf Shifter from a noble lineage. Even if you are of mixed blood, it doesn't negate your potential. We don't always know what we're capable of until the moment calls for it."

KeeKee shook her head. "But I don't have any training or background with magic. Besides, only those purebred wolves who are from your family carry the traces of magic, and even then, it requires rigorous training to wield in any meaningful way."

"Maybe so. But this...this was something different. Micky said the island doesn't heal just anyone. And certainly not using its own snow. To shield, yes. To warm where there should be no warmth, to protect, to cover tracks, even. But to heal?" He let the thought drift into the air between them, his words quiet but impactful.

KeeKee's heart hurt at the thought. She had never been destined for great things. Yes, she was cunning and smart, but she learned at a young age to stay in the shadows, avoiding too much attention. Her strength had always been in her ability to plan, to strategize, to understand people and situations. Magic, even the possibility of it, had never crossed her mind.

She turned toward the town square where a small group of carolers had begun singing, their voices cheerfully cutting through the chill.

The scent of spiced apple cider and pumpkin spice wafted through the air. The normalcy of the festive atmosphere was a stark contrast to the turmoil growing inside her.

"I can't... I just can't believe that I could do something like that," KeeKee said, hating the way her voice trembled as she spoke. "Christmastime is supposed to be one of joy and hope, but the thought of me having some mysterious ability to heal someone frightens me more than anything."

Christian stepped closer, his presence comforting even though she tried to convince herself that it shouldn't be. "It's alright to be afraid, KeeKee. Powers like these, if they do exist within you, can be daunting. But fear does not have to be your enemy. It can be a guide, steering you towards your purpose."

KeeKee's gaze hardened. "And what purpose would that be? To become some... some vessel for magic that I've never wanted, never trained for? What if that magic isn't controllable, Christian? What if—" That last thing KeeKee wanted was to become anything at all like Sherrie, the witch who had turned the gargoyles into living creatures as a way of gaining more magic. She knew that magic in and of itself wasn't necessarily bad, but when mixed with supernatural creatures, it could be intoxicating in a way that drove the supe to crave more and more - like a drug.

Christian took another step closer, gently gripping her shoulders and turning her to face him. "Whatever happens, KeeKee, you won't have to face it alone. Here on Misfit Island, none of us are alone."

Those simple words, coupled with his steady presence, soothed a small part of her. A part that wanted to believe, wanted to trust him and trust that she wasn't destined to be feared or used, but rather something more. Time felt treacherous to her, like each second that slipped away was artificial, revealing only fragments of what was to come.

Misfit Island, despite its name and being shrouded in both mystery and joyous Christmas cheer, was a place where those like her were meant to find peace. Security. Even answers.

The sound of a child's laughter brought KeeKee out of her thoughts, and she looked up to see Abner surrounded by his friends, his arm clearly in no pain, as he showed off his new sledding technique. He looked so full of life and energy, as though nothing had ever happened to him.

"He's just a boy," KeeKee whispered, more to herself than anyone else, "and yet his innocence has a way of making you believe that maybe, just maybe, this island is full of miracles we haven't even begun to understand." She watched him dash down the small slope, his friends following close behind with gleeful shouts. The sight was enough to bring a small smile to her lips, though it was tinged with uncertainty.

Christian followed her gaze, the corners of his mouth lifting slightly. "It seems even in the midst of all this chaos, life finds a way to be joyful. Perhaps that's something we should take comfort in."

KeeKee looked at him, searching his eyes for the sincerity that his voice promised. And she found it—genuine and unguarded. The way the sunlight caught off the snow on the ground reflected in his pale eyes, casting them in a shade of blue that reminded her of an endless winter sky.

"I want to believe that," she said softly. "I do. But there's so much we still don't know, so much left unanswered. Like why Kirill would risk so much, burning every bridge just to get us back. There's more to this than just losing three pack members. No one goes to these lengths unless they're hiding something. Something big."

"Exactly," Christian replied. "Which is why we need to be vigilant. Kirill's actions suggest more than just old grudges. There's a dangerous game being played, and we're not privy to all the rules. Not yet."

KeeKee breathed in, the action grounding her thoughts. "Yet. That's the key. We have to figure out what's motivating him, what he's hoping to gain. And we need to do it before it's too late."

Christian nodded, his demeanor shifting from the gentle reassurance of a moment ago to one of steely resolve. "We will. But we can't rush this, or we risk tipping our hand too early. For now, we focus on gathering intelligence and identifying the spies still hiding right under our noses."

KeeKee glanced over her shoulder at the other supes milling about the square. The backdrop of holiday cheer, coupled with an undercurrent of tension, wasn't lost on her. "Do you think... could they be working for Kirill, or is there another player in this?"

"Both are possible," Christian admitted. "But until we have solid evidence, we need to investigate from all angles. Whoever they are, whether working directly for Kirill or for someone else entirely, we must approach this delicately. Missteps could lead to disaster—not only for us but for the entire island."

KeeKee sighed, a mix of frustration and determination bubbling within her. Every path they needed to follow seemed to twist and turn into a labyrinth of deception and hidden intentions. And yet, she knew, deep down, that allowing herself—or anyone else—to be swept away by fear wasn't an option. It never had been.

She stood taller, a new resolve bracing her spine. "We'll do it together. We'll find out who the spies are and keep Kirill from whatever it is he's planning. This island has become home, and I refuse to let that be taken from us."

A small smile tugged at the corner of Christian's lips. "That's the spirit, KeeKee. We'll protect this place, and each other, no matter the cost."

"Indeed, we will," a voice chimed in from behind them.

KeeKee and Christian turned to find Sofka standing there, her eyes gleaming with that typical fierce determination of hers, and Maxim right beside her, the vampire's expression as inscrutable as ever.

"I couldn't help but overhear," Sofka continued, "and I agree. Kirill isn't the type to do anything without a reason... one big enough to justify his risks. Whether it's us, this island, or something else entirely, we're going to unravel that mystery. And soon."

Maxim's voice was low, almost predatory. "We've got the entire island on alert. It's time we set some traps of our own."

KeeKee felt a shiver run down her spine at the intensity in Maxim's tone. She nodded firmly. "We can't let our guards down. Not for a second."

Sofka adjusted her stance, her presence commanding. "Agreed. Starting tomorrow, I'll be coordinating surveillance with the Sheriff. We're going to tighten the net around these spies, whoever they are."

Christian exchanged a look with KeeKee, a silent acknowledgment passing between them. They were far from done, and the road ahead promised to be perilous. But they weren't alone in this.

"I'll look into the new arrivals again," Christian added. "There's been movement... whispers among them about timing on certain 'deals,' though nothing has been confirmed yet. We need to focus on that too. See if we can sniff out who's involved in this trafficking ring."

"And I'll see what else I can find out from our friends," KeeKee said, determination lacing her voice. "Horatio at the Welcome Center is always a treasure trove of information, especially with all the newcomers."

Sofka nodded, her eyes narrowing slightly as her mind raced ahead. "Good. Let's make sure that by the time Kirill moves his next piece, we're already three steps ahead."

The silent agreement among them solidified their resolve. This wasn't just an impromptu alliance—they were a pack, a family, even with Christian included in that now. Each of their skills and abilities would be necessary if they were to protect Misfit Island from whatever storm was brewing.

As the carolers continued to sing, and the festive ambiance swirled around them, KeeKee felt a warmth inside, one not entirely attributable to Christian's proximity. There was something about this group she had found herself surrounded by. Their shared purpose, their willingness to fight for one another, felt like an extension of the Christmas spirit itself: a commitment to light, hope, and resilience in the face of darkness.

"You're right," she said softly, almost to herself, as she looked around at the friends, the allies, who had gathered around her. "Together, we'll figure this out."

Christian's hand found hers, his grip firm but gentle. "We will. One step at a time."

KeeKee nodded, squeezing his hand back before letting go. "And whatever secrets this island holds, we'll uncover them. We'll be ready for whatever Kirill or anyone else tries to throw our way."

The four of them—KeeKee, Christian, Sofka, and Maxim—stood together, surrounded by the holiday cheer of Misfit Island, but united by a much deeper bond: their shared determination to protect all that they held dear.

Tomorrow they would begin setting their traps, tightening their surveillance, and continuing the hunt for the spies that lingered amidst the snow-covered trees and twinkling lights. Whatever came next, they would face it head-on.

And as the carolers' song lifted high into the cool winter sky, KeeKee found herself holding onto a hope that even in the deepest waters of suspicion and mystery, the light of trust and unity would guide them to shore.

For now, they had one another, and that was something worth celebrating in the heart.

Chapter 11

KeeKee shivered in the cool night air as she slipped into the small workshop they had set up in an abandoned old building on the outskirts of town. The light turned on overhead, illuminating stacks of colorful wrapping paper and glimmering bows: the tools of her newfound passion for giving.

"Are you ready?" Sofka whispered, her excitement barely contained as she joined KeeKee, her breath visible in the nippy air. She wore a festive red hoodie under a warm down jacket, a hint of mischief dancing in her ice-blue eyes.

"More than ready!" KeeKee grinned, adjusting a stocking cap over her hair. "I still can't believe we're actually doing this. Secret Santa on Misfit Island? It feels like a dream."

Sofka chuckled, bouncing on her heels. "It's a 100% true dream. But remember, we have to be stealthy. No one can know this is us, at least for now."

KeeKee nodded, her heart pounding with excitement. "Don't worry; we'll keep it under wraps. It'll be like old times. Just you, me, and a mountain of gifts. Well, almost like old times. If only Ree were here with us."

Sofka put a hand on her best friend's shoulder. "Ree would totally love this. But we agreed that no one else would know."

"I know, I know. It's just that I miss it being just the three of us." Since Sofka and Ree had both mated, KeeKee had been feeling left out of things. However, now that she was a part of this new project, she felt as though things were getting back on track for her.

Before, Secret Santa had left special gifts on certain doorsteps. Tonight, it would be much more. KeeKee had suggested they do something similar to an Easter Egg hunt, she called it a Sugar Plum Fairy Hunt.

As they shifted into action, the two friends worked tirelessly, crafting handmade gifts with boundless creativity. They spent hours decorating gingerbread cookies shaped like little wolves, and painting ornaments cleverly styled after their favorite things from life on Misfit Island. KeeKee, with her knack for details, put together unique charm bracelets using bits and baubles they found around the barn while Sofka worked on cozy knit hats, each embellished with shining bells.

"Do you think the island knows what we're up to?" KeeKee mused, her hands deftly tying a red ribbon around a box filled with cookies.

Sofka shrugged, a mischievous smirk on her lips. "I don't think so. But it would be pretty funny if it did and started helping us out! Can you imagine? Glitter showers and snowflakes appearing every time we tried to deliver?"

KeeKee laughed, picturing the chaos. "Well, let's be glad the island isn't too talkative." She turned serious for a moment, thinking of how much the residents had been through after the attack. "I just hope they enjoy our treats. I wish I could see their faces when they find them."

"They will," Sofka replied confidently, pulling out her knitting needles to tighten the loose ends on one of her hats. "I've seen the way the island residents light up during the holidays. It's like we can sprinkle a little happiness around, even if it's just for a moment."

KeeKee felt a swell of warmth at Sofka's words. "Exactly! This island deserves a bit of magic, especially after everything that's happened."

As they chatted about the gifts, the atmosphere transformed into one of nostalgia and joy as they reminisced about Christmases from their childhood, before their parents had died. When they finished packing the last of their gifts, the excitement was palpable.

"Alright, time to deliver the goods," KeeKee said, her eyes sparkling with anticipation as they prepared to step out into the crisp night.

Sofka nodded, adjusting her scarf. "We should start with the town square first. That way we can easily spread our gifts far and wide without anyone catching us."

Stepping quietly around the old peeling paint and rusted metal, they emerged into the moonlit night, the air fresh and crisp. Each step crunched lightly on the snow-covered paths, making their way toward the heart of Misfit Island.

As they reached the town square, KeeKee took a moment to take in the festive decorations. The snow glittered under the light of the twinkling Christmas lights strung across the buildings, livening the atmosphere. "It's beautiful," she breathed, momentarily awestruck by the decorations adorning every nook and cranny.

"Okay, enough staring; let's get moving!" Sofka urged, sharing a knowing smile with her friend before reaching into her satchel to pull out the first stack of gifts.

They began to carefully lay out their presents, tucking them behind trees, under benches, and near the warm glow of the exterior lights. The last few times they'd left gifts on people's porches. But that way took too much time, they weren't Santa Claus, so this time they left their gifts in places where the local supes would find them on their way into work or to gather supplies for the week.

KeeKee giggled as she left a pile of cookies for the sheriff, knowing that Roscoe would relish the taste of homemade treats.

As they distributed their gifts, a few other residents of the island were out and about. The two Secret Santas kept to the shadows or hid behind buildings in order to keep their identities a secret. KeeKee felt a flicker of joy ignite within her. She wanted everyone to feel this happiness.

"Wait," Sofka whispered suddenly, crouching down as they snuck around a corner. "Did you hear that?"

KeeKee strained her ears, catching whispers that seemed to come from the entrance of the bakery. "Someone's talking. Should we check it out?"

"It sounds suspicious," Sofka warned, though her curiosity flickered in her eyes. They inched closer, blending into the shadows.

The two slipped around the corner, and as they did, the voices grew clearer. "Did you hear about the gifts randomly appearing around the island? The people are starting to wonder who is behind it."

A darker voice responded, laced with contempt, "It's probably some ploy by Santa's family. It's all too good to be true. Or maybe the island itself has begun doing its own kind of magic."

KeeKee and Sofka exchanged a worried glance. Their hearts raced, realizing that whispers of their Secret Santa project had become fodder to the gossip mill, and some members of the supernatural community on the island didn't sound too happy, or thankful.

"I guess we should head back," KeeKee whispered urgently. "We don't want to draw any attention to ourselves. If they're onto us…"

"Then we'll have to be even sneakier," Sofka concluded, more determined than ever. "Our mission is far from over. Besides, I still have more hats to knit."

"Maybe we should make sure those two received special gifts tonight." KeeKee wasn't sure, but she thought that their complaint might stem from the fact that they hadn't received anything yet.

Sofka looked at her accomplice and grinned. "Definitely."

With that, they dashed back to the shadows, their hearts pounding from the thrill of the night and a growing realization that their joyful mission could spiral into something else altogether. As they made their way back to the workshop, KeeKee couldn't shake off the inescapable feeling that they were only beginning to scratch the surface of all that was happening on Misfit Island.

Tomorrow would bring fresh challenges, and as the thought of it settled in, her resolve to keep their secret Santa project running was only strengthened. Christmas cheer wouldn't just spread itself, someone had to be the unseen hands of Christmas Cheer.

Their laughter filled the chilly air as they slipped back into the workshop, the warmth from the evening's excitement mingling with the aroma of fresh pine and sugary treats. KeeKee couldn't help but feel a surge of accomplishment; they had spread a little joy, even if a few of the townspeople weren't exactly buzzing with excitement about the mysterious gifts. Two of them might change their mind come morning.

"Can you believe they're already talking about us?" KeeKee said, shaking her head in disbelief. "We've barely started, and they're already wondering who's behind it."

Sofka grinned as she began organizing the remnants of their gift-making supplies. "They're curious about magic, and this island is known for its surprises. I suppose it's not too shocking that we've drawn interest." She leaned over, meticulously adding a few extra stickers to the decorated boxes they had yet to deliver.

With nimble fingers, KeeKee picked up a couple of spare ornaments. "We could always throw them off our scent. You know, have some small gifts show up on our own doorsteps. It might redirect their attention away from us."

Sofka raised a brow in thought. "That's not a bad idea."

"Exactly! And it could add a dash of fun!" With sudden enthusiasm, KeeKee rummaged through their supplies, collecting all manner of odds and ends. There were confetti-filled baubles, brightly painted wooden trees, and even mini sleighs made from twigs. "What do you think Ree would like?" She held up a red and white striped hat that Sofka had finished a few days back, but hadn't given away yet.

Sofka grinned from ear to ear. "Perfect. And I think I have a matching cap over here for Marcus. Can you imagine him wearing a cap that matches his mate?"

Both of them giggled and looked around for a few more items they could wrap and deliver on their way home.

But as they busied themselves, the underlying tension about Kirill loomed over their heads. They needed joy, but the darkness of their reality was hard to shake off. They both kept glancing toward the doorway, half-expecting to see someone creeping in to confront them about their secret.

"Okay, let's keep our heads down while delivering these," Sofka said after a brief silence. "We can't let them know who we are. Also, as much as I want to gift everyone, we have to keep some for later."

"Right. We can't let Kirill think we're not on high alert, either." KeeKee agreed resolutely, the thought of the nefarious alpha creeping back into her mind. "We do need to check in with Christian and the others to see if there's any news about Aelita's roommates. I wonder if any of them are truly working with Kirill, or if they are just being anti-social?"

Keeping the element of surprise on their side, they slipped out into the night once more. The world around them was laced in a blanket of twinkling stars, and the gaslamps cast a soft glow against the pure white snow. They moved quickly, distributing gifts to every possible nook and cranny without attracting attention to themselves, whispering playful enthusiasm about where they might hide the next pile.

At one point, they decided to tuck a few treats under benches by the town square, near where Abner's friends often played. There was joy in leaving the cookies and ornaments, knowing they would bring smiles to the kids' faces when they found them in the morning.

KeeKee's heart swelled with warmth each time she imagined the laughter echoing through the crisp morning air upon discovery. "What if we left some gifts with little notes too? You know, as if they were written by the island itself?" she suggested, excitement dancing in her eyes.

"Perfect! Just give it a little twisting mystery. A reminder that Misfit Island is magical, rather than us." Sofka's face lit up with an idea. "We can write small notes suggesting whatever they found, was part of the island's magic at Christmastime—giving them a chance to connect to the very spirit of this place."

"We could even ask them to pay it forward. You know, ask them to consider making a gift to give to someone secretly." KeeKee laughed at the prospect. "Now I really think we can solidify our mythos here. You know we'll create a whole legend at this rate!"

As night turned into the early hours of morning, their laughter mixed with the sound of crunching snow beneath their boots. Gift by gift was placed artfully—first near the Frozen Bean, then toward Island Burgers, until they had almost run out.

At one last stop, they placed a large sack filled with goodies underneath the festive gazebo in the town center. The sight almost made her swell with pride. "We did it! The second phase of Secret Santa successfully delivered," KeeKee said, nearly bouncing with happiness.

Sofka grinned, "And no one knows a thing!"

With that secret shared between just them, they turned, ready to make a final run toward the workshop for the special gifts they were going to leave for themselves, to throw everyone off their scent. But as they approached the door, a crisp voice rang out behind them.

"Where do you ladies think you're sneaking off to?"

KeeKee spun around, her heart racing as she spotted Christian leaning against a nearby tree—his arms crossed, an amused grin on his face. "Oh no," she said, glancing at Sofka as panic surged, "I thought we had been quiet as mice!"

"You're quite the stealthy little Santas," Christian replied, pushing off from the tree to close in on them. "But that doesn't mask the friendly magic hovering in the air." He stepped forward, a charismatic glimmer in his ice-blue eyes.

KeeKee exchanged a look with Sofka, and before they could form an excuse, he continued, "Could it be that our very own Arctic Wolves have taken on the mantle of Christmas cheerleaders? I won't tell anyone if you won't. You have my word."

"Um, we can explain." KeeKee started, before curling her fingers into her palm. It struck her then how unChristmas it felt to confess. What they were doing was supposed to be a secret, not something that anyone could praise - or judge - them for. But Christian seemed more curious than anything, his eyes glistening with wonder rather than judgment.

"Relax!" Christian laughed, clearly finding humor in their slight panic. "I'm not here to ruin your fun. I just want to know if you need extra hands. Word has it, you're leaving gifts for the entire island."

"What does it matter to you?" Sofka asked, but her tone held more curiosity than defiance. "Aren't you too busy figuring out who's behind those black-market dealings to bother with us?"

Christian laughed, good-naturedly shaking his head. "I think this island could use a bit of joy amidst all that's swirling through the darkness, especially around the Christmas holidays. I want to help—discretely, of course."

KeeKee shared a quick glance with Sofka, silently deliberating their options. The idea of involving Christian in their Secret Santa project felt both thrilling and worrying. What if he let it slip? But, on the other hand, his charisma and dedication could undoubtedly enhance their mission.

"Weren't you just saying that you couldn't do something like because it would make it obvious to anyone who knew you were doing it that you are the son of Santa?" Sofka asked.

"Hmm." Christian pondered her question for a moment. "You might be right, but I just can't help myself. I need to be involved, somehow."

"Okay, if you promise to keep it under wraps, you can help us." KeeKee finally conceded.

"What are you planning? Will it be more than just cookies and fun trinkets?" His smile widened as he stepped back to create some space.

"Of course! We figured we might leave a few more gifts embellished with some additional holiday magic," KeeKee explained, her enthusiasm building as she spoke. "There will be little notes from the island itself, encouraging the residents that hope is never truly lost."

Christian's eyes lit up with delight. "That's brilliant! The spirit of Christmas could use a more hands-on touch with this dark cloud lurking over us."

"We thought it would spread cheer and distract folks from whatever is going on in the shadows," Sofka said. "Especially given the way the whispers have echoed through town."

Christian nodded, a glint of determination in his eyes. "Count me in. Let me help you build on the magic you're already creating.

Together, we can ensure that the spirit of the season is felt by the entire island."

"Which means we'll have to be stealthy and clever about it," KeeKee cautioned, her heart thumping with excitement. "We need to ensure no one suspects anything while drawing them into the joy that this island holds."

With a new sense of camaraderie, the three of them began to plot their next moves, determined to expand their merry mission even further. KeeKee felt a warmth blossoming in her chest and wondered if, perhaps, a bit of the magic from Christmas would spread beyond gifts and treats, embedding itself in the very fabric of their alliances forged against the chilling shadows that threatened to envelop their beloved Misfit Island.

As they plotted under the moonlit sky, the frost-tipped edges of the island shimmered with promise, and a sense of unity bloomed between them, surging forth with a bright hope that perhaps, just perhaps, they could face the coming storm. Ultimately, no dark schemes could withstand the warmth of love, hope, and friendship that thrived amidst the Christmas season.

Chapter 12

Early morning on Misfit Island brought with it a sense of adventure as a new day began. Mist lay over the freshly fallen snow, almost like something out of a fairie tale. KeeKee and Sofka sat huddled together on a bench in the town square, steam rising from their mugs of hot cocoa as they watched the island slowly come to life.

"I can't believe how well our Secret Santa mission is going," Sofka said, her eyes sparkling with excitement. "Did you see the look on Horatio's face when he found that hand-knitted scarf?"

KeeKee nodded, a smile spreading across her face. "And Carmen's reaction to the tropical fruit basket we left for her? I thought she was going to burst into tears of joy."

"It's not just the gifts," Sofka mused. "Have you noticed how people are starting to talk to each other more? Even some of the grumpier residents are beginning to open up."

KeeKee took a sip of her cocoa, savoring the rich chocolate flavor. "You're right. I overheard Julianna and Nikolai actually having a civil conversation yesterday. Who would have thought?" He was probably trying to get her to go out with him, since he was turning out to be the biggest flirt on the island. But better her than KeeKee.

As they continued to chat, KeeKee couldn't help but feel a sense of pride wash over her. Their little project was doing more than just spreading holiday cheer; it was fostering a deeper sense of community on the island.

"We should probably start thinking about our next round of gifts," Sofka said, pulling out a small notebook from her pocket. "I was thinking we could-"

Her words were cut short as Christian approached, his face a mix of concern and determination. "Ladies," he greeted them, his voice low. "Mind if I join you?"

KeeKee felt her heart skip a beat at the sight of him, but quickly pushed the feeling aside. "Of course not," she said, scooting over to make room. "What's on your mind?"

Christian sat down, his body tense. "I've been doing some digging," he began, glancing around to ensure no one was within earshot. "Word on the street is that Kirill is on the move again."

Sofka's eyes narrowed. "What kind of move?"

"Nothing concrete yet," Christian replied, running a hand through his hair. "But there's been chatter about him gathering resources, reaching out to old contacts. I'm planning to document his movements, see if we can get ahead of whatever he's planning."

KeeKee felt a chill run down her spine that had nothing to do with the cold. "Do you think he's coming back here?"

Christian shook his head. "I don't know. But whatever he's up to, it can't be good."

The three sat in silence for a moment, the weight of Christian's words hanging heavy in the air. KeeKee couldn't help but notice the way Christian's brow furrowed, the tension in his shoulders. There was something else bothering him, something beyond Kirill's potential threat.

"Christian," she said softly, "what else is on your mind?"

He looked at her, surprise flickering across his face before he let out a deep sigh. "Am I that transparent?"

Sofka snorted. "Only to those of us with eyes."

Christian managed a small smile before his expression turned serious again. "It's just... I feel torn," he admitted. "Between my family's legacy and... well, and this place. These people. You."

KeeKee felt her breath catch in her throat. She knew Christian had been struggling with his role as the future Santa Claus, but hearing him voice his conflict made it all the more real. Since he hadn't taken the *hat*, she figured he must have been struggling with his future. Santa always began his term at the ripe old age of eighteen.

"I understand," she said, placing a hand on his arm. "But you know we support you, no matter what you decide."

Christian nodded, his eyes meeting hers. "I know. And that's what makes it even harder."

Before anyone could respond, Sheriff Roscoe's booming voice cut through the square. "Christian! KeeKee! Sofka! We need you at the station, pronto!"

The three exchanged worried glances before quickly getting to their feet. As they made their way to the sheriff's office, KeeKee couldn't shake the feeling that their peaceful morning was about to become a distant memory.

Inside the station, they found Sheriff Roscoe pacing back and forth, his normally jovial face creased with worry. Maxim stood in the corner, his arms crossed and his expression unreadable.

"What's going on?" Sofka asked as they entered.

Roscoe stopped pacing and turned to face them. "We've received an anonymous tip," he said, his voice grave. "Someone's been spotted skulking around the boat dock on the southern tip of Chile, asking questions about Kirill and his old hideouts."

KeeKee felt her heart rate quicken as she exchanged looks with Christian. "Do we know who it is?"

Maxim shook his head. "No positive ID yet. But whoever it is, they're not locals from the continent."

Christian stepped forward, his eyes blazing with determination. "This has to be connected to Kirill's recent activities. We need to step up our defenses, prepare for a potential confrontation."

Roscoe nodded in agreement. "I've already put the word out to be on high alert. But we need to be smart about this. We can't let panic spread through the community."

"Hold up," Sofka spoke above the voices. "If someone is looking for Kirill, it doesn't necessarily mean they are working for him." She arched a brow.

Marcus, who had been leaning against the back wall with leg bent and his foot propped against the wall, kicked off the wall and approached them. "Sofka might be on to something. Think about it. If someone was working for Kirill, wouldn't he know where Kirill was?"

Roscoe rubbed his chin. "You could be on to something here, even more reason we need to keep our guard up."

As the group began to discuss strategies and patrol schedules, KeeKee found her mind wandering back to their Secret Santa project. It seemed almost trivial now, in the face of this new threat. But then she remembered the smiles on people's faces, the way the community had started to come together.

"We can't stop our holiday activities," she said suddenly, causing everyone to turn and look at her.

"KeeKee," Maxim began, his tone cautious, "I'm not sure now is the time-"

"No, hear me out," she interrupted. "The whole point of the variety of Christmas festivities to bring this community together, to create a sense of unity and trust. We need that now more than ever." While she still wasn't ready to let anyone know it was Sofka and her giving out the small gifts, there were plenty of other events the small island had planned for the time leading up to the big day.

Sofka nodded enthusiastically. "She's right. If we let fear take over, if we stop living our lives, then Kirill's already won."

Christian's eyes met KeeKee's, a look of admiration and something deeper passing between them. "I agree," he said. "We need to be vigilant, yes. But we also need to show whoever's out there that we're strong, that we're a community that stands together."

Sheriff Roscoe stroked his chin thoughtfully. "You make a good point. Alright, we'll continue with the holiday plans. But," he added, his voice turning stern, "I want everyone to be extra careful. Report anything suspicious immediately."

As the meeting wrapped up and everyone began to file out of the station, Christian caught KeeKee's arm. "Can we talk?" he asked softly.

KeeKee nodded, her heart racing as they stepped outside into the crisp winter air. They walked in silence for a few moments before Christian spoke.

"I just wanted to thank you," he said. "For reminding us what's really important."

KeeKee smiled up at him. "We can't let fear dictate our lives. Especially not here, not on Misfit Island."

Christian nodded, his expression serious. "I've been thinking a lot about what you said earlier, about supporting me no matter what I decide." He paused, taking a deep breath. "The truth is, I'm scared. Scared of letting my family down, scared of letting this community down. But when I'm with you, when I see the way you care for everyone here... it makes me believe that maybe I can find a way to do both."

KeeKee felt a warmth spread through her chest that had nothing to do with the hot cocoa she'd drunk earlier. "Christian," she said softly, "you don't have to choose. Your family, this island, they're all part of who you are. And who you are is pretty amazing."

Christian's eyes widened slightly at her words, a smile tugging at the corners of his mouth. For a moment, it seemed like he might say something more, but then Sheriff Roscoe's voice boomed across the square, calling for Christian.

"Duty calls," Christian said with a rueful smile. "But KeeKee? Thank you. For everything."

As he jogged off to meet the sheriff, KeeKee watched him go, her heart full of conflicting emotions. She knew that whatever challenges lay ahead, they would face them together. As a community, as friends, and maybe, just maybe, as something more.

With renewed determination, she set off to find Sofka. They had a Secret Santa mission to continue, and a community to uplift. The storm might be coming, but for now, they would create as much warmth and joy as they could. After all, that was the true spirit of Misfit Island, and no threat, not even Kirill, could take that away from them.

Chapter 13

The early morning air was crisp, carrying with it the scent of pine and wood smoke from chimneys dotting the landscape. KeeKee pulled her coat tighter around her as she made her way towards the Sheriff's Office, her boots crunching in the fresh snow.

As she approached, she could see a small crowd already gathered outside. Sofka and Maxim stood huddled together, their breaths visible in the cold air. Christian was there too, deep in conversation with Sheriff Roscoe. The tension in the air was palpable, a stark contrast to the festive decorations that adorned the buildings around them, a recent addition if KeeKee remembered correctly.

"KeeKee!" Sofka called out, waving her over. "You're just in time. Roscoe's about to start the meeting."

KeeKee nodded, joining her friends as they filed into the office. The small space was soon packed, with familiar faces from all corners of the island present. She spotted Horatio, his usual jovial expression replaced by one of concern. Carmen was there too, perched on a chair near the back, her bright eyes a splash of color in the somber room.

Sheriff Roscoe cleared his throat, the sound cutting through the murmur of voices. "Alright, folks," he began, his deep voice carrying easily through the room. "I know you're all wondering why I've called this meeting. Well, I'm not gonna sugarcoat it. We've got trouble brewing."

A ripple of unease passed through the crowd. KeeKee felt Christian shift beside her, his arm brushing against hers. The brief contact sent a spark through her, but she forced herself to focus on Roscoe's words.

"We've received intelligence that Kirill might be planning something big," Roscoe continued. "Now, I know that name strikes fear in many of you, and rightfully so. But I want to make one thing clear: we are not helpless. This island, this community, is stronger than any threat Kirill can throw at us."

Murmurs of agreement rippled through the crowd. KeeKee felt a swell of pride in her chest. This was the Misfit Island she knew and loved – a place where even the most diverse group of supernatural beings could come together in the face of adversity.

"That being said," Roscoe went on, his expression growing serious, "we need to be prepared. I'm implementing new security measures effective immediately. Bart will be increasing patrols around the island's perimeter. Maxim, I want you coordinating with our vampire residents to set up a night watch."

Maxim nodded solemnly, his pale features set with determination.

"The rest of you," Roscoe continued, scanning the room, "I need you to be our eyes and ears. If you see anything suspicious, anything at all, you report it. We can't afford to take any chances."

As Roscoe laid out more details of the island's defense plans, KeeKee couldn't help but notice the way Christian was fidgeting beside her. His brow was furrowed, his eyes distant, as if he was wrestling with some internal conflict.

"Hey," she whispered, nudging him gently. "You okay?"

Christian startled slightly, as if pulled from deep thought. "Yeah," he said, offering a small smile that didn't quite reach his eyes. "Just... thinking."

Before KeeKee could press further, a commotion near the back of the room caught her attention. Ree was pushing her way through the crowd, her face etched with worry.

"Sheriff," Ree called out, her voice cutting through the chatter. "I've got something you need to hear."

Roscoe paused, gesturing for Ree to come forward. The room fell silent as she made her way to the front, all eyes on her.

"It's about Aelita," Ree began, her voice trembling slightly. "I... I've seen her with some strange individuals. From the black hills."

A collective gasp went through the room. The black hills were notorious, a place where even the bravest supernaturals feared to tread. It was known to be a haven for those who dabbled in dark magic and illegal trades. As well as where the darker of the supernatural creatures only wanted to live in peace, or so they say.

"Are you sure?" Roscoe asked, his voice grave.

Ree nodded. "I saw her myself, just last night. She was talking to a group of them, looking... well, looking pretty cozy."

The room erupted into worried whispers. KeeKee felt her heart sink. Aelita had always been a bit of an outsider, but she'd never imagined she might be involved with something so sinister.

"Now, now," Roscoe's voice boomed over the noise. "Let's not jump to conclusions. Aelita's been a part of this community for a while now. We owe it to her to hear her side of the story before we make any judgments. For all we know, she was discussing her barbecue joint."

KeeKee nodded in agreement, but she couldn't shake the uneasy feeling in her gut. She glanced at Christian, expecting to see the same concern mirrored in his eyes. Instead, she found him staring at her with an intensity that made her breath catch.

As the meeting began to wrap up, with Roscoe assigning tasks and setting up patrol schedules, KeeKee felt a tap on her shoulder. She turned to find Marcus standing there, his expression unreadable.

"KeeKee," he said, his voice low. "Can I have a word?"

She nodded, following him to a quiet corner of the room. From the corner of her eye, she saw Christian watching them, a flicker of something – was it jealousy? – crossing his face.

"What's up, Marcus?" KeeKee asked, trying to keep her tone light despite the tension in the air.

Marcus ran a hand through his hair, a gesture that reminded her so much of Christian that it made her heart ache. "Look," he began, his voice barely above a whisper. "I know you and Christian have been getting... close."

KeeKee felt her cheeks flush. "I... we're just friends," she stammered.

Marcus raised an eyebrow, clearly not buying it. "Right. Well, friend or not, I need you to be careful."

"Careful?" KeeKee repeated, confusion coloring her tone.

Marcus sighed, glancing over at Christian before continuing. "He's not just some random supernatural, KeeKee. He's the heir to you-know-who. That comes with a lot of baggage, a lot of expectations. I just... I don't want to see you get hurt."

KeeKee felt a surge of defiance rise in her chest. "I appreciate your concern, Marcus, but I can take care of myself. And Christian... he's a good person. Whatever decisions he has to make about his future, that's between him and his family."

Marcus held up his hands in a placating gesture. "I'm not trying to cause trouble. I just... I care about you, KeeKee. You're Ree's family, and now mine. I don't want to see you caught in the middle of some cosmic family drama."

Before KeeKee could respond, Christian appeared at her side, his presence warm and comforting. "Everything okay here?" he asked, his tone carefully neutral but his eyes fixed on Marcus.

"Just fine," Marcus replied, a tight smile on his face. "I was just leaving." With a nod to KeeKee, he turned and made his way back to Ree, who was watching the exchange with a worried expression.

As soon as Marcus was out of earshot, Christian turned to KeeKee. "What was that about?" he asked, unable to keep the edge out of his voice.

KeeKee sighed, suddenly feeling very tired. "Nothing important," she said, offering him a small smile. "Just... family stuff."

Christian didn't look convinced, but before he could press further, Sofka's voice rang out.

"Alright, everyone, one last thing before we wrap up," she called. "I know tensions are high right now, but I want to remind you all of something important. We're not just a bunch of misfits thrown together on this island. We're a community. A family. And families stick together, no matter what."

A murmur of agreement ran through the crowd. KeeKee felt some of the tension leave her shoulders as she looked around at the faces of her friends and neighbors. Sofka was right. Whatever challenges lay ahead, they would face them together.

As the meeting dispersed, KeeKee found herself walking alongside Christian, their steps falling into sync as they made their way out into the chilly air toward the small pier.

"So," Christian began, his breath visible in the morning air, "what do you make of all this?"

KeeKee shook her head, her mind still reeling from everything that had been discussed. "It's a lot to take in," she admitted. "I'm worried about Aelita. And Kirill... well, I hoped we'd seen the last of him."

Christian nodded, his expression grim. "Kirill isn't the type to give up easily. But KeeKee," he paused, turning to face her, "I want you to know that no matter what happens, I'm here. For you, for this island. For all of it."

KeeKee felt her heart skip a beat at the intensity in his eyes. "Christian, I..."

But before she could finish her thought, a commotion near the docks caught their attention. A group had gathered, pointing and shouting at something out on the water.

Without a word, KeeKee and Christian took off running towards the commotion. As they neared the docks, KeeKee could make out a small boat approaching the island, its occupants obscured by the misty air.

"Who is that?" someone in the crowd called out.

"Could it be Kirill?" another voice added, panic evident in their tone.

As the boat drew closer, KeeKee felt Christian tense beside her. She reached out, almost instinctively, and took his hand in hers. He squeezed it gently, a silent acknowledgment of her support.

The air was thick with tension as the boat finally docked. A figure stood up, tall and imposing, and for a heart-stopping moment, KeeKee thought it might indeed be Kirill.

But as the mist cleared, a collective gasp went through the crowd. It wasn't Kirill at all, but a face many of them recognized from ancient texts and legends.

"Queen Mab," Christian whispered, his voice a mix of awe and apprehension.

The Queen of the Unseelie Court stood regally in the small boat, her ethereal beauty at odds with the rough surroundings of the dock. Her eyes, cold and calculating, scanned the crowd before landing on Christian.

"Well, well," she said, her voice carrying easily despite its soft tone. "It seems I've arrived just in time for all the excitement."

As Queen Mab stepped onto the dock, KeeKee felt a shiver run down her spine that had nothing to do with the cold. Whatever challenges they had been preparing for, she had a feeling they had just become much more complicated.

Christian's hand tightened around hers, and KeeKee knew in that moment that everything was about to change. The calm before the storm had passed, and now, they would need to face whatever came next – together.

Chapter 14

A tense silence blanketed the docks as Queen Mab's presence unsettled everyone gathered. Her lithe figure moved with an ethereal grace that kept everyone on edge, as though she were something not quite of this world, which of course she wasn't. Mab was a Queen from the Land of Faerie, not a human realm. Her platinum hair spilled like liquid silver over the dark velvet of her cloak, and her eyes—a piercing shade of ice-blue, not unlike Christian's but with none of their warmth—scanned the crowd dispassionately.

KeeKee's heart pounded furiously in her chest. She fought the instinct to step back, tightening her grip on Christian's hand instead. She could sense the ripple of tension running through him, but his expression remained calm, carefully guarded. This was the Queen of the Unseelie Court, and all their instincts screamed that this was no ordinary visitation.

"Well, well," Mab's melodic voice echoed softly through the crowd, ice lacing every word. "I didn't expect such a warm welcome." Her lips curved into a sardonic grin, her eyes flicking toward Christian.

"Mother." Marcus's voice rang out low and clear, cutting through the tension like a knife. He knew how much she hated it when he addressed her as anything but Your Majesty. It was immature, but he couldn't help himself.

Marcus stepped forward, placing himself between Mab and the others, his face showing the careful neutrality he'd perfected over centuries of political maneuvering as a prince of the Unseelie Court. KeeKee could see the tightness in his shoulders, the flicker of unease in his usually assured movements.

"Roderick." Mab addressed Marcus by his full name, her tone cold. There was no warmth, no familial recognition in her gaze, only the expectation of obedience.

"What brings you to our island, Your Majesty?" Marcus asked, carefully avoiding the familial address, now that he'd got his dig in. He couldn't afford to show any weakness in front of her.

A silence fell, thick as the morning mist curling off the water. Those who knew the history between the Claus family and Queen Mab—between Christian's family and Marcus's—held their breath, unsure of what would happen next.

Mab's gaze flickered with amusement as she noticed the restrained hostility in each of the gathered supes. "Oh, come now, Roderick. Can't a mother simply want to visit her beloved son?" Her words were laced with venom, mocking the very idea of maternal affection.

Marcus's spine stiffened at the intentional jab. KeeKee knew the Queen's so-called 'affection' was often no more than veiled threats and manipulations. Their relationship was notorious for its dangerous undercurrents.

"I can't see any reason why you'd suddenly have an interest in visiting me, certainly not after centuries of staying away," Marcus responded, suspicion thick in his voice.

Mab tilted her head, an eerie smile dancing on her lips. "Why, I've heard such fascinating things about this little island you've found yourself attached to. How could I resist? Besides, there are developments within the supernatural world that require attention—critical gatherings of interest if you will."

Christian, his posture rigid but composed, finally spoke up, his voice hard. "We've heard nothing about any such gatherings, Mab. If you're here to toy with us, you'd be wise to reconsider your strategies."

Mab shot him a cold glance. "Ah, and who but the son of Santa Claus should lecture me on strategy?" Her tone was gratingly sweet, dripping with derision. "You would do well to remember, Christian, that your family's position has always been fraught with precarious alliances, none more so than mine."

Christian's expression darkened. Mab and the Claus family had a long and troubled past—one fraught with bloodshed, betrayal, and a tenuous peace that was held only by the skin of its teeth and the intervention of powerful intermediaries. But here, on Misfit Island, that fragile peace wasn't worth much. In this place, they couldn't simply rely on the vague rules of the supernatural world to protect them.

Before Christian could form a reply, another figure stepped off the boat, moving with a presence so imposing that the crowd instinctively parted to make room. He was a giant of a male, towering at nearly eight feet tall, with skin the color of midnight sky and eyes like smoldering embers. His hair, long and jet black, hung loose around his bare shoulders, and from his ears hung thinly spun silver chains.

Instantly, the crowd tensed. Though no one moved, KeeKee could feel the energy around her shift as the people of Misfit Island braced themselves for whatever new threat had just arrived in their midst.

"And who might this be?" Sheriff Roscoe's voice rumbled from behind the group, his massive, bearish form cutting a path toward the docks. "We weren't expecting guests today."

Roscoe's deep voice momentarily drew Mab's attention away from Christian. "This is one of my personal guards, Daimon," Mab answered smoothly, not betraying even a flicker of the tension her arrival had caused. "He will be accompanying me during my stay."

"Your stay?" Marcus's voice took on an edge of incredulity. "You can't be—"

"Of course," Mab cut him off, her smile widening, showing glimmering white teeth. "Surely, as my son, you would not deny your mother a place to rest?"

KeeKee's eyes widened, a sense of dread creeping over her. Mab staying on the island could only mean trouble. It was a known fact that wherever she went, she instigated discord, turning allies against one another with nothing more than poisonous words and thin veils of politeness. She worried what Mab would do when she discovered Marcus had married Ree.

"Forgive me, but Misfit Island doesn't usually accommodate—" Marcus struggled to maintain his composure.

"Oh, but I insist," Mab purred, her tone brooking no argument. Her eyes flicked over to KeeKee, lingering there for a moment as if she were something to be dissected and studied.

Then Mab looked back to Christian, her smile sharp and insincere, like a polished blade. "And I must say, Christian, it seems you've been making quite the influence on this island. Is it true? The future Mrs. Claus is among us?"

Christian's jaw set tightly, his voice a low, controlled growl. "That's not up for discussion, Mab."

"Oh, but everything is up for discussion in my world," Mab responded sweetly. "Wouldn't you agree, Roderick?"

A muscle ticked in Marcus's jaw, but he didn't give her the satisfaction of a reply.

Sheriff Roscoe, sensing the glaring storm of tension building like a physical presence, said quickly, "Queen Mab, if you insist on staying, I'll be sure accommodations are made. I'll have Horatio show you to—"

"Nothing but the best, Sheriff," Mab interjected smoothly, her gaze sliding back to Christian, then KeeKee. "After all, I wouldn't want my sojourn here to be anything less than memorable."

KeeKee felt a shiver run down her spine, and a part of her screamed internally to get this dangerous woman as far from the island as possible. But with the current stakes rising and tensions already high, any wrong move could lead to a catastrophic fallout.

Christian straightened, as if preparing for an invisible blow. "We'll show you to your quarters, Queen Mab," he said coldly. "And we'll ensure you have everything you need. But make no mistake, you will be under strict observation while you're here. Misfit Island is neutral ground, and any act against that neutrality will be met with equal force."

Mab's laughter sang out, light and airy, but the malice behind it sent a fresh wave of unease through all present. "How delightfully quaint," she said mockingly, but she made no further remark as she gestured gracefully for Daimon to follow.

As Mab moved off the docks and toward the island's interior, Marcus took a quiet, resigned step back and cast a glance at KeeKee. His usually composed face was laced with something nearing desperation, but he kept it in check.

Keenly aware of how many eyes were on them, including the daggers darting from Ree's glare, KeeKee turned to him and whispered, "Marcus, what does your mother want here? What is she really after?"

"She doesn't do anything without reason," Marcus replied, voice low. "But one thing is certain—whatever she plans, it's not going to benefit anyone here."

"And Ree, your mate? Does Mab know about her?" KeeKee thought she knew the answer, but had to ask anyway. Ree was one of her very best friends and didn't want anything bad to happen to her.

Marcus looked at Ree with such longing, that KeeKee felt bad for him. "I honestly don't know." He left KeeKee where she stood and made his way to his mate.

KeeKee felt a gnawing sensation in the pit of her stomach, but before she could speak further, Christian gently tugged at her hand. "Come, we should ensure she's properly escorted."

There was no need for discussion; KeeKee knew now that they would all have to keep a much closer eye on Mab's presence, even if it meant delaying their other preparations.

But as they walked toward the island's main buildings, Maxim, who had remained silent up until now, leaned over to Sofka. "We should be careful in assuming she didn't come with more than one ally."

Sofka nodded grimly. "I had a similar thought. Something feels off, and it's not just Mab's presence here. The timing... everything."

Maxim's hand, cold as usual, brushed against KeeKee's arm as he moved closer to Sofka. "Trust is going to be in short supply for the foreseeable future," he warned, his tone grave. "We should take nothing at face value from now on."

KeeKee nodded, the weight of his words settling heavily in her mind as she and the others followed Mab, who strolled as if she owned the very snow beneath her feet.

Hours later, after Mab had been safely ensconced in a special cabin made up for her on the spot by the Island—and after ensuring that Daimon's quarters were adjacent, limiting his ability to sneak around unnoticed—KeeKee, Christian, Marcus, and the rest of their new-found team reconvened in the warmth of the Sheriff's Office.

Outside, the evening snow had begun to fall more heavily, pulling the light of the soon-dimming day into a soft blanket of silence. It only added to the pressured quiet inside as each of the Misfit Island leaders processed the weight of their new... "visitor."

"You know this isn't just a visit," Sheriff Roscoe began, breaking the heavy quiet. "Queen Mab's arrival means something much more complicated for all of us."

"Her track record of fostering havoc wherever she goes isn't inspiring much confidence for any of us," Maxim remarked dryly, his gaze moving across the concerned faces.

"She's testing us," Marcus said, his brows knitting together in familiar concentration. "There's something specific she wants here. The question is... what?"

"We don't have time for guessing," Sofka responded, folding her arms. "We need to figure out her agenda before it's too late. It can't just be coincidence that she appears on the exact same day we get wind of Kirill's movements."

"There's no such thing as coincidence when it comes to Queen Mab," Christian agreed, his voice carrying the burden of his own family's history with her. "She moves pieces on the board with intent—and if she's here, it means she's already calculated a strategy with a purpose we don't yet know."

"The bigger problem," Sheriff Roscoe added, "is that while we're keeping an eye on her, we've got scores of other issues to deal with—like Kirill's alliance movements that could give us a real battle here."

Marcus inhaled sharply. "Her timing... it almost feels like she wants us distracted by her so that Kirill can move more freely."

At those words, a heavy realization settled over them. Christian exchanged a weighted glance with KeeKee, whose mind raced with the possibilities and dangers lurking beneath the surface.

"We've been preparing to face Kirill, and now Mab's entrance demands we switch our focus. That's exactly what she wants," KeeKee said softly as Maxim's earlier warning echoed in her mind.

"We'll need to divide our attention carefully," Christian said, his tone grim. "We can't afford to slip up on either front. Especially not now."

The silence that followed hinted at the same fear in everyone gathered; they were walking a treacherous path with devastating consequences at every turn.

"It's time," Sofka began, breaking the silence, "to trust the network we've started building. I know blocks are being set up all around us, and more than one infiltrator must have made their way here. It's the black market ringleaders we need to flush out, and that means we need more than just eyes and ears—we need people willing to be underestimated as distractions, and people who can separate the truth from lies under pressure."

"You're not talking about a response team," Roscoe noted, eyebrows raised. "You're talking about a strike team handling operations concurrently."

"That's exactly what she's talking about," KeeKee confirmed, her voice steadying as the tension in the room translated into action that she could wrap her head around. "I might not be a strategist by title, but I do have a knack for seeing people's true intentions. If we go at this like disjointed links in a chain, that's how Mab and Kirill will sever us. We need a unified plan that pushes our objectives forward without giving them any obvious weaknesses to exploit."

Christian nodded, a shadow of admiration passing his icy gaze as he locked eyes with her. "KeeKee's right—and if we're going to win, strikes that impose careful, strategic pressure will be key."

"And we should find more allies who want to assist us," Sofka pointed out. "There have to be others that want to put a stop to the supernatural trafficking ring, at the very least."

Her suggestion drew thoughtful nods, knowing that adding more supes to their numbers would provide strength that would be crucial.

Before falling into planning specifics, Marcus spoke up, his tone laced with the lingering tension of earlier. "If my mother is hiding her true objective here, there's a strong possibility she isn't working alone. We're going to need to identify her 'helpers' on this island quickly if we want to avoid being blindsided."

KeeKee nodded, finally releasing the breath she hadn't realized she'd been holding since their encounter with Mab on the docks.

The room's mood darkened as each of them realized the necessity of every split-second decision in the hours and days to come. With the warning of betrayal hanging heavy in their minds, the island's fate felt more fragile than ever.

In this complicated web of shifting allegiances, where Christmas cheer was being underscored by deadly intentions, the Misfit Island team knew this was their true battle—one that could define them—and possibly break them.

For every face they trusted, there would soon be two more lurking in shadows they couldn't yet see, some manipulating with power they couldn't begin to comprehend.

But as the group continued forging ahead with plans, one thing remained undeniably steady—there was still a quiet, hopeful resolve taking root.

United and unwavering, they would ensure that no foe—be it Queen Mab, Kirill, or anyone else—could tear down the bonds they were building or the future they wanted to protect on this island. Together, they would brace for the storm, determined to see its worst unraveled—with their spirit intact.

And ultimately, they couldn't afford to treat this simply as a battle for survival; it was a fight to keep belief alive—in their purpose, their island...and each other.

When the tell-tale sound of a screen rolling down the back wall sounded, all present turned their attention to what the Island had to say.

I've sent out a request to supes who are to be trusted.

Expect Gabriel and his shifter delegation to arrive in the next few days.

Then the screen rolled up and everyone looked around with wide eyes.

Chapter 15

KeeKee stood at the window of her small apartment over the Welcome Center, staring out at Main Street below. The island was peaceful at this hour, the early morning light casting long shadows that stretched like fingers across the landscape. But the peace was deceptive, masking the tension she could feel simmering beneath the surface. The events of the last few days had been a whirlwind—Queen Mab's arrival, the ominous warnings about Kirill, and now the Island itself going so far as to request help from an outside delegation.

She sighed, pressing her fingers against her temple. Sleep had been elusive since Queen Mab's appearance. There was too much to think about, too much that could go wrong. And amidst it all, Christian's presence had become a comforting constant, even as their relationship grew more complicated with every passing day.

The sound of footsteps crunching on the outside steps leading up to her apartment caught her attention. She pulled herself away from the window just as a knock echoed through the small apartment.

When she opened the door, Christian stood on the other side, his breath visible in the frigid morning air.

"I didn't wake you, did I?" he asked, his voice soft, though it carried concern.

KeeKee shook her head. "I couldn't sleep anyway," she admitted, stepping aside to let him in.

Christian entered, rubbing his hands together to fend off the cold. Despite everything, a smile tugged at the corners of his mouth as he looked around her apartment. The interior, though modest, was cozy and warm, with bookshelves packed to the brim and the scent of cinnamon lingering in the air.

"You've made this place feel like home," Christian observed, his tone admiring. "It suits you."

KeeKee smiled faintly, but the expression didn't reach her eyes. "I'm not sure how much of a home it'll be if things keep unravelling the way they have been," she said quietly. Not bothering to remind him that the Island is the one who decorated her place, including all of the books shoved into every nook and cranny in her floor to ceiling bookshelves. It was every reader's dream, and one KeeKee had always had, but never voiced aloud to anyone, except for the Island.

Christian's expression softened as he moved closer to her. "KeeKee, I know things look bleak right now, but we'll figure this out. We've faced difficulty before, and we've always managed to get through it."

She nodded, wanting to believe him. But there were too many unknowns, and the stakes felt higher than ever. "It's just... Mab's presence here. The fact that the Island itself sent out a request for help. It feels like the ground is shifting beneath our feet and we can't find our footing."

Christian reached out, gently placing his hand on her shoulder. "I won't let anything happen to you," he promised, his ice-blue eyes locking onto hers with an intensity that made her heart stutter.

KeeKee felt a warmth settle in her chest, even as her thoughts remained tangled. There was so much to consider, so much she didn't understand. That included her own abilities, which had seemed to manifest without any explanation.

"It's not just me I'm worried about," she whispered. "It's everyone. The Island. All the people here who've finally found a place to belong."

Christian's expression grew thoughtful. "That's why we have to fight this, KeeKee. Not just for survival, but for the idea that Misfit Island can exist in peace. That it can be a safe haven for those who need it."

KeeKee nodded, feeling some of her resolve returning. "You're right. We can't let fear defeat us. We need to be proactive—to uncover whatever Kirill, Mab, and any other unlikely allies might be planning."

Christian pulled her into a gentle hug, the warmth of his embrace warding off the anxiety that had been gnawing at her chest. For a moment, she allowed herself to simply savor the feeling of being close to him, to let the world drift away. But reality had a way of intruding, and ultimately, they had work to do.

"We should get moving," she said after a moment, stepping back from him reluctantly, before she could give in to her desire to kiss Christian. "There's a lot to do, and I'm tired of waiting for the other shoe to drop."

Christian nodded, his expression hardening with determination. "I agree. We should start with figuring out more about Mab's real agenda. But we also need to follow up on that anonymous tip about Kirill's movements."

KeeKee grabbed her coat and scarf, wrapping herself up against the cold. "Let's split up. You talk to Sofka and Maxim about following up with the Sheriff and making sure that the security measures are solid. In the meantime, I'll head down to the Welcome Center and see if I can gather any more information about Kirill."

Christian arched an eyebrow. "Horatio's been one of our best sources for intel, but be careful. If Kirill really is gathering forces, there's no telling who might be involved."

KeeKee inhaled deeply. "No, Horatio would never..."

She was cut off when Christian's eyes widened and he shook his head vehemently. "I didn't mean Horatio, I meant you need to be careful with anyone else who might be inside of the Welcome Center, if it's open."

KeeKee nodded. "Of course. I doubt it's open yet, but I will be careful." She hesitated for a moment before asking, "What about Marcus? Do you think he's okay after Mab's arrival?"

Christian's expression darkened slightly. "He's... handling it. Marcus is a survivor, but dealing with Mab isn't easy, especially knowing how she's played with the lives of her own family members before. I'll check in on him after we finalize the security setup."

KeeKee felt a pang of concern for Marcus. Though he often played the part of the aloof, undisturbed prince, she knew there was more to his story—especially when it came to his mother. "Alright," she said softly. "Stay safe, Christian."

"I will," he promised, leaning down to press a gentle kiss to her forehead. "And you too."

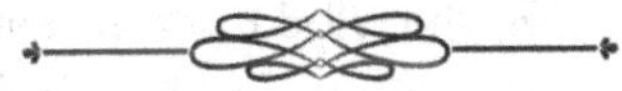

The walk downstairs to the Welcome Center was quick, the morning air biting at KeeKee's exposed skin as she trudged around the side of the building to the front door where she stopped and looked out over Main Street. The decorations set up in the town center looked a bit out of place against the tension surrounding the island, but she found the familiar sight oddly comforting.

When she walked inside, she was greeted by the warm glow of lanterns and the sight of Horatio bustling about inside, his large frame making the interior look comically small. The polar bear shifter was easily the most jovial being on Misfit Island, always ready with a joke and a smile even in the most difficult of times.

"KeeKee!" Horatio boomed as she entered, his face lighting up at the sight of her. "What brings you by this fine morning? Looking for some good news, I hope?"

KeeKee managed a smile. "I'm always ready for good news if you've got any. But I was actually hoping you might have some information on Kirill. I heard there were new faces asking about him on the mainland of Chile."

Horatio's expression sobered slightly, his usual jovial demeanor dimming in response to the subject matter. "Ah, yes. I've heard some whispers. The small groups who have left the island lately to shop on the mainland, then come home, have heard whispers that I'm not comfortable with. Some of them even seem a bit too interested in our previous encounters with Kirill." He chuckled. "Course they could just be drumming up old gossip to pass the long, cold nights."

While the southern tip of Chile was part of the human world, there were still plenty of supes who called that region home. It was them who helped Bart to get the supplies that the Island didn't generate itself.

KeeKee felt a chill that had nothing to do with the weather. "Do you think they're working with him? Perhaps trying to recruit more allies, or just to gather intel from gossipy Island residents before making a move?"

Horatio stroked his chin thoughtfully. "Hard to say. What I do know is that there's been a few who've arrived here who aren't as forthcoming about their reasons for being here. Now, it's not unusual for some folks to want to keep to themselves, mind you—this place attracts misfits for that reason. But this last batch of new arrivals… they've got an air of urgency about them."

KeeKee nodded, processing the information. "Have they mentioned anything specific? Connections to the supernatural black market, perhaps?"

"Aelita namedrops this black-market ring, but I don't think she actually knows who's involved," Horatio rumbled, shaking his head. "I haven't heard anything direct, but there are bits and pieces floating around. Deals being made under the table, mentions of other 'interested parties'… But I'll tell you this, KeeKee, whoever these people are, they're keeping it quiet."

KeeKee frowned. "We've got to dig deeper. And we need to see if anyone's willing to let something slip, even if it's just by accident."

Horatio leaned closer, his massive figure casting a shadow over her. "I'll do some asking, shuffle things around, see if I can't get certain tongues wagging. But you be careful, KeeKee. Whoever's behind this doesn't want to be found out. And they won't hesitate to silence anyone who gets too close."

KeeKee met his gaze, appreciating the concern there. "I'll be careful, Horatio. And thank you for always looking out for us."

Horatio snorted, his grin returning. "Looking out isn't a chore for this old bear. It's more of a pleasure. You take care, little wolf."

"Old bear? Yeah, right. Somehow I doubt you're much older than I am." KeeKee chuckled and felt the tension drain from her shoulders as she and Horatio bantered back and forth.

As KeeKee left the warmth of the Welcome Center and returned to the cold outside, her mind raced with possibilities. Kirill's network was already more expansive than she'd predicted, and the notion of unknown agents among them was both terrifying and frustratingly vague. After the big battle a few weeks back, she would have sworn that anyone who had been on Kirill's team was gone. Today? She wasn't so sure.

She had no doubt now that the island was playing host to more than saboteurs or spies—it might just be the latest front for a battle none of them were fully prepared to fight.

Even as these realizations grew darker in her mind, she couldn't afford to let them slow her down. There was too much at stake to give in to fear. The island, the people she loved—they were all depending on them to weather the storm.

Just as she was about to cut across the town square, a faint, familiar scent caught her attention, something almost metallic in the crisp air. Frowning, KeeKee followed it, her senses leading her toward a quiet alley behind a row of shops.

Her pulse quickened as the scent grew stronger—blood. Using her wolf senses to heighten her awareness, she advanced cautiously, her heart pounding with each step.

To her horror, she found Maxim kneeling beside a familiar figure on the ground—a young female supe she recognized as Serena, one of the newcomers to the island. The snow around Serena was stained crimson, and she lay limply in the cold, her eyes wide open in terror.

"Maxim!" KeeKee gasped, rushing over to his side, her breath catching in her throat as she surveyed the scene.

Maxim's eyes glinted with concern, his earlier stoicism melting away at something more vital. "She's been badly injured," he murmured, while he worked to staunch the bleeding with a makeshift bandage. Though he was a vampire, KeeKee had known him long enough to recognize the intensity in his eyes as something more than thirst. "We need to get her to Sherrie. But she'll need a lot more than just ordinary care."

KeeKee could barely hear him over the rush of blood in her ears as adrenaline coursed through her. She dropped to her knees beside Serena, trying to grasp how this had happened. "But she's only been here a few weeks," she whispered. "Why would someone do this?"

Maxim shook his head. "I don't know, but I can only assume someone didn't want her to talk. KeeKee..." He looked up at her, his face ashen. "There's something we need to consider. What if Mab brought more than just chaos with her? What if she brought... assassins?"

KeeKee swallowed hard, the realization settling over her like a lead blanket. "I—we need to move her, now."

As she got ready to move the girl, Maxim's eyes met hers, something in them reflecting both stark necessity and compassion. "She won't make it to Sherrie's place on the other side of the island. You might be the only one who can save her, KeeKee. We don't have much time."

KeeKee hesitated. If anyone could tell how much longer a body had, it would be a vampire. "But... I don't know if—"

"You don't have time to doubt that now," Maxim interrupted gently but firmly. "Your power might be able to save her, but you have to trust in it."

It was true that she'd already used her fledgling healing abilities before... but this was different. This injury was severe, deliberate, and would likely kill Serena if not treated immediately.

Taking a deep breath, KeeKee allowed herself a moment to center, focusing inward as she placed her hands on Serena's wounds. She knew the care needed here—caution so as not to damage anything further, but there was a critical wound just above the heart torn through her flesh like a penetrating stab wound, freshly enough that the blood was still bright and oddly fragrant.

Closing her eyes, KeeKee let the world around her dissolve as she reached inside, feeling for the threads of power that had surfaced before. They flared to life underneath her touch, pulsating almost painfully through her, as though the world itself was pushing back.

But KeeKee could also draw strength from her surroundings—the iced ground beneath her, the frigid air with each controlled breath. She sank deeper into this sensation as the energy flowed more freely into Serena's body, washing warmth over the frozen pallor of her skin.

Under Maxim's watchful eyes, KeeKee worked feverishly, her concentration unbroken as energy coursed from her through Serena, knitting torn flesh together, stemming the bleeding, and guiding Serena's body back toward stability.

After what felt like an eternity, KeeKee finally pulled back, shuddering with exertion as the power ebbed away. Serena's breathing, once shallow and punctuated by silence, gradually steadied—a healthy flush of color returning to her cheeks as the wound had closed up as if it had never been there.

KeeKee panted, trying to catch her breath as the world drifted back into focus. She felt Maxim's hands gently gripping her shoulders to steady her.

"You did it," he whispered, awe coloring his voice. "KeeKee, you saved her life."

Somewhere deep in KeeKee's chest, both relief and horror mixed in equal measure. The lingering dread she'd felt since their last encounter with danger threatened to tear her apart at the seams, but at that moment, all she could do was nod numbly.

As she gently rose to her feet, Maxim eased Serena into his arms, preparing to carry her somewhere safer. "We need to tell the others, KeeKee. This was an attack, and I suspect it won't be the last."

KeeKee nodded, willing herself to remain composed. They still had battles to fight, and she would have to reconcile her fear with the need to use her abilities—to be the person who could keep this island and its people safe, despite the cost it might demand from her.

"Let's go. I'll keep an eye out while we move her," KeeKee whispered, her mind spinning with all that had just transpired. Yet beneath the storm of thoughts was the cold, hard truth: the time for hesitating had evaporated like mist in the snow. Their enemies, like shadows, moved quietly in the distance, waiting for them to falter.

As they carried Serena to safety, past festive decorations and snowy paths that nervously whispered of an ominous future, KeeKee felt a resolve solidify within her—a resolve born not of fear, but of purpose, intertwined with the identity she had tried for so long not to acknowledge.

Whatever the next steps demanded, KeeKee would face them alongside Christian, Sofka, Ree, and the others. And she would use whatever strength the island and its magic offered her to protect Misfit Island until the bitter end. Together, they would wrestle back the certainty of peace amidst the storm, even if the cost proved greater than they'd ever imagined.

Chapter 16

Once Serena was settled into a safe house, KeeKee headed over to Ree and Malcom's house. This attack and the arrival of Queen Mab couldn't be coincidence, Mab had to have something to do with this. Maybe Serena saw Mab meeting with one of Kirill's agents, or discussing Kirill with her security guard. While KeeKee couldn't imagine all scenarios, she did believe that Serena saw, or heard, something that caused her to be attacked the way she had been. Marcus might have a better idea.

As KeeKee approached Ree's house, the hair on the back of her neck stood on end. Then she began to hear snippets of an argument. She turned around to see who would be arguing outside, but she didn't see anyone. Not even a child playing in the area. The closer she got to Ree's house, the louder the voices. But that was impossible, he houses were sound proofed. No sounds ever left a supe's house unless their door was open. And Ree's door was not. Neither were any of the neighbor's doors.

Every now and then, a voice spoke to her. Not out loud, but inside her head. She always thought it was her mother or father warning her about something dangerous. Now, that voice was telling her to get to the side of the house, and quickly.

The moment KeeKee ran to the side of the house, the door opened and out walked Mab herself. "I'm telling you Roderick, if you don't put your little plaything to the side, or better yet, kill her, then I'm removing my protection from you!" She pointed her finger so close to Marcus' face that from KeeKee's perspective from around the corner, the tip of Mab's fingernail was pushing against his nose.

"Mother, I don't need your so called "protection". If you had ever put it on me, then why did Kirill attack the island a few months ago? Why am I constantly in danger?" Marcus stepped outside and stood between Mab's security guard and his mother.

Mab scoffed and shook her head. "Oh, what a baby. You were never in any danger from Kirill. He could never harm a single hair on an Unseelie Prince." She tapped her long, red-painted nail on her chin. "He might be able to hurt a Seelie Prince, but not you. The Seelie are weak."

"That's besides the point. I'm mated to Ree and that's the end of it. No one is going to hurt my mate. If they do, I'll release the Unseelie Prince inside of me and let it kill anyone who might have been involved in hurting her. And that includes you, or your security guards." He puffed his chest out and rested his fists on his hips. Above his head the ethereal crown appeared like a ghostly rendition of a three-foot crown hovering above his head.

KeeKee had heard about Marcus' anger management issues, and even witnessed some of it when everyone thought that Ree might be seriously injured, but she'd not seen the crown. Lots of witnesses spoke about it after the first battle with Kirill, but this looked larger somehow than before.

Mab snarled and turned from her son. "I'm done with you and this island. Don't expect me to help when Kirill comes to destroy you all." Her black and red dress flowed behind her as though a mini fan was underneath it, giving it the look of something one might see on a runway in Milan.

KeeKee stayed where she was until she could no longer see Mab and her security guard. After she took a deep sigh, she headed to Ree's front door.

KeeKee quickly approached Maxim's and Sofka's house the next day. The crisp morning air had become synonymous with urgency, each breath sharp with the foreboding sensation that clung to the island like mist. Every step toward Sofka's door echoed KeeKee's lingering exhaustion from the night before. Despite having saved Serena's life, a sense of dread pulsed in her chest, growing with every heartbeat.

And it wasn't all due to Mab's dramatic departure from the Island, either.

Maxim's sharp eyes scanned the surroundings with the precision of a vampire well versed in the art of vigilance when he opened the door to KeeKee's loud knock. She couldn't shake the lingering sensation from her exertion the day before—an uneasy weight resting in her bones as if some part of herself had been left behind during the healing. The energy she'd channeled might have saved Serena, but it left

KeeKee feeling adrift, more aware than ever of the unknown power within her.

"Everything in check?" Maxim's smooth voice broke the silence, as his gaze scanned the horizon behind KeeKee.

KeeKee nodded, though uncertainty wove through her thoughts. "As far as I know. Sofka's been preparing the island for whatever Kirill might have up his sleeve. But after Serena's attack, I'm sure there are things we're missing. We need to cover every angle."

Maxim hummed in agreement. "These attacks seem to follow Kirill's wave—but there's something more than just his grudge driving them."

Sofka stepped up beside her mate, and she wrapped a possessive arm around his waist.

"More pieces on the board than we've seen," KeeKee murmured, recalling Christian's words. Last night's reconfirmation of her healing capabilities had only deepened the mystery, and the shadow cast by Queen Mab's presence, and sudden departure, felt heavier with every passing day.

Sofka opened the door and waved for KeeKee to enter. Ree's face peeked around the couple with a mixture of surprise and concern. The partially open door offered a glimpse into Sofka's and Maxim's living room, now co-opted into an informal command center, complete with maps, books, and weaponry laid out on every available surface.

"KeeKee," Ree greeted, pushing the door fully open to let her in. "Marcus and Christian are inside. They've been talking tactics. After what happened with Serena, we need to adapt fast."

The mention of Serena sent a pang through KeeKee's heart. With a tight hug, Ree turned to check on Marcus, the two rarely went anywhere without the other these days. The door shut softly behind her, sealing KeeKee into the large open living room with the others.

After checking to make sure no one was listening, KeeKee leaned in toward Ree. "How is Marcus handling the confrontation with his mother?"

Ree pursed her lips. "He's doing fine. Although, he says that she is mot likely not involved with Kirill. But that makes no sense to me."

"Me, either. We can talk more about this later, let's join the rest." KeeKee nodded to the other side of the room where Sofka was looking around.

KeeKee's gaze settled on Sofka, whose expression was fiercely focused. Sofka was never someone to back down from a challenge; her resolve was as strong as the icy winds that howled against Misfit Island's rugged landscape. Christian sat beside her, his forehead creased with concentration as he reiterated points on a detailed map of the island laid out on the coffee table.

"We've increased the night patrols, roped more people in wherever possible," Christian was saying as they approached. "But we won't be able to sustain the level of vigilance we need without overextending ourselves."

"Particularly with Queen Mab's dramatic departure," Sofka added, her eyes flicking toward the window as if the Queen's mysterious influence could slip like a wisp of smoke into their hearth. "She's up to something, and I don't doubt it's calculated down to the last breath."

Christian's gaze flicked upward as KeeKee entered the living room, and the concern—the tension—etched into his features softened slightly at the sight of her. "You're here," he noted, pulling his chair back to make room for KeeKee.

She slipped into the seat beside Christian while Maxim positioned himself against the wall closest to his mate, folding his arms in a watchful manner. KeeKee could feel the lingering echoes of her earlier use of healing magic, like a warning note played too long on a haunting tune. But there wasn't the time to nurse her uncertainty or pause to process her newly awakened abilities. Not yet. When she did have the time, she'd need to carefully consider how this new ability fit into her distrust of magic use. Although, she knew that all of the previous Mrs. Clauses had this ability and while it was a form of magic, it wasn't like a witch's magic. It was more of a gift from Christmas itself.

While she doubted she had the same ability as a Mrs. Claus would, she knew she didn't have the type of magic that an actual witch possessed. Since KeeKee was an Arctic Wolf Shifter, it only made sense that she'd have something similar to the magic Mrs. Claus wielded, if only she knew for certain.

"We've had some unusual frost activity on the island's western shore, near the cliffs," Sofka informed them as if continuing the meeting seamlessly. "It's hard to say whether it's related to Kirill, something else, or just a trickle from the island's own defenses. We've sent a small team to investigate. Sheriff Roscoe and Bart are overseeing that right now."

KeeKee absorbed the news. The island was alive, breathing, thriving—protecting them in ways they scarcely understood and wouldn't dare take for granted. But even the island's latent magic couldn't be everywhere at once—especially when the tension simmering beneath the surface felt as if it could burst around them at any moment.

Christian's wary eyes returned to KeeKee, and his voice dropped to a conversational tone that didn't lose its urgency. "Can you tell us all in your own words what happened yesterday with Serena?" He put his hand on one of KeeKee's and left it there for a moment, before pulling it back.

The touch left a warmth on her hand that spread throughout her entire being, giving her the strength to tell everyone in the room what she witnessed, and more importantly, what she did.

KeeKee recapped her and Maxim's discovery of Serena, including her encounter with what appeared to be a stab wound from a knife that wasn't very sharp. "Maybe it was claws and not a knife?" That thought only just hit her and she saw the way Sofka's fists subtly tightened as she spoke. Christian's sharp inhale didn't escape her notice, either.

"Well, that settles it," Sofka said darkly, avoiding the gaze of her friends as she adjusted the brass knuckles peeking out of the pocket of her jacket. "These attacks—they're coordinated, directed at our weakest members. But they're not aimed at outright destruction. Not yet. They're trying to destabilize us before launching something bigger that will require the full assault."

KeeKee's voice trembled as she spoke. "I agree that Serena isn't one of our stronger members, but I think she either saw something she shouldn't, or overheard an important conversation. Serena was defenseless, Sofka—if I hadn't been there..." She trailed off, the memory of Serena's limp body replaying in her mind.

Christian jumped up. "You might be on to something there. We'll need to talk to her when she's up for it. Until then, we have to assume everyone is in danger."

Sofka's eyes softened for a fraction of a second before they returned to their steely determination. "I shouldn't have let her walk alone.

We're only as strong as our weakest members, and that's where our defenses have holes. We should pair up. No one should wander alone anymore, not until we have a tighter grip on this mess."

Christian agreed, noticeably tense. "And we can't forget Queen Mab—her minions may be more scattered and hidden among us than we realize." He turned his gaze to the second son of the Unseelie Court Queen.

KeeKee barely registered his words as a wave of dizziness washed through her as if the room itself were spinning. Whether it was exhaustion or the remnants of her magic, she couldn't be sure. But Christian's steadying hand coming to rest on her shoulder brought her back, grounding her just as the crisis hammer had too many nails.

"There's something else," KeeKee whispered, looking up toward them, her gaze taking in both Sofka and Christian. "There's one more thing we need to consider—Kirill's motivations. Why would he go to such lengths now? What has changed?"

Maxim's calm voice echoed his darkly observant nature. "We're missing something. An advantage that Kirill has gained more recently, considering the risks he's taking by edging closer to the island. There must be another factor at play—something larger than just the grudge against you three."

"KeeKee's right," Marcus acknowledged. "Every step he takes has been planned, not just by him, but potentially under the influence or encouragement of others. Maybe even my mother. After all, something else must be motivating her arrival. She certainly wouldn't be here just to visit me."

While Ree hadn't said much, she had something to add now. "I think she heard about me and that's what brought her here. You saw how quickly she left when you refused to divorce me."

Marcus put a comforting arm around his mate. "That may be why she came when she did, but I still don't trust her."

Sofka stared at the map of the island, as if willing the answers to reveal themselves on the paper. But it was clear no simple answer was forthcoming, no matter how they wracked their minds.

"For now," Sofka continued, her tone reining them back toward action, "our priority remains twofold—defense and damage control. The rest will have to wait until we have more intel."

Maxim leaned forward, his eyes more intense. "We need to draw Kirill out—force him to reveal what he's been planning. If it's just him, we'll neutralize his threat quickly. If it's more than him...well." He shrugged, a coldness lurking behind his casual manner. "Then we'll simply have to be more deadly in our response."

Maxim's words carried a weight that reminded KeeKee of how little time they truly had.

"He won't just walk into a trap," Christian pointed out. "Not unless we make him."

"Then we'll create the perfect bait," Sofka said, determination writhing through her voice. "We'll prepare for a confrontation Kirill can't ignore, one that will draw him close enough for us to strike."

KeeKee listened as the others talked strategy, her mind straying between reality and an abstract drift of ideas—the island, the magic, Kirill's sudden aggression, and the enigmatic threat represented by Mab. Somewhere in all these tangled threads lay the truth of what they would need to do next.

Her gaze met Christian's again, and he offered her a small, reassuring smile—the steadiness and care in it giving her a comfort she didn't want to risk losing.

Finally, Sofka stood, pacing the room. "We don't have time to waste," she declared. "Let's put these plans into action. KeeKee, Christian—I need you two to help spread the word and finalize arrangements with the sheriff and Bart tonight. Maxim and I will start the patrols early and focus on drawing Kirill's attention."

KeeKee nodded, commitment surging back through her veins like adrenaline. They didn't have all the answers they needed yet, but they would have to make do with what they had.

Shortly after, they dispersed to fulfill their respective roles, all with the same silent hope, steadfast determination, and brittle worry supporting their decisions—the future of the island hung on these immediate actions, and they had to win every skirmish, every chess move. Or they would lose the war.

Night had fully settled over Misfit Island, and with it, an icy breeze that seemed to carry the whispers of distant storms across the inky black ocean. KeeKee and Christian walked side by side, making their way toward the end of Main Street where the sheriff's office stood like a sturdy beacon.

"All we have to do now is hold everything together," Christian murmured. His tone was light, but the tension in his shoulders belied the deeper concern beneath his words.

"Easier said than done," KeeKee responded, though she tried to keep the edge out of her voice.

Christian gave a low chuckle. "We've endured worse."

"Barely."

His smile faded, and he stopped, turning to face her with solemnity in his ice-blue eyes. "KeeKee..."

But before he could say more, a rustling sound caught their attention; both KeeKee and Christian spun quickly to face it, instincts on full alert. A moment later, the sheriff emerged from the shadows, walking briskly toward them with a grim expression on his face.

"KeeKee, Christian, I need a word," Sheriff Roscoe said in a low tone.

They exchanged a brief glance before nodding and closing the gap to meet the sheriff. A faint tension seemed to hover in the air between them, especially with the frost settling heavier now that night had encased the island.

"What is it?" Christian asked, his voice cold and precise, much like the air that surrounded them.

"Just got word from Bart," Roscoe began, his eyes shadowed under his furrowed brow. "He's heard there's movement inside the black market corridor. We've received confirmation that it's not just Kirill working from afar. Someone else is definitely working with him on Misfit Island."

"What did Bart find out?" KeeKee asked, pulse picking up.

"There's been a run on the Chilean docks after sunset," Roscoe explained. "They thought they could slip through the Island's magical barrier, but Bart had some of his gargoyle friends on night watch. A group of unfamiliar supes were sniffing around, maybe looking for someone—or something. One of Bart's contacts overheard them talking about trying to punch through the barrier, but not having any luck."

Christian's jaw clenched, teeth audibly grinding. "Were there any other signs of aggression?"

"There wasn't time to engage the barrier, not properly," Roscoe growled quietly. "But whatever they were doing, they've fled before we could learn more. We're not sure if they gained any valuable intel. But we'll need to double our patrol efforts tonight."

KeeKee's thoughts spun quickly—Kirill's attempts were becoming more audacious, with the mystery of this new collaborator deepening the puzzle. But now there was no more doubt; something was definitely spiraling out of control.

Her gaze landed on Christian. "We need to warn Sofka, Maxim, the others...we should be on full alert. They need to know what's happening."

Christian nodded sharply, his expression unreadable. "We'll tell them first thing in the morning, but it's likely too late to gather anyone else safely after dark."

His words hung like a sharp point in the cold air, signaling how much of the chessboard was already covertly shifting beneath them.

"I'll rejoin Bart's group," Sheriff Roscoe grunted, turning to leave.

KeeKee felt Christian's grip tighten slightly, as if suddenly needing reassurance, but she looked back with a nod—now was the time to trust their team.

"We'll prepare for the worst, and we'll patrol until morning," Christian murmured as they began to move silently through the nighttime streets.

Together, they vanished into the night—armed with a fragile sense of hope and a steel-hard resolve to outlast whatever Kirill and his new-found conspirators intended to unleash upon their beloved island. And whatever came next—they would face it together.

For as long as they could endure.

Chapter 17

KeeKee stood at the edge of the island's one and only pier, staring out over the gray-blue waters that lapped lazily against the pilings. Normally, the sight would bring her a sense of peace, but all she felt now was a gnawing anxiety that rested uneasily in her chest.

Every day felt like a new ordeal, every breath a little more labored under the weight of impending disaster. She couldn't shake the vision of Serena's blood-stained snow from her mind, or the way Maxim had looked at her when she used that raw, unfamiliar magic to heal the young supe. It was as though the island itself had demanded more from her, pulling every ounce of energy from her body to make something good out of something terrible. How much more would she have to give before this was all over?

As she stood there, lost in thought, a familiar voice tugged her back to the present.

"KeeKee." Christian's voice carried over the cold, cutting through her thoughts, grounding her back to the reality of what lay ahead.

She turned to find him approaching, his expression an unreadable mask. The flawless beauty of his ice-blue eyes stood out against the pale gray of the morning. In that instant, she could see the worry and concern—a mirror image of her own.

"Hey," she said softly, offering him a small but weary smile that she immediately regretted when his expression tightened.

"Hey," Christian replied, stepping closer and pulling her into a warm embrace, his grip a little tighter than usual, as if he too was haunted by the weight of their situation.

She allowed herself to let go just for a moment, to melt into the comforting embrace and forget everything else. But there was no time for that, no time to pretend everything would be fine just because they wished it so. With a resigned sigh, she pulled back, her heart sinking with the realization that their brief foray into peace had only amplified the storm that now brewed around them.

"We need to get moving if we're going to cover the ground we've planned," she said, her voice steady despite the tremor beneath.

Christian nodded, his gaze lingering on her for a moment as if he wanted to say more. But instead, he simply took her hand and pressed a small, comforting squeeze into it, grounding himself in the contact. "We'll do what needs to be done," he assured her, voice filled with resolve.

Their walk towards the barracks where Sofka and Maxim were stationed was silent, the tension between them thick as the frost coating the trees. The gravity of today was bearing down on them all, and there was no hiding from it anymore.

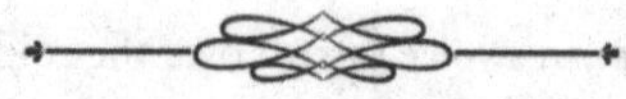

The barracks were a small but sturdy structure—another creation of the island that had solidified into place when they first began preparing for Kirill. Now, the building served as the heart of their operations, a hub where every plan and every decision converged into one final push for survival.

As KeeKee entered the barracks with Christian beside her, they found Sofka and Maxim already pouring over a map splayed out on a long table strewn with notes and markers. The room was filled with low murmurs, the atmosphere thick with anticipation.

Sofka looked up as they entered, her ice-blue eyes narrowing slightly as she took in their weary expressions.

"You both good to go?" she asked, though the question was laced with unsaid worries that had no place in this dire situation.

KeeKee nodded, forcing confidence into her voice. "As ready as we'll ever be. What's our current status?"

Maxim leaned over the table, his imposing frame cutting a shadow over the map as he pointed to specific locations. "We've got the western shore secured for now, but the sheen of frost there is unusual. Could be a sign of something bigger brewing—it doesn't match the pattern of the island's usual defenses."

Sofka's tone took on an icy edge as she added, "Bart's team encountered nothing on patrol last night, but activity at the Chilean docks is escalating. We've tightened our defenses, but they're probing us—looking for a way in."

KeeKee clenched her jaw. "Kirill is trying to wear us down. He and his allies are preparing us for something big, and we're not even sure what it is yet."

Maxim shot her a thoughtful look. "They won't have the luxury of catching us off guard. We've already started fortifying our borders—anything that gets close to shore won't leave without our say-so."

Christian gave a curt nod. "Good. We need to stay one step ahead of them."

Sofka sighed heavily. "But here's the problem—the way they're operating, it feels like they're waiting to see where our weakest point is. It's not just about breaking our defenses; they want to see how we'll react to pressure and where we'll crack. This time, I know they won't be so obvious with their attack on the Island."

KeeKee's gaze flicked toward the map, absorbing the marked regions that now represented more than just areas of the island but a lifeline to everything they were trying to protect. "We should throw a wrench in their plans. Divide their focus, force them to regroup."

Christian's eyes sparked as he met her gaze. "Agreed. Sofka, Maxim—how do you see us doing that?"

Maxim glanced at Sofka, an unspoken understanding passing between them before Sofka turned back to Christian and KeeKee. "We set up traps, foxholes, decoys—everything. We can make the island itself our ally in this. There are parts of the island that react to certain threats—we only need to coax that power where we need it."

Sofka's words brought a surge of cautious hope through KeeKee's chest. They might still be on the defense, but the island itself was a force they couldn't ignore—a force they could harness.

"There's one more thing we need to consider," KeeKee said, her voice steady as she mentally steeled herself for the pushback she knew was coming. "The people on this island—they're frightened. We need to make sure they understand what's at stake, and how to stay safe. We can't allow panic or confusion to break us apart."

Sofka nodded firmly. "I've already started coordinating with Sheriff Roscoe. We're organizing drills, setting up emergency shelters, and making sure everyone knows where to go if things turn south."

It wasn't a perfect solution, but it was all they had. KeeKee knew there was something more they could do, something born not just of strategy but of the very strength that had made Misfit Island the sanctuary it was today. Yet, how could she unlock that potential—her own potential—if she didn't fully understand it?

Her thoughts were interrupted when Marcus entered the room, his usually confident stride heavy with tension. Ree followed behind him, her eyes darting from face to face as though gauging the collective mood.

Marcus didn't mince words. "We've confirmed some movement among the new arrivals. A few of them have been seen in places they have no business being—like near Bart's lookout. Whoever's working with Kirill is probably using them for reconnaissance."

Ripping a hand roughly through his blonde hair, he leaned forward on the table, his expression deeply troubled. "But this isn't just about the black market—it's bigger than that. Kirill's trying to forge something that will pull in as many of our allies as possible. And he wants to do it under our noses."

KeeKee's chest tightened at this revelation. "What kind of alliance? I mean, what does he even have to offer them out there?"

"Aside from control over Misfit Island?" Marcus's voice dripped with sarcasm. "He's using fear and power to draw them to him. But there's more—he's promised them something else, something that everyone here fears will come to pass. A new reign."

The air in the room grew heavy as Marcus's grim words sank in. A reign of fear and dominance across Misfit Island would undo everything they had fought to protect—turning it from a sanctuary into yet another realm of darkness ruled by power and terror. Misfit Island could easily fall, barely fighting back, if Kirill and his allies succeeded.

When a knock sounded at the door, KeeKee jumped. This was the place where the leadership met, and they were all there, save a couple of supes who were out patrolling or standing guard in town, like Horatio who manned the Welcome Center.

Maxim and Sofka exchanged a nod and then the vampire walked to the door and opened it. A strange male no one had seen before stood before them grinning. He held out a hand. "I'm Gabriel, the Island sent for me and my team." He motioned to the six supes standing behind him.

Every single one of them could have easily passed for human special forces. They were all over six feet tall, one looked to be a head taller than the rest, and if KeeKee wasn't mistaken, they weren't all the same Supernatural race, either. Gabriel had short light blond hair, if she wasn't mistaken, the humans called it a "high and tight". Something she'd seen many times on military men. While he wore snow gear, it was all snug and she could tell he had a very broad chest. His chiseled facial features told her he was very fit. She expected him to be in the best shape of his life, probably better than most on the island.

The males behind him all had different color hair and skin, but they all had that chiseled face that military men had. One had longer hair, but the rest wore a high and tight style. Every single one of them had broad shoulders and stood in a way that told anyone looking they were confident, not only in their good looks, but also in their ability to fight, and kill. These were the types of supes that KeeKee would never want to meet in a dark alley.

Exactly what the island needed more of if they were going to successfully defend against any attack.

Maxim's grin showed his sharp canines, and he stepped back welcoming them inside. "We were expecting you. Thank you for coming."

KeeKee wasn't quite as open to welcoming them, but when Marcus smiled and headed toward the newcomers, she wondered if Gabriel and his allies had been Marcus' friends before they left the island.

"Gabriel, it's so good to see you again, my friend. How has life off-island treated you?" Marcus patted the male on the back and then shook hands with the rest in his group.

"I think better to me than you, although, I heard a rumor about you. Is it true you finally took a mate?" A spark entered Gabriel's eyes as he searched the room, looking for something KeeKee wasn't sure about.

"Ah, yes. I've been shackled. But once you get to know Ree, you'll understand why I succumbed to her so easily." Marcus chuckled and motioned for Ree to join him.

Once introductions were over, everyone moved back to the center of the room where the map was located.

"I have news about the Chilean docks." All friendly expression vanished the moment Gabriel went into military mode. "We were approached by an envoy from Kirill. They are actively seeking allies of the Island to join them. In fact, when they learned we were coming here, they offered us quite the boon to spy for them."

Marcus' brows rose. "Really? And what did Kirill have to offer you that you couldn't turn down?"

Maxim's eyes reddened and his fangs came out.

Several others growled and waited for Gabriel's response.

The supes with Gabriel didn't seem to worry about the rising tension in the room. They just grinned and waited for their Alpha to explain.

"It seems Kirill just assumed we'd be interested in running security here on the Island once he took it over. Someone must have given them some bad intel on us. They thought we were power hungry shifters who left he island because we weren't allowed to rule." Gabriel and his friends chuckled.

Marcus snorted. "Little did they know, you left because the last thing you wanted was to play Sheriff, or security detail." His features changed and he narrowed his brows. "Tell me, when you left it was because you were seeking peace and enlightenment. After your years of fighting other packs, you wanted to get away from any chance of fighting. Why are you back here now?"

Gabriel nodded. "You're right, we did want to seek enlightenment. And I think we found it in a small church run by missionaries from America." He looked to his buddies who all nodded. "When you've seen the sort of death and destruction we have, there comes a time when you need to find absolution, or forgiveness."

"Are you talking about religion?" KeeKee had heard others talking like this, but with the way she grew up, religion wasn't something she ever studied. Especially not the human's type of religion with one All-Knowing God.

One of the others with Gabriel, Rakabi, spoke up, "We did. While we scoured the jungles of Bolivia, we found a small village where a group of human men were witnessing to the residents about God. We stayed there for a few years and helped them. In the process, we found the peace we all needed."

Christian asked Gabriel, "does this mean you won't fight?"

All six supes shook their heads. And all of their eyes glowed with a fierceness that pierced KeeKee to her very soul.

"We have come to help defend the Island that is home to any and all who seek a peaceful existence. If this Island is defeated, then evil will win. We can't have that." Rakabi took his jacket off and when he crossed his arms over his chest, the large biceps bulged and KeeKee almost gasped.

His arms were larger than her thighs.

Ree's voice broke the silence, her tone solemn. "We need to focus on disrupting his alliances. If we can keep them from pulling together, it might shatter the momentum he's been building."

Christian nodded. "We need to get intel on whoever's already sided with him. And to do that, we'll have to lure them out."

Before KeeKee could respond, a sudden, sharp clatter sounded from outside the barracks—like something heavy had been thrown against the wall.

The entire group stiffened, instantly on edge. With Gabriel's team here, there weren't any other expected arrivals.

Maxim's eyes flashed crimson, his fangs elongating slightly as he moved towards the door with the speed of a predator ready to attack. Sofka followed quickly behind him, a low growl rumbling in her throat as she extended her claws.

Christian's hand instinctively tightened around KeeKee's, pulling her behind him even as they approached the door with cautious silence.

Maxim pushed open the door, revealing the cause of the noise—a figure slouched against the wall of the barracks, one hand clutching their side as blood seeped through worn clothing, staining the snow beneath them.

It was Carlotta, one of the newer arrivals who was living with Aelita on the island, and her gray coat—normally sleek and elegant—was matted with blood. Her eyes were wild with panic, darting between the faces of the group gathered at the entrance. A shimmer glowed around her eagle form as she shifted back into her human body.

"Help... he's coming, I couldn't—there was nothing... Please..." Her words came out in gasps, broken and frantic.

KeeKee dropped beside Carlotta, ignoring the shockwave of dizziness that threatened to pull her under as she reached out towards the girl's wounds. She pressed her fingers against the torn fabric, trying to stanch the flow of blood, but it just kept coming.

Carlotta's breathing was erratic, like it was taking every ounce of her strength just to cling to life. KeeKee knew that look—she'd seen it just yesterday with Serena—and it sent fresh fear snaking through her veins.

Maxim knelt down beside them, his face a mask of concentration as he held Carlotta's hand, trying to center her and calm the terror threatening to overwhelm her.

"Who did this?" Maxim asked urgently, his voice a low rumble.

Carlotta's eyes fluttered weakly, and for a moment, KeeKee thought she wouldn't answer. But then she took a shuddering breath and whispered a single word: "Kirill."

KeeKee's blood ran cold. This was the confirmation they had all dreaded—the threat had arrived, and she couldn't allow this girl to die before revealing what she knew.

But the questions KeeKee wanted to ask fell away as she noticed the wound at Carlotta's side—it was deep and jagged, unlike anything she'd seen on a supe before. This wasn't just a random attack. It was deliberate, violent—like a message sent in blood.

KeeKee could feel the rising panic in her chest, threatening to overtake her logical mind. But she couldn't let it—she had to focus on healing Carlotta, on stopping the life from ebbing out of the girl before their eyes.

But even as KeeKee began to draw on her fledgling healing powers for the second time in two days, it was as if something resisted—an impediment deeper than the physical wound itself. The magic buzzed under her skin, crackling with raw energy that threatened to lash out unpredictably. She hadn't fully recovered from healing Serena, and now, here she was again, called upon to perform a miracle she didn't fully understand.

Heat flared through her body, spreading from her chest outwards, pulsing with a rhythm that echoed something older, something primal within her. The world around her blurred as she began to funnel her magic into Carlotta's wound, attempting to knit the flesh together and mend the damage with every ounce of strength she could summon.

But this time, the power wasn't gentle—it was wild, fierce, battering against the terrible wound like a storm battering against the side of a cliff. KeeKee struggled to control it, trying to refocus her mind on the task at hand. The pattern of the magic seemed chaotic, erratic, and unpredictable, as if it had grown stronger since yesterday's use and refused to bend to her will.

Maxim watched her in silent awe, keeping his hand on Carlotta's head as KeeKee's magic surged and fought against the wound. Before his very eyes, the raw magic seemed to almost tear at KeeKee's control before somehow drawing itself back, creating an all-too-thin but crucial bond that began to close Carlotta's wound just enough to stabilize her condition.

Christian knelt next to KeeKee and added his strength to hers when he put a comforting hand on KeeKee's shoulder.

Finally, after what felt like a wrenching, exhausting eternity, KeeKee felt the energy ebb away, retreating back into her chest as if satisfied. She slumped forward, panting, her arms trembling with the effort it had taken to keep the power from overwhelming her.

The silence that followed was heavy with tension—an unspoken understanding among them all that KeeKee had just performed another task thought to be far beyond a typical Arctic Wolf Shifter, especially one that wasn't purebred. Once again, she had used that strange, instinctual magic, a gift connected to who she might become.

Christian's arms caught her before she could collapse fully, his touch warm and grounding against the cold, though she was barely aware of it. For a moment, all she could do was breathe—as if every breath had to be fought for like a hard-won battle.

"You did it," he whispered, deep admiration and concern coloring his voice. "KeeKee, you're…"

But before he could finish, Carlotta's voice, weak and barely audible, threaded between them like a dark warning. "He's coming... Kirill... planning something big..."

KeeKee struggled to regain her focus, blinking back the remnants of dizziness as she forced herself upright. "What is he planning? Carlotta, tell us."

Carlotta's breathing was shallow, her eyes glassy, but some fragment of strength remained within her as she clenched Maxim's hand one last time. "He's... he's leading them here... all of them... soon. But there's more... he's got something... something that can... nullify magic..."

The final word left her in a sigh, and as the last of her consciousness slipped away, a quiet gasp filled the room—Carlotta had passed out, either from the wound or perhaps exhaustion.

"That's it," Christian said, his tone steely. "We're done waiting for Kirill to make the first move. We can't leave this to chance or react too late. We need to hit him hard, make him realize who he's dealing with."

Marcus, who had been standing silent next to Ree, clenched his fists tightly, finally nodding in agreement. "Kirill isn't going to stop until Misfit Island is nothing more than a memory. We need to prepare everything—every defense, every bit of magic, every trick."

Ree, usually calm and measured in demeanor, stepped closer to Marcus, her voice low but filled with determination. "We'll protect each other, and we'll fight together."

For the first time in a while, KeeKee felt a surge of belief through the haze that had gripped her tightly. To fight back. To survive. To win. No matter how random or chaotic the pattern seemed to be, they would prevail.

"Alright, then," Sofka said, her voice clear above the tension-filled room. "Let's settle it. We've seen enough to know what we're all up against. We may not have everything in place yet, but we'll have to be prepared for whatever comes next. We go with our plan, and we strike before they can."

A chorus of agreement followed, and the group quickly split ways to follow through with the defense strategy they had spent hours piecing together. But this time, they did so not just with knowledge, but with the desperate urgency that came with knowing their enemy was not only on their shores but plotting a destruction that would threaten their very existence.

KeeKee watched as the group moved swiftly, setting into motion the steps they had outlined. But even as she prepared to follow, Christian's hand on her arm pulled her back.

"KeeKee," he murmured, concern pooling deep in his gaze as he searched her face for answers, "tell me how you're really doing. This magic... it's—"

"New," KeeKee finished for him. "But it's more than that. It's like something's changed in me since... maybe even before I came to the island. And now it's pushing back, asking... no, demanding that I use it, that I control it. But I don't know how much longer I can keep doing it before it overwhelms me."

Christian's thumb brushed her cheek, offering her a solace that made time stand still for just a moment—the temptation of resting, sharing the burden, lingered on her lips as the harsh reality of what they were up against shadowed everything else.

But there could be no stepping back. Not now. Only forward.

"We'll figure it out," he finally said, his voice as sure as his well-honed instincts in battle. "We'll take on Kirill together. And when the time comes... we'll tear down every alliance he's built."

It was a vow, unspoken as any breath shared in love or war, but one that set their focus to the task at hand.

KeeKee squeezed Christian's hand one last time before nodding. "Let's make sure we're ready. Lead on."

Chapter 18

The room was lit by the warm flicker of lantern light, casting shadows that danced along the walls of the barracks, turning the scattered papers and maps into something almost sinister. The quiet hum of tension filled the space as KeeKee, Christian, Sofka, and Maxim huddled together, reviewing their latest reconnaissance reports.

After the battle when Sofka went all crazy drill sergeant on everyone, most supes complained. Now? They were all grateful for the drills and exercises that have helped them to hone their battle skills. KeeKee doubted she'd hear anyone complain any time soon about Drill Sergeant Sofka.

KeeKee's fingers drummed lightly on the table, her mind absorbing the information laid out before her. They had gathered all the available intel, mapped out Kirill's suspected movements, and drafted their strategies. And yet, something still felt off, like they were missing a critical piece of the puzzle.

"So, we can confirm another of Kirill's spies?" Marcus's voice cut through the silence as he entered the room with Ree at his side.

KeeKee nodded, looking up from the map. "I heard Maxim and Sofka discussing Julianna this morning. She's been hiding in plain sight this whole time."

"Not hiding very well in the end," Sofka muttered, a trace of bitterness lacing her tone as she crossed her arms, her piercing gaze narrowing.

"She wasn't hiding," Maxim added, his voice low and deliberate. "She was waiting—keeping an eye on us, likely reporting back to Kirill."

Ree bit her lower lip in concern. "Julianna had the perfect cover. We all thought she was just another misfit running from a bad alpha. We should have seen it sooner."

"We're not half as bad at spotting spies as Kirill is at making them," Sofka remarked bitterly. "He's had years to perfect the art, while we've been playing catch-up since the moment we arrived here."

"Right now, we need to secure Julianna immediately," Christian interjected, his tone businesslike and cold. "If she catches wind that we're onto her, she'll alert Kirill."

Maxim exhaled sharply. "I'll confront her, but Sofka, I want you to stay close. If she's more dangerous than we anticipate, I might need backup."

"You know I'm not letting you run off alone," Sofka replied, her eyes flashing with protectiveness for her mate.

Ree glanced at Marcus, her face set in a determined frown. "We'll spread the word and keep everyone else on high alert. If Julianna has allies we haven't identified yet, they might try to get to her before we do."

KeeKee couldn't shake the sense of unease that lingered between them. Only a few short months ago, it was Sofka, Ree, and KeeKee. They formed their own little pack. Now that pack was growing—a family now, more or less with the five of them, or was it six now? Even the smallest threat to that balance could unravel everything they had worked for. But with the tension only growing, they couldn't keep their guard up forever.

Sofka's eyes caught KeeKee's, and though they were filled with the same fierce determination she'd admired for so long, there was also something KeeKee hadn't seen often—caution. Sofka wasn't one to second-guess herself, but at this moment, even she was aware of how precarious their situation had become.

"We secure Julianna tonight," Sofka added. "But we'll need to keep up appearances until we're ready to confront her. That means keeping our plans under wraps until the last possible moment."

Christian nodded, his expression hardening with resolve. "If Mab's presence here is anything to go by, Julianna isn't the only one we need to worry about. Mab loves to play both sides of a conflict if it benefits her. If that's the case, we'll need eyes on everyone. Who knows who she had made an alliance with before she left. Or who she was already allied with before she arrived. She may have been here to pass on vital info to a spy or gather intel from one, or more."

The mention of Mab made Marcus stiffen. His mother's arrival on the island had struck a chord deep within him, a chord that reverberated with mistrust and a lifetime of complicated feelings. He had been distant since her arrival, wrapping himself in a shell of carefully calculated indifference, but KeeKee could tell it was wearing on him.

As if sensing her gaze, Marcus met KeeKee's eyes and offered her a small nod, acknowledging her silent concern.

"We'll be ready," Marcus assured, his voice taking on that smooth, almost regal edge he used when he needed to pull from his royal upbringing. "And if Queen Mab set up any traps before leaving, well, she won't be catching us unaware."

Ree stepped up close to her mate and KeeKee saw something she'd not seen in her best friend before - a level of confidence fit for a queen.

"It's not just us she's after," Sofka said quietly, her eyes reflecting the lantern light with a sharp resolve. "She wants Misfit Island—wants it for herself or for someone else. If the island falls, it's not just Kirill we have to worry about. We'll be facing a far darker threat."

Silence settled over the group, the gravity of those words sinking in like jagged stones pressing on their collective chest.

"Then we need to move quickly," KeeKee urged, trying to keep her voice steady. "We can't wait for them to come to us. We have to take the fight to them."

"They may have their spies," Maxim added, his voice cutting through the tension in the room, "but so do we—Julianna isn't the only one who knows how to play this game."

With the decision made, the group broke off and went their separate ways to begin their preparations. KeeKee felt a weight lifting off her chest, tempered with the knowledge that this night would likely set the course for everything that followed. Everything hinged on whether they could contain Julianna without tipping off any of Kirill's other potential allies. If they could nip this in the bud, they might just stand a chance.

As KeeKee and Christian headed toward the door, she paused just before stepping outside.

"Christian, I'm worried," she admitted. "About Mab's involvement. About what comes next."

Christian's hand found hers, and this time he didn't pull it away. "I am too," he admitted, his voice low enough that only she could hear it. "But whatever comes, we'll face it together."

She nodded, taking comfort from his words, though the unease still gnawed at her heart. Together. It was all they could count on right now.

Later that evening, KeeKee and Christian stood in the shadows outside Julianna's small cottage, their breaths visible in the frigid air. The plan had been set into motion as soon as the sun dipped below the horizon. Sofka and Maxim were nearby, patrolling the perimeter with the same quiet focus they had carried throughout their preparation.

"We wait for the signal," Christian reminded her, his voice barely above a whisper.

KeeKee nodded, watching the cottage with baited breath. To an outsider, it looked like any other home on the island—modest, cozy, and filled with small comforts. She wondered how many of those comforts had been carefully constructed by Julianna to throw off suspicion. A deep sense of betrayal stirred within her, mingling with the ever-present fear.

They waited in silence, the minutes ticking by with excruciating slowness. Finally, the signal—a faint, almost imperceptible flash of light from the far reaches of the cops of twigs that passed as a forest on the island—appeared. Sofka was in position.

Careful not to make any noise, KeeKee and Christian crept toward the cottage door. Christian pressed his ear against the wood, listening intently for any sign of movement within. After a few tense moments, he straightened, nodding to indicate it was safe to proceed.

He reached for the handle, and with a gentle push, the door creaked open.

The interior of the cottage was just as KeeKee imagined—cozy and lived-in, with small trinkets on shelves and a fireplace crackling soothingly in the corner. But what struck KeeKee was the lack of any sign of recent activity. The place felt too still, too empty.

Christian's muscles tensed beside her, his senses on high alert. "Something's not right," he whispered.

KeeKee nodded, feeling the same unease. Moving into the room, she quickly scanned the space, her eyes narrowing as they landed on a small door at the back of the cottage. She pointed to it, and understanding passed between them wordlessly.

Christian moved forward, his hand hovering over the hilt of a dagger at his side as he slowly opened the door. KeeKee held her breath.

The door swung open to reveal a small, narrow hallway that led to a basement stairway. A faint light flickered from below, casting eerie shadows along the stone walls.

KeeKee's heart pounded as she descended the stairs with Christian. Each step brought them closer, the tension growing with every inch they covered. The air grew colder, the temperature of the basement starkly contrasting the warmth they had left behind upstairs.

At the base of the stairs, they found themselves in a small, dimly lit room, illuminated by a single lantern on a wooden table. The shadows danced erratically across the walls, and at the far end of the room, a figure stood with their back to them.

Julianna.

Her long, black hair cascaded down her back, hiding her face from view. But the tension in her posture told KeeKee that Julianna was fully aware of their presence. The air in the room grew thicker with the coming confrontation.

Christian's voice was calm, controlled. "We know what you've been up to, Julianna."

For a moment, Julianna didn't respond. All KeeKee could hear was the crackling of the lantern flame and the faint hum of the island vibrating around her.

Then, slowly, Julianna turned to face them. Her expression was unreadable, her green eyes cold and calculating. There was no trace of guilt or remorse—only a steely resolve that sent a shiver down KeeKee's spine.

"It took you long enough," Julianna said, her voice dripping with contempt. "I was beginning to think you'd never catch on."

KeeKee fought to keep her voice steady. "You've been feeding Kirill information, haven't you?"

Julianna's gaze shifted to KeeKee, a smirk playing at the corners of her lips. "Of course I have. But you've already figured that out, haven't you? So, tell me, what exactly do you plan to do about it?"

Christian's grip tightened around the hilt of his dagger. "You'll be coming with us. You're not leaving this island."

Julianna's smirk widened. "You think you can stop what's coming? Kirill's plan is already in motion, and there's nothing you can do to undo it. You're all too late."

"You underestimate us," KeeKee retorted, feeling her own resolve harden. "Misfit Island won't fall to you or Kirill. We've fought for this place before, and we'll fight to protect it again."

Julianna's expression darkened, her amusement fading into something far more dangerous. "That's the problem with you runaways—so full of hope and foolish dreams. But this island isn't a sanctuary—it's a prison. And soon, it will be a grave."

Before KeeKee or Christian could react, Julianna's form shimmered, morphing into her leopard form with a speed that left them momentarily stunned. Within seconds, she charged toward them, teeth bared, and claws extended, driven by both primal instinct and desperate circumstances.

But before Julianna could reach them, Christian was already in motion, deflecting her attack with a sharp slash of his dagger. The blade grazed her side, drawing blood and causing her to recoil with a snarl.

KeeKee's pulse quickened, adrenaline flooding her system as she prepared to defend herself. But before she could move, a flash of movement from above caught her eye, and she realized with a jolt that Sofka and Maxim had dropped into the basement from a concealed entrance above the stairs.

They flanked Julianna, circling her with practiced precision, their eyes blazing with the intensity of mates working together to defend each other and those they cared about.

Julianna's eyes darted between the four of them, calculating her odds. But even she knew she was outnumbered, her only hope of escape cut off by the very island she had betrayed.

"This isn't over," Julianna hissed, her voice a low growl as she shifted back into her human form, clutching her side where Christian's blade had drawn blood. "You think you've won? You've only delayed the inevitable."

Maxim stepped closer, his eyes cold and unyielding. "You'll answer for your involvement with Kirill. And if there's anyone else working with you, we'll find them."

Julianna's lips curled into a defiant sneer. "You think you can stop what's coming? Kirill is stronger than any of you. And when he comes, not even this pathetic island will protect you."

"It doesn't matter how strong Kirill is," Christian said, his voice deadly calm. "We'll do whatever it takes to protect Misfit Island from him—and from you."

KeeKee felt a surge of pride at Christian's words. They may still be facing overwhelming odds, but they were united. And together, they would stand against whatever Kirill had in store for them.

As they led Julianna out of the cottage and toward the jail where she would be held until they could extract more information from her, KeeKee's mind raced with the implications of what they had learned.

Kirill's plan was in motion, and the clock was ticking. But they had managed to secure one of his spies, taking a critical step toward understanding the full scope of his intentions.

"We'll have to act fast," KeeKee murmured to Christian, her voice filled with resolve. "Every moment we delay gives Kirill more time to advance his plans."

Christian nodded in agreement. "We've gained an advantage tonight, but this is only the beginning. The real battle is still ahead of us."

As they passed by the town square, where the festive decorations glowed softly against the night sky, KeeKee felt a renewed sense of purpose. Misfit Island was more than just a place—it was a sanctuary, a beacon of hope for those who had nowhere else to go.

And she would fight for it.

Together with Christian, Sofka, Maxim, Ree, Marcus, and the rest of their allies, KeeKee would confront whatever dangers lay ahead, no matter the cost.

As they reached the jail, where Sheriff Roscoe stood waiting, his eyes narrowing with determination, KeeKee knew one thing for certain:

She would not let Misfit Island fall.

Chapter 19

KeeKee, Christian, Sofka, Maxim, and a small group of other Misfit Island inhabitants gathered near the water's edge. KeeKee looked out at where the water should be and watched as the fog moved all around and swirled into peaks and valleys. She felt as though the Island was sending them an ominous message, but she didn't understand what it was trying to convey. The long journey ahead weighed on their minds, but it was a necessary step if they were to gather the information they desperately needed about Kirill's plans. The stakes were too high to sit idly by while he orchestrated his next move. They needed answers, and they needed them now.

Bart, the gargoyle who had ferried countless souls to and from the island, stood at the helm of his boat. His stocky frame was almost dwarfed by the wheel he gripped with stone hands. Despite his age, Bart's keen eyes, capable hands, and years of experience made him one of the safest bets when navigating the treacherous waters between Misfit Island and the mainland.

KeeKee adjusted the puffy parka that hung over her shoulders, its weight a comforting reminder of the island she was leaving behind, however briefly. This trip to the mainland would only be her second time off-island since she arrived. She wasn't worried about the boat ride itself, that was rather short and other than traveling through a portal, it was uneventful. The unknown was what had her wanting to bite her nails.

Marcus gave Ree a tender kiss on the forehead as Ree clung to his arm. "Sofka, are you sure you don't need us to come along?"

"Yes, I'm sure. We need supes we can depend on to stay here and keep an eye on things. Gabriel and his team are solid, but they haven't been here in a while." Sofka glanced at Marcus, thinking about his mother, then gave Ree a tight smile. Maxim waved his mate over to his side and she hugged Ree before moving away.

KeeKee watched Sofka and Maxim, who were exchanging a private conversation just a few feet away. The closeness between them—the way they moved in sync, understanding each other without needing words—was something KeeKee deeply admired. It was a bond forged by love and tempered by the harsh trials they had faced together.

"The boat will be ready soon," Christian commented beneath his breath from beside her. His voice was calm but laced with the ever-present undercurrent of tension everyone had been living with since Kirill's shadow first darkened their doorstep.

KeeKee nodded, staring out at the silver-hued waves that lapped gently against the shore as the blanket of fog ebbed and flowed showing snippets of the ocean they would soon traverse. "We can't afford any mistakes, Christian," she murmured, her voice barely carrying over the sound of the water and the distant screech of seabirds.

"I know," he responded, a hint of resolve deepening his tone. "We've been holding our breath too long, waiting for the next wave to hit. It's time we took control."

Bart's gravelly voice broke through their private moment. "All aboard who's goin' aboard! It'll be a rough trip 'cross the pond, so hold fast if ye don't want to lose yer lunch."

KeeKee grinned as she realized that Bart was trying to down play the tense situation with a bit of salty pirate speak. She knew she liked that gargoyle and was glad he'd be aboard to help them.

The group moved to board the boat, leaving Marcus and Ree behind on the rickety old dock. As KeeKee reached the gangway, she gave them a small wave. Ree waved back, though her expression was weary with concern.

"Stay safe," Ree called out. Marcus added a sober nod, his silent wish for their safety conveyed in his piercing gaze. "We'll be waiting for your return."

KeeKee's heart swelled with the knowledge that this just might be their final goodbye. But she wasn't about to let her mind go in that direction. With a final glance at the island, she turned and stepped aboard the small boat, joining the others on the deck.

The boat rumbled to life beneath them, its powerful engine thrumming beneath their feet as they eased out into the crisp water. The Dark Hills loomed in the background, their snow-dusted peaks blending with the misty horizon. There was a strange tranquility in the moment—the calm before the storm.

As they sailed further out into the open ocean, Bart guided the boat with expert precision to a location where the air seemed to shimmer with a faint, otherworldly light. KeeKee recognized the spot immediately—where the portal to the mainland resided, concealed by the island's magic and accessible only to those with permission to visit the island.

Christian moved closer to her, his warmth a welcome contrast to the cool wind that bit at her cheeks. "We'll be on the other side soon," he said, his voice steady with a confidence that KeeKee found infectious. "It won't be long now."

KeeKee nodded, but couldn't shake the anxious knot in her stomach. But there was no turning back now—they had to find the warehouse where Kirill's agents were last seen, and quickly.

Bart's voice rang out again. "Stand tight, misfits. Yer 'bout to embark on a journey unlike any ye've faced before." He spit water to the side, as he usually did. For some strange reason, this small piece of Bart's normal behaviour gave KeeKee a smidgeon of peace and she grinned.

Just as he finished speaking, the faint shimmer in the air intensified, wrapping around the boat like a cocoon. KeeKee felt a curious sensation—as though her skin was tingling with electricity—before the world around them seemed to twist, fold, and dissolve. The water beneath them rippled with strange motion as the skyline bent and wavered like a mirage.

And then it was over.

The shimmering air cleared and KeeKee found herself squinting into the brilliant light of the southern hemisphere's sun, a stark contrast to the magical dome sky of Misfit Island. They had arrived in Southern Chile, far from the safety of home.

The harbor they now drifted toward was bustling with activity—human fishermen hauling in nets, seagulls squabbling overhead, and the distant hum of village life just beyond the shore. But there was something else KeeKee noticed—a tension that made the air feel almost electric. Though to most, it would seem like just another day at the docks, KeeKee could sense the undercurrent of danger lurking beneath the surface.

Maxim was the first to ask, "Is this the place?"

Bart, still at the helm, nodded. "Aye, this is it. The heart of Punta Arenas—the mouth of the southern continent—and where we should find the warehouse in question." He was still continuing with a bit of his salty seadog speak, and did seem to spit a lot less. KeeKee wondered if this was his way of dealing with the tension that seemed to suck the joy out of being in the water on this trip.

She looked to Maxim, the only vampire in the group, and wondered how he was doing with the direct sunlight. He caught her look and winked. "Don't worry, I can handle the sunlight."

Sofka narrowed her eyes, scanning the horizon. "We're not alone here," she muttered, her intuition painting invisible lines of threat and opportunity across the scene before her. "We should split up...and stay sharp."

KeeKee's pulse quickened at the suggestion. For as long as she could remember, the idea of splitting up had a sense of finality to it. Splitting up had always been a precursor to disasters in the past. But there wasn't time to protest.

Maxim gently took Sofka's hand, and she leaned in to hear his whispered words of encouragement.

Christian stepped closer to KeeKee. "We'll cover more ground this way," he explained softly, his breath warm on her temple. "You and I will head for the shipyard near the warehouse our spies warned us about. Sofka and Maxim can scan the outer regions, make sure we don't have any unwelcome surprises. And the rest will walk through town and see what they can discover."

KeeKee met his gaze, the cold blue of his eyes reminding her of the frigid waters around Misfit Island, tempered by the warmth she knew was in him. When she nodded her assent, it wasn't just out of obligation—it was trust in him, and in the bond they had begun to forge together.

"Fine," she said, her voice firmer than she felt. "Let's get to it."

With a brief glance and nod between them, the group disembarked, splitting into pairs as they hit the docks. Bart remained aboard, securing the boat and preparing to be their means of escape if the situation took a turn for the worse. KeeKee looked back and felt a smile tug at her lips when she witnessed Bart turn his head toward the water and a long waterfall left his mouth and emptied into the harbor.

The shadowed alleyways and bustling streets of Punta Arenas unfolded before them like a maze. The narrow junctions led to the more industrial areas, where the heart of trade pulsed through every shipyard, warehouse, and container terminal.

As KeeKee and Christian moved deeper into the heart of the shipyard, the atmosphere darkened. The din of working machinery faded in the distance, replaced by the clink and grind of heavy metal being moved and shifted, orders barked out in Spanish by workers hurriedly loading and unloading crates.

They kept their pace brisk, edging closer to a collection of newly arrived cargo ships that had only recently been moored in the bustling port. Wooden crates littered the area, some stacked as high as the surrounding buildings, creating enough cover to act as hiding spots.

Christian led them closer, his posture a perfect fusion of predatory grace and quiet lethality.

Suddenly, vibrations rumbled up from their feet, stirring dust that shimmered through stray beams of light, highlighting a hidden group lurking behind a wall of shipping containers. KeeKee's pulse quickened as she spotted them—vague figures clad in dark, nondescript clothing, their faces obscured.

Christian motioned for KeeKee to take cover as he moved silently forward, positioning himself along a row of stacked crates. He gestured for her to stay hidden, his features locked in steely concentration.

Heart pounding, she crouched behind the containers, straining to catch fragments of their conversation in the rapid, clipped tones of Spanish. KeeKee only managed to understand a handful of words, but it was enough to send a shiver down her spine—Kirill's name came up more than once. These weren't just ordinary workers. They were performing what seemed to be a clandestine transaction, exchanging packages and information dangerous enough to warrant hiding in the shadows.

A sickening knot of dread coiled in her stomach, and her thoughts immediately shot to the island. If these were Kirill's agents operating unchecked, then the situation was far worse than they could have imagined.

Christian's gaze met hers, and with a slow, deliberate nod, he crept closer to the group, his training and instincts ignited as he focused on catching an earful of crucial details. KeeKee felt terror and admiration battle within her in equal measure as she watched him. Despite the clear danger, she knew he was doing this to protect them all, and she couldn't help but respect his determination.

A stray word drifted to her ears—"Misfit"—spoken by a man who appeared to be in command of the small group.

That was all she needed to hear.

Christian must have heard it too, because he tensed and motioned for KeeKee to retreat farther back, just as one of the men began walking toward the crates.

KeeKee instinctively pushed herself into the small alcove between two containers, her breath caught in her throat as the approaching footsteps drew nearer. Christian melted into the shadows, an embodiment of stealth as the leader passed by, a dull thud echoing through the alley as he tapped a wooden crate with his boot, apparently searching for something—or someone.

KeeKee's pulse drummed an erratic rhythm in her ears, her muscles coiled like springs as she weighed her options. It wouldn't take much for the man to discover their presence—one false move, and the entire operation would be compromised.

Time seemed to stretch out endlessly until, finally, the man stepped away, his attention dragged back to the rest of the group as they continued their transaction.

Christian waited just a moment longer before creeping back to her side, his expression unreadable but his focus sharp. "We need to find out more," he whispered, his voice barely audible. "Whoever they are, they're tied to Kirill, and that means they have to know something important."

KeeKee nodded, slowly releasing the breath she had been holding. "Agreed. But how do we get to them? If these guys are working with Kirill, you can bet they're prepared for this."

"We don't fight them here," Christian replied, considering their options carefully. "We follow them. We find out where they're hiding and what they're transporting. If we can, we'll intercept the ship itself and make sure nothing leaves this port that could help Kirill."

KeeKee couldn't help the apprehension that rippled through her. She had expected a fight, yes, but not a quiet game of cat and mouse in a foreign land where their every move could be observed, where an unseen enemy might unmask them with ease. But if Christian had a plan, she would follow it.

"Okay," she resolved, the fear tightening her grip on the hilt of her dagger as she readied herself to follow their leader. "Let's do this."

As they busied themselves with circling around to continue their surveillance of the group, Christian sent a brief text message to Sofka, relaying the shift in strategy. While back on Misfit Island their mobile phones rarely worked, but the with knowledge they'd heading back to the human world, it made sense for them all to charge their phones and bring them on this journey.

They agreed to reconvene near the docking areas when they could. The warehouse they were searching for might be found just by following these agents of Kirill.

The tension crawled up KeeKee's spine, making her hyper-aware of every sound, every movement along their path. Christian's shadow guided her through narrow alleyways, bringing them closer to the edge of the shipyard and up on top of a high stack of crates as their targets started moving toward the water, where a small cargo vessel waited in eager anticipation of its clandestine load.

It didn't take long for the men to begin boarding the boat, their actions suspiciously deliberate—a sign they were well aware of the cargo's value. Every instinct within KeeKee screamed at her to take them down, but the moment wasn't right. They needed information first.

From an elevated position overlooking the vessel, KeeKee and Christian watched as the men arranged the crates on board, their actions calculated and precise. The leader remained at the helm, issuing orders with stern authority that reminded her of Kirill himself. Whoever this man was, he had experience and confidence—two traits that only strengthened KeeKee's resolve to see him brought down before he could reconnect with Kirill.

They remained hidden until, finally, the ship's engines roared to life, and the vessel began to pull away from the dock with the aid of several tug boats.

"It's time," Christian said in a low tone, his eyes flaring with determination. "They'll lead us right to Kirill's operations if we stay close." He motioned for them to climb back down to the ground so they could try and follow the path of the ship.

KeeKee's heart pounded as they began their quiet pursuit, moving silently along the shoreline to avoid detection, careful not to lose the ship from view. If they played their cards right, they might be able to discover the exact location of Kirill's base on the mainland. Knowing where he was operating from, as well as his supply routes, could give them a strategic advantage.

Yet, even with this glimmer of hope, KeeKee could not shake the weight of dread hanging over her heart. Keeping her focus on the ship and the mission before them, KeeKee made a silent vow: she would not allow their home—Misfit Island, or the people she loved—to fall into the hands of the enemy. They had come into enemy territory, but they would leave it with the information they needed to win this fight.

Whatever it took.

Chapter 20

The low hum of the cargo vessel's engines had KeeKee's hackles raised as she and Christian crouched behind a large stack of wooden crates near the edge of a cliffside overlooking the shore. As the ship they had been following inched closer to its destination, KeeKee's stomach knotted with both anticipation and apprehension. They had stayed as close as they could during the time the vessel spent navigating the fog-heavy waters, and now they were being led right to the base they had been looking for.

"Isn't it strange that they moved further inland, and not out to the open sea?" KeeKee asked as they continued their trek along the shoreline. "This channel can't be deep enough to traverse much longer, can it?"

Christian shook his head. "We have to be close now. While those tugboats can deal with shallow waters, the smaller container ship won't be able to go much further. I'm actually surprised it has been able to go this far inland. My guess is that they dredged the bottom of the channel to give them the ability to go…" he waved his hand in the direction of the ship, "somewhere over there."

"I'm going to text Sofka and give her our location and an update." KeeKee pulled her cell phone out of her pocket and began texting.

"There," Christian whispered, his voice so low it barely registered above the insistent crashing of the waves below. "The channel ends at the highest point of the cliffside." He pointed to a cave-like structure in the back of the rocky cliffside, mostly hidden from view by natural overgrowth. But now, with the ship mooring carefully beside it, it was clear that this wasn't just any cave—this was Kirill's hidden base.

KeeKee narrowed her eyes, silently admiring Christian's sharp instincts. She wouldn't have spotted the hidden entrance without his guidance. Her heart raced as she took in the sight before them. The cargo vessel was now unloading numerous crates and barrels—carefully concealed within each container rested potential weapons, resources, and most disturbingly—smuggled supernatural goods.

"Looks like we found it," KeeKee murmured in return, her breath catching in her throat. It was deeply unsettling to see the magnitude of Kirill's operation. There was no denying the scale of what they were witnessing.

Without looking at her, Christian pressed a hand on her arm, steadying her. "We can't act yet," he muttered, his voice tight. "Going in without a plan will get us killed or worse—it'll tip off Kirill that we're onto him, and he'll move faster."

KeeKee nodded, the gravity of their situation pressing down on her. "I just can't shake the feeling that this is bigger than we thought," she whispered. "Whatever's in those crates isn't just to bolster Kirill's forces. This is the foundation of something… larger, darker."

Christian's ice-blue eyes flicked toward her, the steel resolve behind them as unwavering as ever. "There's no turning back now. But we need to play this smart, KeeKee. We'll report what we found, and when we strike, it'll be from a position of strength."

KeeKee understood his caution, but a cold shiver ran down her spine at the thought that with every passing moment, Kirill was strengthening his grip over the supernatural black market and gaining influence that could disrupt much more than just Misfit Island.

The distant creaking of boxes and shouted orders caught their attention as more and more crates were hoisted from the cargo vessel into the cave, disappearing into the shadows like whispers into the void. KeeKee strained her wolf hearing and vision, trying to catch every detail of the movements below them.

"They'll have guards," she whispered, her gaze shifting back to Christian. "We should scout the perimeter, see if we can get better intel on the cave's layout."

Christian gave a sharp nod, his eyes already scanning their surroundings for the best vantage point. "Good idea. But remember—stealth is our strength right now. We need to get this intel back without being spotted."

Silently, they slipped away from the cliffside, keeping low to avoid detection as they circled the area in search of any additional openings or patrols. The further they moved, the clearer it became that the cave wasn't just a temporary hideout—it was a well-defended, strategically placed stronghold.

"I count at least four guards near the entrance," Christian said quietly, as they observed from a ridge overlooking the cave mouth. "Two more are stationed along the cliffside, watching for any approach by sea."

KeeKee's stomach tightened. They were right to be cautious. Trying to engage the guards would only alert Kirill's men before they could get the full scope of what they were dealing with.

"We should keep moving," she whispered, glancing toward a rock formation that jutted out along the ridge. "Let's see if we can get closer to the storage areas and figure out what they're hiding."

With Christian leading the way, they weaved through the narrow pathways and natural cover offered by the rugged landscape. Every muscle in KeeKee's body was taut, her heightened senses picking up every creak, every breeze, every out-of-place sound. She could feel the weight of the magic surrounding them too, a dark tangle of power that clung to the air like a heavy fog.

Finally, they reached a position where they could see into the cave more clearly. Hidden by thick foliage, they watched as several workers—humans intermixed with supes, likely coerced into Kirill's service—unloaded the cargo into the inner recesses of the cave. Lamps were strung throughout the cavern, casting long shadows across the stone. And then...

Her breath caught when she saw it.

Dragon eggs.

A small collection of them had been placed inside heavily guarded crates, each shimmering faintly with golden light even beneath the layers of protective coverings. KeeKee's heart lurched in her chest. Dragon eggs weren't just illegal—they were priceless. More than that, they held immense magical power. If Kirill was trafficking dragon eggs, that meant he had access to a resource that could tip the balance of power in his favor. Worse still, it meant he was working with someone very powerful from the black market—and possibly from a dragon house itself.

"Christian..." KeeKee murmured, her voice barely a breath. "Do you see them?"

Christian, whose eyes had already zeroed in on the precious cargo, dropped into a crouch beside her. "I see them," he replied, his voice tight with barely contained frustration. "This is far worse than we thought."

KeeKee could feel her pulse racing in her throat, her wolf instincts practically howling at her to do something. Destroy the eggs, destroy Kirill's black market deal, stop this madness before they had a chance to lose everything.

But she couldn't afford to be rash.

"Why dragon eggs?" She asked, her voice still barely above a whisper, as she tried to make sense of it. "What's Kirill planning that requires magic this strong?"

Christian's jaw tightened. "Whatever it is... it's bad news. Aelita mentioned the black market ring—this must be what she was referring to. There's someone out there profiting from the sale of dragon eggs. With that kind of power, they could destabilize entire regions of the supernatural world, not to mention only one egg could take down the barrier protecting our island."

KeeKee inhaled deeply through her nose, trying to steady her wild emotions. "We need more intel on this buyer, or buyers. And we need to send word to Marcus and Ree immediately. They should start preparing the island for combat because this is only going to escalate."

Before they could move, a sound from behind sent a jolt of terror down KeeKee's spine.

Footsteps.

KeeKee and Christian both froze, their gazes meeting for a heartbeat before Christian gestured for her to stay hidden. A shadow loomed behind the nearby rocks, creeping closer to their position.

With merciless precision, Christian slipped out of their hiding spot and into position, his movements as silent as the wind itself. KeeKee could hear him breathing, could feel every muscle in his body tense as he prepared to strike if necessary.

But just as the figure rounded the corner—Christian struck, pulling the intruder to the ground with lightning speed and pinning them beneath his weight.

KeeKee crawled forward carefully, heart in her throat.

To their surprise, the intruder was neither a guard nor a patrolling soldier. It was a girl—a teenage girl, perhaps no older than sixteen or seventeen. Her wide, fearful eyes stared up at Christian from under the authority of his dagger, her breaths shallow with terror.

"Hold on," KeeKee whispered sharply, stepping quickly to Christian's side and motioning for him to lower his weapon. "She's not one of them. Look at her."

Christian hesitated a beat before loosening his grip. The girl gasped in relief, trembling with visible fear.

"What are you doing out here?" KeeKee asked, kneeling down to meet the girl's panicked gaze, but keeping her voice soft, reassuring.

"I-I was j-just... trying to... escape," the girl stammered, her body quaking.

"Escape?" Christian's voice softened, as if surprised. "From who?"

The girl's breaths came in ragged waves as she gestured toward the cave's entrance with trembling hands. "I... I was brought here. Forced to work. They said they'd kill me if I didn't do what they wanted."

KeeKee's heart shattered at the fear woven through the girl's words. She reached out, laying a soothing hand on the girl's shoulder. "You're safe with us now."

The girl's fear-riddled eyes locked with KeeKee's as she whispered, "They have others... Supes. Half-breeds. They're planning to move them... Soon. To Kirill."

KeeKee and Christian exchanged an urgent look.

This wasn't just about dragon eggs. Kirill was trafficking people—supernatural beings. KeeKee knew this, but she didn't realize he had brought them here, to Chile. So close to Misfit Island. And if they didn't act soon, they'd lose the chance to free the supes and half-breeds who had been illegally trafficked to do things KeeKee didn't know if she could handle.

Chapter 21

KeeKee and Christian knew they had to act quickly. The young girl they had just rescued from Kirill's clutches, whom they learned was named Anastasia from a small town in Eastern Europe, was trembling with a mixture of fear and relief. She looked at them with wide, tear-stained eyes, her thin frame shaking under the weight of her experiences.

"Anastasia," KeeKee said softly, placing a comforting hand on her shoulder. "We need to get you to safety. Will you come with us?"

Anastasia's eyes widened further, and she hesitated for a moment before nodding slowly. "Yes," she whispered, her voice barely audible. "I want to be safe."

Christian nodded firmly, his grip on his dagger tightening. "We'll make sure you're safe. But first, we need your help. Can you tell us more about Kirill's plans and where the other prisoners are being held?"

Anastasia took a shaky breath and nodded. "They're keeping everyone in the caves not far from here. Supes, half-breeds... some of them are very sick. Kirill's planning to move them soon, maybe in a few days, when a big ship comes."

KeeKee's heart raced at the urgency in Anastasia's words. Time was indeed running out, and they needed to act swiftly. They had to relay this information to Sofka and Maxim and get back to Misfit Island as fast as possible.

"Alright, we'll move quickly," Christian decided, his voice steady and confident. "We need to get back to the others and warn them about Kirill's plan. It looks like we might have a window of opportunity to strike before the big shipment is moved."

KeeKee pulled out her phone and sent a quick message to Sofka and Maxim, outlining their discovery and the urgent need to rendezvous at the boat. Then they messaged the rest of the teams telling them to rendezvous at the dock. The response was swift, acknowledging the gravity of the situation and assuring them that they would be there soon.

With Anastasia tucked safely between them, KeeKee and Christian made their way back to the docks, taking care to avoid any potential guards or lookouts. The journey was tense, every shadow seeming to hold a hidden threat, every sound echoing the impending danger. Anastasia was a real trooper and she kept up with them the entire way back.

As they approached the boat, they saw Bart waiting anxiously, his stone face betraying none of the tension he must have felt. Sofka and Maxim were already there, their expressions a mix of urgency and relief.

"What's the situation?" Sofka asked immediately, her eyes sweeping over Anastasia with concern.

As Christian began to explain the situation, the rest of the their fact-finding team began to trickle in.

"We found Kirill's base," Christian explained rapidly. "They're trafficking dragon eggs and have other prisoners, including half-breeds and several different supes. Kirill plans to move them to another base in the next few days."

Maxim's gaze darkened, both from the seriousness of the situation and the limited time they had to act. "We need to strike now, before they have a chance to move them. But we need a solid plan."

Anastasia, who had been silently observing the exchange, suddenly spoke up, her voice stronger than before. "I know the layout of the base. I can help guide you through the tunnels and the holding areas."

KeeKee nodded, grateful for Anastasia's willingness to help. "Thank you. That will be invaluable."

Christian turned to Bart. "Can we get back to the island quickly? We need to gather more allies and prepare for the strike."

Bart nodded solemnly. "Of course, I'll get you back as fast as the wind, and the portal permits."

Without further delay, they boarded the boat. As they set sail, KeeKee couldn't help but feel a sense of foreboding. They were on the brink of a dangerous and decisive battle, one that could determine the fate of Misfit Island and everyone they held dear.

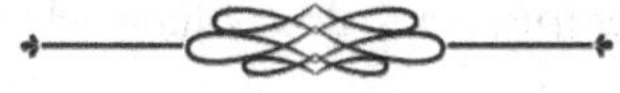

Back on the island, the atmosphere was electric with anticipation and determination. Messages had been sent out calling for allies to rally in support of the upcoming battle. The island itself seemed to thrum with energy, as if sensing the impending conflict.

In the main square, KeeKee, Christian, Sofka, and Maxim gathered with Marcus, Ree, and a growing number of allies who had answered their call for aid. Anastasia stayed close to KeeKee, her eyes wide but filled with a newfound resolve.

"Thank you all for coming," KeeKee addressed the crowd, her voice steady and clear. "We've identified Kirill's Chilean base and discovered his plans to traffic dragon eggs and prisoners to another location in a day or two. We need to act swiftly and decisively before we lose the chance to free the abducted supes."

Murmurs of agreement rippled through the crowd, everyone keenly aware of the stakes.

Sofka stepped forward, her eyes scanning the gathered allies. "We have a narrow window to strike before Kirill moves his prisoners. Anastasia has agreed to guide us through the base. We need volunteers ready to fight and secure the prisoners and dragon eggs."

Maxim added, "This won't be easy. Kirill has guards and we can expect resistance. But together, we can outsmart and overpower them."

Marcus, standing beside Ree, his expression grim and determined, spoke up. "Remember, Kirill isn't working alone. We need to be on high alert for any sign of Queen Mab's involvement." He shook his head, still not convinced his mother was working with Kirill. However, he would never trust her to do anything right. She's always done what is best for her, and no one else. "She's cunning and won't hesitate to exploit any weakness."

Ree nodded, her eyes reflecting the same resolve. "We'll be ready for whatever comes our way."

The crowd buzzed with energy and determination. KeeKee could feel the solidarity, the united front they presented against the encroaching darkness.

Christian, standing beside KeeKee, his eyes locked onto hers, added, "We fight not just for Misfit Island, but for all those who have no voice, no power to resist Kirill's tyranny. Together, we stand strong."

As the final preparations were made, KeeKee couldn't shake the uneasy feeling in her gut. She knew they were facing an uphill battle, but the island's magic seemed to pulse through her veins, giving her a strength she hadn't known before. They were bound together by a common cause, a belief in justice and freedom.

Sofka took Anastasia to get cleaned up and some fresh clothes, and Christian pulled KeeKee to side. "KeeKee, are you sure we can trust Anastasia? Doesn't it seem too easy how we found her and got away with her?"

KeeKee bit her lower lip and considered what Christian asked. She shook her head. "No, I can feel in my gut that Anastasia is on our side." She tilted her head. "What does the future Santa think? Is she on the nice list? Or the naughty list?"

Christian chuckled. "Sticky candy canes! I should have thought to see where she stood on the lists." He thought for a moment and a sly smile crossed his features before he cleared all emotion on his face. "She's on the nice list."

KeeKee took his arm and grinned. "Then we go to battle with a new ally."

They would fight all for Misfit Island, as though Christmas itself was on the line.

Chapter 22

As night fell, the final group of allies boarded Bart's boat, armed with both physical and magical weapons, their resolve unwavering. The waterways between Misfit Island and the mainland were quiet, the moon casting a silver glow over the waves as if guiding their path. After so many traverses through the magical portal that took them quickly across the Southern waters between Chile and Antarctica, the voyage was beginning to lose some of the awe KeeKee had once felt.

Or maybe it was just the upcoming incursion into enemy territory that dulled her sense of excitement as she traveled through the magical portal, covering hundreds of miles of sea in an instant.

Once they reached the shore, they moved swiftly and silently, following the route Anastasia indicated. KeeKee kept close to her, ensuring her safety while also relying on her guidance.

As they approached the hidden base, KeeKee could feel the tension rising. They exchanged hand signals, preparing to breach the entrance.

Silently, they spread out, each group taking a different section of the base to ensure they could cover as much ground as possible.

Kirill's first line of defense was taken by surprise, swiftly and silently dispatched by the skilled supes on Team Misfit Island. KeeKee used her newly acquired healing powers to immobilize rather than kill, ensuring they had the element of surprise on their side.

Inside the base, the chaos began. Kirill's men, unaware of the intrusion, were caught off guard.

Aelita, who still hadn't shown her shifter form, charged in with a gun in one hand and a large sword in the other. KeeKee and Anastasia watched in fascination, and maybe a bit of horror, as the powerful supe easily sliced the head off of one guard before he even had a chance to shift, or pull his weapon out of his belt.

"Stick behind me and watch my back." Aelita called out over her shoulder at KeeKee.

Since KeeKee didn't have much experience with battles, she fell in line. She told herself that someone needed to keep an eye on Aelita's back. And she really didn't want Anastasia to have to fight, either. The poor thing wasn't even a full supe, she had shifter blood running through her veins, but she'd never been able to shift like her mother did. Her father was the human, and Anastasia told KeeKee that she feared she'd forever be just like him.

Before KeeKee had a chance to respond, a guard had come in from behind a large set of racks that were full and snuck up on Aelita. This was KeeKee's chance to show she could pull her own. The little Arctic Wolf Shifter shifted as she flew in the air toward the male supe who had a large hunting knife poised to stab Aelita in the back. KeeKee's large paws clawed at the supes back and she pushed him down on his face.

Her muzzle leaned down against the guard's neck and she snapped her large teeth together before growling. He didn't move.

Anastasia quickly found some rope and helped tie the supe up so he couldn't do any harm to their teammates. "You really should let me dispatch him. If he's on Kirill's team, he's evil."

"I think we should keep a few to question. They might provide some good intelligence." Besides, KeeKee didn't like killing someone who had in essence surrendered.

Christian, who had been close by, dragged a shifted bear by his hind leg. The supe was knocked out, but his weight was proving to be difficult to manage. "KeeKee, can I get some help?"

"Of Course." KeeKee turned to Anastasia. "Any more rope?"

"On it." A small grin began on the young woman's face as she helped to secure yet another of her captors.

KeeKee realized that by letting Anastasia help, she was helping the girl deal with the trauma she'd suffered at the hands of Kirill's supes. This action was enabling Anastasia to take back the power that had been so callously stolen from her, and the others who were still trapped.

She also realized that had she and her two packmates allowed Kirill to sell them on the supernatural black market all of those months ago, they'd most likely be forced to fight Kirill's battles. In fact, they could have been on the other side of the fight several weeks back when Kirill made his first attempt at attacking the island. Before she would let that thought take root, she shoved it aside and focused on the here and now.

Prisoners were quickly liberated, two dragon eggs carefully secured, and the facility turned into a battlefield.

KeeKee, her senses heightened, felt a surge of power from within as she realized they were nearing victory. Each step they took, each enemy they defeated, brought them closer to the end of Kirill's reign.

But the victory came at a cost. Many allies were injured, some severely. Carmen the Toucan shifter, took a knife to her side as she attempted to stop one of the guards from sounding the alarm. In the end, another guard was able to sound the alarm, but the fact that Carmen distracted the first guard, gave them precious minutes to get in a defensive position before the bulk of the fighters came out of the cave. KeeKee used her healing powers to tend to the supes on her side, feeling the energy within her expand and grow stronger with each life she saved.

KeeKee stopped her forward momentum when she discovered Carmen. One look from her was all it took for Christian to replace her and watch Aelita's back. The female was a fierce warrior, but she still needed help when they were outnumbered by at least three to one.

Once she was sure Aelita was covered, KeeKee leaned over Carmen's prone body and wiped a drop of sweat from the female's forehead. "You did great, Carmen. Now we just need you to do one more thing."

When Carmen attempted to scoff, she broke out in a fit of coughs instead. KeeKee feared the knife punctured one of the Toucan Shifter's lungs. She put her hands on Carmen's injured side and closed her eyes. A moment later she opened them and nodded to Anastasia. "I'm going to need you to pull the knife out when I say. Keep it straight and go slow. Can you do that?"

Silently, Anastasia nodded and found a comfortable position next to Carmen.

"Carmen, I'm sorry, but this is going to hurt. Would you like a stick to bite down on?" KeeKee looked around for something small enough to put between the injured supe's teeth. While KeeKee had never done anything like this, she had seen it done before. Back when she, Sofka, and Ree were all part of Kirill's pack. The three of them may not have participated in many fights, but they had seen enough attacks, and training accidents, to have a decent understanding of first aid.

Gritting her teeth, Carmen breathed out an agreement. Once the small stick was in place, KeeKee nodded at Anastasia who put her hands on the hilt of the knife.

"Alright, prepare yourself, I'm going to have Anastasia pull on the count of three." KeeKee looked at the young woman who was assisting her and shook her head. Then she held up her forefinger to indicate she wanted the girl to pull on the count of one, and not three. When Anastasia nodded, KeeKee started the count, "one..."

Anastasia pulled slowly, but the knife coming back out earlier than expected, caused Carmen's eyes to open wide and her nostrils to flare. With fighting going on all around them, no one worried about the noise their patient made. KeeKee's hands were next to the hole the knife left and she closed her eyes again, focusing her power to close up the damage the knife made. She was so in tune with her newfound power, that she felt the tiny puncture wound in Carmen's lungs begin to close and the edges melded together as though a surgeon's ghost hand was in there stitching up the wound. Once the lung was closed, then the magic made its way out toward KeeKee's hands. It closed up every wound and slice it came near. When it finally closed the skin where the knife had been, KeeKee would have sworn Carmen had never been injured.

Although, the Toucan Shifter would have told her how much pain she was still in if she hadn't passed out in the process.

By the time KeeKee looked up, only a couple skirmishes remained. She could see many bodies lying around the base. Even though she didn't know for sure, she estimated that the enemy lost a lot more than the Misfits did. As she stood up to see where her friends were, KeeKee wobbled. "Whoa." She put a hand to her head and stood still while the world around her swirled and swayed.

Anastasia jumped to her feet and put a steadying hand on KeeKee's shoulder. "Are you alright? Can I help?"

"No, thank you. I'm fine. I just need to recharge." KeeKee bit her lower lip as the scene came more into focus. Bodies were everywhere. She'd have no trouble recognizing her own supes, but should she try and help those on the other side? A part of her said that all supes deserved medical treatment, but another part of her felt that only her allies should benefit from her gift. As she warred with herself on what was best to do, Christian came to her side and made the choice for her.

"KeeKee, you need to rest. You can't heal them all. The one thing I've learned from my mother about this gift of healing is that it isn't an endless pool of power. You've healed a lot of supes already. Take a break and we can triage the wounded. When you're ready, I can help you to find those you feel the call to heal." Christian led her to a crate not far from where she had healed Carmen. He helped KeeKee sit down and then took a water bottle from his pack and handed it to her. Then he pulled out a protein bar. "I also learned that my mom needed a lot of water and protein after healing others. Be sure to drink it all and finish at least two protein bars." He pulled another from his pack and set it on the crate next to her.

Finally, after what felt like endless hours of battle, they stood victorious. The base was in ruins, their enemies defeated, and the prisoners—both half-breeds and supes—were free.

Exhausted but triumphant, KeeKee looked around at her allies, seeing the cost of their battle etched in their faces. But they had won. They had struck a blow against Kirill's tyranny and freed countless souls from his grasp.

But as they prepared to return to Misfit Island, KeeKee knew this was only the beginning. Kirill would not take this defeat lightly. The true battle for the island's future was yet to come.

It was that thought that gave her the courage to do what she did next.

Not caring that at least two dozen of her compatriots from Misfit Island were in watching distance, KeeKee walked up to Christian and without a single word she took his face between her hands and pulled a confused, and dazed, Christian close to her. She looked into his eyes, almost asking for permission for what she was about to do. KeeKee had never initiated a kiss before, but she wasn't about to let that stop her. She'd seen plenty of human women do this, so she had no clue why it was so tough to do.

With their faces only centimeters apart, KeeKee closed her eyes and tilted her head just enough in anticipation of his warm lips touching hers. When she didn't feel the anticipated connection, she opened one eye only to wish she hadn't. Maxim stood there with both of his hands wrapped around Christian's neck. The vampire's eyes were red and his fangs had already elongated so much, they were forced to rest on the outside of Maxim's mouth and down along his chin.

"Maxim! What in Frosty's name are you doing?" She moved closer to the vampire and reached for the hands that were wrapped so tightly around Christian's neck, that he was beginning to turn purple. "You'll kill him if you don't release him. And you do not want Santa coming here. Not now." Her nostrils flared and she pulled the vampire's fingers back from Christian's neck as much as she could.

Maxim simultaneously released Christian and pushed him down to the ground. "Never kiss my little sister. We don't need you playing with her emotions and then abandoning her." The vampire shivered with anger and something KeeKee couldn't identify - fury or was it hatred?

"You fool, I pulled *him* in for the kiss, not the other way around." KeeKee put her hands on her hips. "And who said you had the right to choose who I may or may not kiss? That's my prerogative, not yours." Normally, KeeKee would have been happy that Maxim was working overtime trying to protect her heart, but not this time. More than anything she wanted to kiss the future Santa.

With Maxim, and Marcus, playing big brother, would she ever get the chance to kiss her prince?

Chapter 23

The group stood amidst the ruins of Kirill's base, the air thick with the scent of battle and the faintest hint of triumph. They were gathering the remnants of the defeated enemy, trying to decide what to do with the captured supes, when a sudden rustling in the surrounding foliage caught their attention. Every muscle tensed, and weapons were drawn as they braced for another attack.

All thoughts of kissing KeeKee left Christian's mind as he stepped in front of her in order to protect her from whatever was coming next.

From the shadows emerged a group of panther shifters, their sleek black forms melding with the darkness until they were all close to the Misfit Island troops. Then, in an instant, the air around the panthers misted and out came tall males.

At their head stood what everyone assumed was their leader, a commanding figure at 6'2", his deep black hair reflecting the moonlight with an almost ethereal glow. His piercing green eyes surveyed the scene with a mixture of curiosity and caution.

"Who are you and what are you doing here?" The leader's voice was deep and authoritative, yet tinged with a subtle warmth, hinting at a protective nature rather than hostility.

Christian stepped forward, his posture straight and confident. "We are from Misfit Island, fighting against Kirill and his black market operations. We've just freed prisoners and seized his base."

The commanding male at the head of the group searched those standing in front of him, taking in the wounded and the weary, before settling back on Christian. "I see. We, too, have been fighting against Kirill's influence. We offer you sanctuary and healing." He bowed and then introduced himself, "I'm Luca Morata."

Before anyone could respond, Sofka interjected, her tone sharp with suspicion. "How do we know we can trust you?"

Luca offered a small, reassuring smile. "We have a sanctuary deep in the jungle. It's a place of healing and protection for those who stand against Kirill. You may join us if you wish, but we mean you no harm."

After a moment of tense silence, KeeKee spoke up, her voice soft but firm. "We should go with them. We need to heal and regroup before we can make our next move."

Anastasia, who had been quietly observing, nodded her agreement. "I've heard Kirill swear he would kill the panthers if he could ever find them. They are trustworthy."

With that, the decision was made. Led by Luca and his panther shifters, the group ventured deeper into the jungle, away from the desolation of the battlefield. The path was dark and winding, but the panthers moved with a grace and surety that inspired confidence.

As they walked, the jungle began to change. The dense, wild growth gave way to a more cultivated area, marked by the distinct scent of herbs and the soft glow of bioluminescent plants. The sanctuary was hidden behind a wall of greenery, which parted to reveal a serene clearing where a large campfire burned brightly.

Around the fire, dozens of supes from various backgrounds were gathered, all bearing the marks of past conflicts. They looked up as the newcomers entered, their expressions ranging from hopeful to wary. Luca introduced the group, explaining their victory against Kirill's base, and a murmur of appreciation and relief rippled through the gathering.

"We welcome you to our sanctuary," Luca said, addressing the entire group. "Here, we offer healing and unity to those who fight against tyranny."

A wise elder, her face lined with age and wisdom, stepped forward and began to chant softly. The words were in an ancient language, but the melody was haunting and beautiful, resonating deep within each listener's soul. The fire seemed to dance in response, casting shimmering lights that swirled around the gathering like protective spirits.

KeeKee felt a warmth spread through her, a soothing balm that eased the aches and pains of the battle. Beside her, Christian's gaze was fixed on the fire, his expression thoughtful. She could sense his unspoken emotions—a mix of determination and doubt that mirrored her own feelings.

One by one, the members of the group began to share their fears and hopes, their voices blending with the elder's chant. Sofka admitted her worry about losing those she loved in the ongoing conflict. Maxim spoke of his constant struggle with his past and his desire to protect those he cared about. Marcus shared his fears of failing Ree and his own potential for darkness. Ree confessed her doubts about her own strength and worthiness, especially after her confrontation with Marcus' mother.

Anastasia, her voice barely above a whisper, revealed her fear of never finding a place to truly belong. Aelita spoke of her sense of isolation and the burden of her current situation. Even Bart, whose stone face rarely showed emotion, shared his fear of being left behind, forgotten in his immobile state.

As each person spoke, KeeKee felt a deepening connection to her allies. Their vulnerabilities laid bare, they found solace and strength in their shared experiences. The elder's chant seemed to weave their words together, creating a tapestry of community and resolve.

When it was KeeKee's turn, she took a deep breath and looked into the fire. "I fear... that I'll never find out the truth about my parents. That I'll never truly belong anywhere. And most of all, I fear losing those I love, especially when we face Kirill again."

Christian, sitting beside her, reached out and took her hand. His touch was gentle but firm, conveying a sense of unwavering support. "KeeKee, you are one of the bravest people I've ever met. Your determination and kindness have inspired all of us. You have a family here, no matter what happens."

KeeKee looked up at him, her eyes shining with unshed tears. "Thank you, Christian. But I still... I still don't know if you'll stay. If you'll choose to be with m...us, or if you'll return to the North Pole." Since they hadn't admitted any real feelings for each other, she decided to keep her words more neutral. While she did fear he would leave her, she also knew that the island residents had come to care for him, and welcomed him just as much as they did her. Everyone would be sad if he left.

Christian's gaze softened, and he squeezed her hand. "KeeKee, no matter where I go, you will always be in my heart. But I promise, I will do everything in my power to stay by your side. You mean more to me than anything, and I can't imagine my life without you."

Tears rolled down KeeKee's cheeks and she squeezed his hand tightly. "I can't imagine the island without you." She wanted to ask him to stay, to stay with her, but everyone was watching them so she bit her lip and didn't say what everything inside of her was screaming to come out *I love you*. She would tell him, but not until they were alone and wouldn't be interrupted by meddling brothers.

A hushed silence fell over the gathering, broken only by the gentle crackling of the fire. The elder's chant reached a crescendo, and a cascade of shimmering light swept through the crowd, filling each person with a sense of renewed strength and purpose.

As the light faded, Luca stepped forward once more. "Your courage and unity are inspiring. Together, we will face whatever comes next. But for now, rest and heal. Tomorrow, we plan our next move against Kirill."

The group dispersed, seeking the comfort of rest and the warmth of the sanctuary. KeeKee and Christian found a quiet spot near the edge of the clearing, where they could be alone. As they sat down, KeeKee leaned against Christian, his arm wrapping protectively around her shoulders.

"Christian..." she began, her voice barely above a whisper. "Do you really mean it? That you'll stay with me, no matter what?"

Christian looked down at her, his ice-blue eyes reflecting the soft glow of the distant fire. "I mean it, KeeKee. I love you, and I want to be with you. But I also have responsibilities to my father and the legacy he's built. It's a difficult choice, but I promise, we will find a way to make it work."

KeeKee sighed, her shoulders relaxing slightly. "I understand. I just... I don't want to lose you. Not after everything we've been through."

Christian leaned down and pressed a soft kiss to her forehead. "You won't lose me, KeeKee. We'll face whatever comes next together. And who knows? Maybe there's a way for me to fulfill my duty to my father and still be with you."

KeeKee looked up at him, hope shining in her eyes. "You really think so?"

Christian smiled, his thumb gently tracing the curve of her cheek. "I believe in us, KeeKee. And I believe that together, we can overcome any obstacle."

As they sat there, the soft glow of the fire casting a warm light over their faces, KeeKee felt a sense of peace settle over her. Despite the uncertainty of the future, she knew that with Christian by her side, she could face whatever came next.

The rest of the night passed in a blur of healing and preparation. The sanctuary was a place of tranquility, where the wounded were tended to and the weary found rest. The panther shifters offered their knowledge and resources, sharing strategies and insights that would prove invaluable in the coming battles.

As dawn broke, the group gathered once more around the fire, their faces determined and their spirits renewed. Luca stood before them, his expression resolute.

"Today, we stand united," he said, his voice carrying over the assembly. "Together, we will strike a blow against Kirill's tyranny and free those who have suffered under his rule. The Creator of All brought us together last night for a reason. I believe it is so that we may all combine our strengths and defeat this evil once and for all."

A murmur of agreement rippled through the crowd, and KeeKee could feel the collective strength of their new bonds. Beside her, Christian stood tall and proud, his hand clasped firmly in hers.

"We will strike at the heart of Kirill's operations," Christian added, his voice steady and confident. "Using the intelligence we've gathered, we will disrupt his supply chains, free more prisoners, and ultimately, bring him to justice."

What was left out was the most important thing, discovering who was behind Kirill. Who had the power to pull Kirill into their circle and provide everything he needs to operate on such a global scale? Christian wasn't certain it was Queen Mab, but he wasn't going to rule her out. They all needed to keep an open mind about who the mastermind really was.

The group nodded in agreement, their faces reflecting the same determination that burned within KeeKee's heart. Together, they would face whatever came next, guided by the bonds of friendship and love that had brought them this far.

As the sun rose higher in the sky, the group prepared to depart. They gathered their weapons and supplies, their movements precise and purposeful. KeeKee looked around at her friends—Sofka and Maxim, her unwavering protectors; Marcus and Ree, their love a beacon of hope; Anastasia, a symbol of resilience and courage; Aelita, a warrior with a hidden heart; and Christian, her steadfast companion and love.

Together, they would face the encroaching darkness and bring light to those who needed it most. Their journey was far from over, but with each step, they drew closer to the day when Kirill's tyranny would be nothing more than a distant memory.

As they left the sanctuary, KeeKee felt a surge of energy coursing through her veins. The healing ceremony had not only mended her wounds but also imbued her with a renewed sense of purpose and strength. She knew that the battles ahead would be difficult, but with her allies by her side, she was ready to face whatever came next.

When they finally reached the shores of Misfit Island, they were greeted by a crowd of eager friends and family, ready to join the fight against Kirill. The island was buzzing with energy, a collective determination that could not be dampened by fear or doubt.

As the group disembarked, KeeKee felt a sense of belonging wash over her. This was her home, her family, and she would fight to protect it with every ounce of strength she possessed. Beside her, Christian's grip on her hand tightened, his eyes reflecting the same resolve that burned within her.

As they stood on the shores of Misfit Island, their faces turned toward the horizon, KeeKee knew that the true battle for their future was about to begin.

Chapter 24

Aelita stood before the leaders of Misfit Island—Sheriff Roscoe, Deputy Sofka, Maxim, Ree, Marcus, KeeKee, and Christian. Her auburn hair shimmered in the soft light filtering through the Welcome Center's windows, her green eyes sparkling with determination. She had called this meeting to discuss a bold new strategy, one she believed would give them a crucial edge in their battle against Kirill.

"Thank you all for gathering here," Aelita began, her voice steady and clear. "We've made significant progress in our fight against Kirill, but we need to step up our game. I believe that what's good for the goose is good for the gander—"

Sofka raised an eyebrow, a hint of skepticism in her voice. "You mean we should start playing by Kirill's rules?"

Aelita shook her head. "Not exactly. What I'm suggesting is that we infiltrate Kirill's army. We need to understand his connections, his inner workings, and then we can turn some of his followers against him."

Christian leaned forward, intrigued. "How do you propose we do that? Kirill's ranks are tightly knit, and loyalty isn't something you can buy or fabricate easily."

Aelita nodded, acknowledging the challenge. "True, but every organization has its cracks. Kirill has made alliances with various supernatural factions—vampires, shifters, and even some from the dragon houses. If we can identify those who are disillusioned or disgruntled within his ranks, we can offer them a way out. Sometimes, all it takes is a nudge in the right direction."

Ree, sitting beside Marcus, looked thoughtful. "That makes sense. But how do we approach them without raising suspicions? We can't just walk into Kirill's stronghold and start recruiting."

Marcus, his eyes reflecting the blue tint of his Fey heritage, chimed in, "We need someone on the inside, someone who can move undetected and gather information. Perhaps one of Aelita's contacts could help with that?"

Aelita nodded. "Exactly. I have a few contacts within Kirill's ranks who could serve as our initial entry points. Most are low level operatives. But we'll need to be strategic and cautious. One wrong move could jeopardize everything."

KeeKee, who had been listening intently, spoke up. "This sounds risky, but it's worth trying. If we can turn even a small portion of Kirill's army against him, it could significantly weaken his position."

Christian turned to Aelita. "Can you give us more details on your contacts and how you plan to approach them?"

Aelita took a deep breath, her eyes scanning the group. "One of my contacts is a vampire named Lucius. He's a high-ranking member in Kirill's inner circle but has grown tired of Kirill's tyranny. He's the only high-ranking contact I have in Kirill's forces. Another is a wolf shifter named Lyra, who has been coerced into serving Kirill but secretly longs for freedom. Both have expressed interest in finding a way out, but they need assurance that they won't be left to fend for themselves."

Maxim's eyes narrowed, a mix of concern and curiosity in his gaze. "And how do we offer them that assurance? What can we provide that Kirill can't?"

Aelita's lips curved into a small smile. "Protection, a safe haven, and a chance to live freely without fear. We can offer them a place on Misfit Island, a community where they can start anew."

Sheriff Roscoe, who had been quietly observing the discussions, finally spoke up. His deep voice carried a sense of authority and wisdom. "I agree with Aelita's plan. But we need to be careful. We can't just bring anyone into our community without thorough vetting. We need to ensure that our offer is genuinely accepted in order to maintain the safety of our island."

Sofka nodded in agreement. "We'll need to establish a system to vet potential defectors. Perhaps a probationary period where we can assess their loyalty and intentions."

Aelita nodded. "Of course. We'll work closely with Lucius and Lyra, ensuring they understand the terms of our offer. They'll serve as our initial contacts and help us identify other potential allies within Kirill's ranks."

Christian leaned back in his chair, his gaze thoughtful. "This is a high-risk strategy, but it could be the key to dismantling Kirill's operations from within. Let's proceed with caution and preparation." He didn't add that any type of probation would be reliant on his Dad's approval, especially for the shifter community. The Vampires had their own Council who would most likely want to add their two cents, but since they weren't too big on punishment, unless a vamp attacked one of the Council members, they usually stayed out of everyone's business.

"Did you say dragons were involved with Kirill?" All of a sudden, one of Aelita's comments hit Christian straight in the gut. He was related to the dragon royals through his Aunt's marriage. Christian doubted any dragon would be allowed to live after partnering with Kirill, no matter what the island offered.

Aelita bit her lower lip, then nodded. "Yes, I know of one dragon who was lured away from his clutch, but I think he regrets it now."

Marcus and Christian shared a look. More than anyone else on the island, Marcus would know how the dragons would react to this defector. "I can't speak for the dragon king, but I highly doubt he'd allow any defectors to go without some sort of punishment, even if they did regret their actions. It wouldn't send a good message to the rest of the dragon kingdom."

With a sigh, Aelita nodded her agreement. "I think the dragon king will have to deal with Callum, himself. I know we don't have the ability to speak for the dragons, or any other race, but if you'll all agree to offer him asylum, I think we can deal with the king after we take down Kirill."

Horatio entered the room before Aelita had finished her pitch and he had stayed quiet, until now. "We don't even have the ability to offer up the island without the Island's approval. Have any of you thought of that?" He arched a brow.

"Of course, you're right, Horatio. We should wait and see what the Island has to say." Sofka looked around the room for the usual signs of communication from the island, but no screen moved to convey its message.

"I say we move forward with the plan, and if the Island doesn't like it, it will let us know." Horatio stood and made to leave, then stopped and nodded at Aelita. She returned his silent greeting with a smile.

As the group continued to discuss the details and logistics of Aelita's plan, a sense of unity and determination filled the room.

Luca Morata, the leader of the panther shifter pack, called a meeting of allies at his camp in the Reserva Nacional Magallanes in Southern Chile, near Punta Arenas. The message had reached the group on Misfit Island, and they knew the importance of attending. Aelita's plan to infiltrate Kirill's ranks needed cooperation and coordination from all their allies.

The journey to Luca's camp was swift, aided by the magical portal that Bart navigated with expertise. As they stepped through the portal, they found themselves in a dense, lush jungle, the air filled with the scent of damp earth and exotic flowers. The panther shifters' camp was well-hidden, a sanctuary nestled within the heart of the wilderness.

Upon arrival, they were greeted by Luca, his deep black hair reflecting the dappled sunlight filtering through the canopy. "Welcome, friends," he said, his voice warm and strong with a strong Spanish accent. "We have much to discuss and prepare for. Follow me."

Luca led them through the winding paths of the jungle, the sound of rustling leaves and distant calls of exotic creatures filling the air. They reached a clearing where a large gathering of supes awaited—representatives from various factions who had united in their shared goal to defeat Kirill.

The meeting commenced with introductions and updates on recent developments. Luca outlined the progress they had made in securing alliances and gathering intelligence. Aelita presented her plan to infiltrate Kirill's ranks, explaining the strategy and the potential benefits it could bring.

The group listened intently, each member weighing the risks and possibilities. One by one, they voiced their support and offered their resources and expertise. The collective strength and determination of the alliance were palpable, a united front against a common enemy.

As KeeKee listened, she realized that they had a good shot at getting rid of Kirill for good, this time. The last time, it was just the residents of Misfit Island who had to fend off Kirill's masterfully planned attack. He had used some of the residents on the island as well as a large army that he'd secretly stashed on an uninhabited island just outside of the Island's magical dome. They weren't expecting such a large attack, but they were still able to fend off the intruders.

This time, KeeKee and her friends knew that Kirill would bring a much larger army along with more firepower, like the anticipated dome killer powered by the dragon egg. Which Kirill just lost, if they had taken the only two dragon eggs Kirill's team had abducted. Something in her gut told her these weren't the only ones missing. They would have to expect that Kirill had at least two more he could use to destroy the magical shield that protected the island and its inhabitants.

Just as the meeting reached a pivotal point, a sudden rustling in the underbrush caught everyone's attention. Tension filled the air as the allies braced for an unexpected intrusion. To their shock, emerging from the foliage was none other than Kirill Antonovich, the very alpha they had been planning to defeat.

Kirill's eyes scanned the gathering, a smirk playing at the corners of his mouth. "What a charming assembly," he drawled, his voice laced with sarcasm. "Plotting against me, are we?"

Christian stepped forward, his voice steady and controlled. "Kirill, your reign of tyranny ends now. We will not stand by and watch you exploit and enslave others for your own gain."

Kirill chuckled, his gaze flicking over the group. "Ah, the prodigal son returns. Still clinging to your father's legacy, I see. What a pity. But tell me, do you really think you can stop me? You're all just pawns in a much larger game, you know."

Sofka growled, her eyes flashing with anger. "We may be pawns, but we're not yours to control. You've underestimated us, Kirill. And that will be your downfall."

Kirill's smirk widened, but there was a hint of uncertainty in his gaze. "We'll see about that, my little wolfling. But for now, I have a message for you. A warning, if you will. Your island, your sanctuaries, they're all temporary. You can't hide forever. I have allies, powerful ones, who share my vision. And they will not be stopped."

With that, Kirill turned and vanished into the jungle, leaving behind a mixture of anger and unease. The group exchanged glances—they had been caught off guard, but their resolve remained unshaken.

It was Marcus who stopped the group from going after him. "Don't bother, he will have used magic to either hide his trail, or take him away. There is no way he would have come in here without a safe way to escape quickly."

Luca punched his left hand with his right fist. "How did he find my sanctuary?"

Christian winced. "There are a lot of us who came tonight, he probably followed out tracks. Not all of us are good at hiding."

"I'm so sorry if we brought him to your sanctuary. That is unforgiveable." KeeKee looked to Sofka, who nodded. "Why don't you bring all of your tribe to the island? We can all stay together until this is over."

Luca shook his head, and all of the members of his tribe, joined him. "This is our land, just like the island is yours. We know how to protect it. We will join you on the island when the time comes, but until then, we will make our own preparations to fend off an attack and protect our families."

KeeKee couldn't help but admire Luca, and his entire tribe, for their fortitude. He was right, this was just like their island, and they needed to protect it. She could support these supes in their desire to continue living here.

The face-off with Kirill in the jungle left the group shaken but undeterred. They reconvened, their determination stronger than ever. Aelita's plan to infiltrate Kirill's ranks had become even more crucial, and they knew they had to act swiftly.

"Do you think he overheard us talking about our plan?" Aelita's shoulders rose, and her nostrils seemed to send out smoke with every breath she released.

Luca looked to where the shifter had left and then back to his second-in-command. Julio Villareal was almost as tall as Luca, but he didn't smile nearly as much as the leader did. The little KeeKee knew of him, she liked. So far, the second-in-command had proved to be very loyal to Luca and not once had she seen him disobey or argue with his Alpha. Julio shook his head and KeeKee agreed that it was highly doubtful Kirill had heard anything. Even if he did, Aelita didn't mention names, only that she knew a few supes in Kirill's employ. Keeping the names a secret had been the decision from the start, no one wanted to put those supes in any danger - or any extra danger.

Luca, his voice steady and resolute, addressed Aelita's concerns. "The canopy around the circle of elders wields special magic. No one can hear on the outside what we speak on the inside." He turned back toward the rest of the group. "We cannot let Kirill's threats deter us. His appearance only underscores the importance of what we're doing. We need to proceed with caution but also with urgency."

Christian nodded, his gaze unwavering. "We'll need to strengthen our alliances and fortify our defenses. We can't afford any lapses in security. Every step we take must be calculated and deliberate."

KeeKee, her mind racing, spoke up. "We should divide our efforts. Some of us should stay on Misfit Island to ensure its safety, while others focus on infiltrating Kirill's ranks. We need to coordinate our actions carefully."

Sofka agreed, her eyes reflecting her resolve. "Maxim and I will remain on Misfit Island to oversee its defenses. We'll work with Sheriff

Roscoe and the other residents to ensure no one can breach our barriers."

Christian turned to Aelita. "You and I will work on infiltrating Kirill's ranks. We'll need to make contact with your informants and gather as much intelligence as possible."

Aelita nodded, her expression serious. "Agreed. I'll reach out to my contacts immediately. We need to establish a secure line of communication and start gathering information."

Marcus and Ree exchanged determined looks. "We'll stay on Misfit Island to help Sofka and Maxim," Marcus said, his voice firm. "Our combined strength will ensure the island remains protected as long as the shield remains active."

With the plans set, the group prepared to disperse. They knew the road ahead would be challenging, and fraught with danger and uncertainty, but they were united in their cause. The face-off with Kirill had only solidified their resolve—they would not let fear or doubt hold them back.

As they made their way back through the jungle, Luca pulled Christian aside. "Remember, Christian," he said softly, "the path you walk is not an easy one. But know that you have allies who stand with you. Together, we will bring an end to Kirill's reign."

Christian nodded, grateful for the support. "Thank you, Luca. We'll need all the help we can get."

The journey back to Misfit Island was filled with a mixture of anticipation and trepidation. Each member knew the stakes and the challenges that lay ahead. But they also knew the strength they gained from their unity and their shared commitment to justice and freedom.

Upon returning to Misfit Island, they immediately set to work. Sofka, Maxim, Marcus, and Ree began fortifying the island's defenses, ensuring every nook and cranny was secure against potential threats. They coordinated with the island's residents, rallying them to stand together and protect their homes.

Meanwhile, Christian and Aelita began their meticulous preparations for infiltrating Kirill's ranks. They carefully crafted their plans, considering every possible contingency. Aelita reached out to Lucius and a wolf shifter named Lyra, establishing secure channels of communication and starting the delicate process of gathering intel.

KeeKee, though not directly involved in the infiltration, played a crucial role in supporting both efforts. She used her unique insights and sharp intellect to offer advice and strategic input. She also continued to explore her healing powers, ensuring she was ready to aid any wounded allies.

Christian, despite the urgency of their mission, found moments to be with KeeKee. Their connection had grown stronger, and the shared sense of purpose deepened their bond. Yet, the uncertainty of Christian's future loomed over them—the prospect of his someday returning to the North Pole to take up his father's mantle.

One evening, as they walked along the shore of Misfit Island, Christian took KeeKee's hand, his fingers lacing with hers. "KeeKee," he began, his voice soft but firm. "I know the future is uncertain, and I can't promise you I'll always be by your side, even though I want to. But I want you to know that no matter what path I take, my heart will always belong to you."

KeeKee looked up at him, her green eyes reflecting the moonlight. "I understand, Christian. And I'm willing to face whatever the future brings, as long as we're together."

Christian smiled, a warmth filling his eyes. "Together, we can face anything."

As the days turned into weeks, the allies worked tirelessly to prepare for the impending battles. The plans for infiltration progressed steadily, and the island's defenses were strengthened. Each day brought new challenges and new insights, but their unity and resolve remained unwavering.

And through all of this, KeeKee's Secret Santa mission continued. Sofka had become too involved in the planning and training to help, so KeeKee worked on her own. Her own personal mission was to ensure that every supe on the island had a Christmas present all their own before the battle took place. It was the night before they were to depart, and she had only a handful of gifts left to deliver.

The first one of the night, Anastasia. Even though she was new to the island and wasn't technically a supe since she didn't shift or have any powers, she was a half-breed and a welcome resident to the island.

As KeeKee looked around to ensure no one followed her, or noticed what she was up to, she snuck up to the new house that several of the refugees from Chile had moved into. They had all received their gifts already. KeeKee knew that Anastasia was sad when she didn't receive one, but KeeKee wanted this gift to be special. It took some doing, but she was able to procure exactly what she wanted for the young woman.

Quietly, KeeKee placed the brightly decorated package with a handmade gold bow on the porch, right in front of the door so as not to be missed, then as silent as the night, she moved into the shadows to watch. It wasn't late, and lights were still on inside the house. Chances were good that someone would come home soon from the final planning meeting/dinner that had gone later than KeeKee would have liked. But she didn't want to end anyone's celebration on what might be their last night here.

It didn't take long, only twenty minutes, or so, and a dark figure walked up the steps, leaned over and picked up the package. He checked the tag and then walked inside the house. A huge smile spread over KeeKee's face as she imagined how happy Anastasia would be with the gift. She'd have to wait until morning to know if it went over as well as she had hoped.

Chapter 25

Anastasia was walking toward KeeKee, a glimmer of excitement in her eyes that replaced the fear and uncertainty that had shadowed them for so long. The morning sun cast a soft glow over the island, hinting at the tranquility that belied the undercurrent of tension.

"KeeKee, I have to show you something! It's amazing!" Anastasia said, her voice brimming with enthusiasm, clutching a small, brightly wrapped package in her hand.

KeeKee smiled, glad to see the young woman excited about something besides the constant preparation for battle. "What is it?"

Anastasia handed the package over eagerly, her eyes sparkling with anticipation. "I found this on the porch last night. It's a Secret Santa gift!"

KeeKee took the package, feigning ignorance as she carefully unwrapped the gift. Inside was a special tactical belt equipped with a small knife and a taser. "This is incredible, Anastasia," she said, trying to suppress a grin.

Anastasia beamed. "I know! I've never had anything like this before. Whoever sent it knew exactly what I needed. I feel... safer now."

"It's important to stay safe," KeeKee agreed, handing the belt back to Anastasia. "And this looks like it will help you do just that."

As they continued their conversation about the gift, a sudden, sharp clatter sounded from the Northeast side of the island, echoing through the morning air like a portent of doom. The ground shook slightly, and distant shouts could be heard.

KeeKee's heart leaped into her throat. "What was that?" she breathed, her senses going on high alert. Anastasia's eyes widened in fear, and they both knew that the sounds were not natural.

Without a word, they ran towards the Northeast side of the island, where the noise seemed to originate. As they approached, the sight that met them was one of chaos—Kirill's forces had somehow managed to launch a retaliatory strike on the island while Christian and Aelita had taken a large group off the island to search for the rogue alpha. It seemed he had taken advantage of their absence.

"He knew." KeeKee said to no one in particular. Her voice floated on the breeze as she assessed the situation.

Marcus and Ree were already there, fighting valiantly against a horde of Kirill's agents. Sofka and Maxim moved in perfect sync, their grace and power evident as they tried to shield the residents from harm. The attackers came in droves, armed and determined to bring down Misfit Island.

"Anastasia, stay behind me!" KeeKee shouted, shielding the younger woman as they moved closer to the skirmish. Her heart pounding, KeeKee realized that she could not be the healer to-day—she had to be the fighter.

"What about the protective dome?" Anastasia asked as she fell in behind KeeKee, gripping her taser and wishing she had more than one.

KeeKee looked up and realized for the first time that it was gone. "Argh, frozen fruitcake! He's already killed a dragon egg and used it to take down the dome. That must have been that loud sound we heard." More than anything, KeeKee was now furious. All she wanted to do was wring Kirill's head for killing an unborn dragon. They were so rare as it was, plus - baby dragons, hello.

Without even thinking, she reached for the first enemy she could get her hands on and started pummeling the life out of him. Then, from out of nowhere, Anastasia yanked the supe from her hands. "I'll take care of him." Anastasia used her knife for the first time that day.

KeeKee's eyes widened, and her mouth opened, but then shut when she sensed someone coming up behind her. She whipped around and ducked, just barely missing the machete that was headed her way. While she was in motion, she swept the legs out from under the supe who was still in his human form. When he fell on his back, his lungs expelled the air it held, and he dropped his weapon.

Once again, before she could get the weapon and kill her enemy, another supe from her team, Micky, picked it up and jammed it down so hard into the male's chest, that only the hilt showed through his chest.

"Thanks Micky, I appreciate it." KeeKee said as she moved on to the next supe. And just as before, someone else came along and took the kill from her before she even had a chance to think about it.

After about the fifth no-kill, she felt a tugging behind her. Not that someone was actually touching her, but more of a magical pull that she tried to ignore, but couldn't. She looked around at all of the bodies on the battlefield and tried to identify her family and friends. They all seemed to be holding their own. Then she searched for Anastasia, who was also holding her own. When it dawned on her what was magically calling out to her, she headed in that direction and called for Anastasia to join her.

It took five long strides to identify the supe who needed her healing magic -Chodrak. He was a peaceful Tibetan Wolf Shifter who never wanted to fight, but had agreed in order to save their island. It was the only safe place he'd known since leaving the monastery in the Himalayan Mountains as a child.

"Chodrak, look at me," KeeKee ordered.

Wild eyes looked everywhere but at her. "Chodrak, you're going to be alright." KeeKee took his hand in hers and felt the magic almost moving on its own down through her arm and into his hand.

When her fingers began to tingle, he looked her directly in the eye. "Thank you," he breathed before closing his eyes. His erratic breathing slowed, and she felt his hand relax. Some would think he was dying, but KeeKee knew better. When a major healing took place, it not only drained her, but the patient. Chodrak would sleep for hours, if not days.

Once she felt the magic had stopped, she had Anastasia help her move the healing supe over to a building that hadn't been there before the battle began. Somehow, the island always knew what they needed and when. Before either of them could reach the door, it flew open to reveal a first aid center that was staffed with some of the supes from the island who couldn't fight well.

"Here, we'll take him. You get back out there." Sienna took Chodrak from KeeKee and Anastasia and smiled. "Thank you for all of your help." Then the door closed behind her and a shimmer masked the opening.

The two stood there looking at each other and then back at the shimmering wall that resembled the side of a mountain more than the opening to a first aid hut. "Okay, that was strange." Anastasia was learning not to ask too many questions. Since arriving she'd learned that the island was unpredictable and did things that always surprised the residents, even those who'd been there for decades, but it was also sentient.

"Let's get back to it." KeeKee led her new friend out into the fighting but kept the location of the first aid hut in the back of her mind in case they needed it again.

As the battle raged on, Anastasia suddenly stopped, her face contorted in pain. A terrible, primal sound erupted from her throat, and she collapsed onto the ground, her body convulsing. KeeKee rushed to her side, her hands instinctively reaching out to offer comfort and protection.

Anastasia's transformation was brutal and agonizing—her limbs elongated, and fur erupted along her skin as she shifted for the first time. The process was excruciating to watch, and KeeKee held her close, offering what comfort she could as Anastasia endured the slow and painful metamorphosis.

Finally, a sleek, powerful leopard stood where Anastasia had been, her eyes still holding the trace of fear and pain. KeeKee marvelled at the transformation—she had never seen a shift like this, especially not for a first-timer. She had thought Anastasia would never shift, even the young woman thought she'd never shift. Which was why KeeKee had gifted her the weapons. A shifter who couldn't shift on an island full of dangerous supernatural creatures needed something to protect themselves.

"Stay with me, Anastasia," KeeKee murmured, moving to keep the leopard safe as they continued to engage the enemy.

The battle was fierce, with Marcus, Ree, Sofka, and Maxim, along with over two hundred fighting supernatural creatures from all races, fending off waves of attackers. The ground shook with the impact of each clash, and the air was thick with shouts and cries. KeeKee's determination shone through, her magic flaring to life as she defended her home and friends with everything she had. But she was careful not to end any lives—instinctively, others moved in to finish what needed to be done, protecting KeeKee's nature as a healer.

Despite the ferocity of their resistance, Kirill's forces seemed endless, pushing them back inch by inch. Just as KeeKee and her allies began to feel the strain of the battle, a chilling realization struck them—Kirill himself was among the attackers.

With a roar, the rogue alpha appeared at the helm of his forces, his eyes burning with malicious determination. "You cannot hide forever!" he shouted, his voice echoing over the chaos. "Your island will fall, and you will all be mine!"

KeeKee met Kirill's gaze with unwavering resolve. "Never," she retorted, her voice steady as steel. "We will protect Misfit Island, no matter the cost."

As they fought, a crucial realization hit them—Kirill was not just attacking out of retaliation. He wanted something specific from the island, something that would give him immense power. His desperation was evident in the sheer force and scale of his assault. Was it the dragon eggs? Whatever it was, they couldn't let him have it. Thankfully, the Island had taken possession of the dragon eggs when they brought them home. Even KeeKee didn't know where they were.

But the most shocking revelation came when they noticed that among Kirill's ranks stood a familiar figure—Marcus's mother, Queen Mab. She stood by Kirill's side, her eyes cold and calculating, her loyalty seemingly twisted towards the rogue alpha. The betrayal cut deep, especially for Marcus, who had always hoped that deep down, his mother might still care for him despite all her machinations.

With renewed urgency, KeeKee rallied her friends, her heart pounding with the knowledge that this battle was more than just a fight for survival—it was a struggle for the very essence of Misfit Island. The revelations continued to unfold, painting a picture of a larger enemy watching behind everything... pulling strings for their own use. Somehow, they needed to gather all this knowledge to stop whatever Kirill was doing.

"We have to hold out until Christian and Aelita return with their army," KeeKee called out, her voice laced with determination. "We must protect what Kirill seeks until reinforcements arrive."

Their resolve bolstered, the defenders of Misfit Island redoubled their efforts, fighting with every ounce of strength they had. The tide began to turn as they pushed back against Kirill's forces, driven by a shared commitment to protect their home and each other.

As the battle unfolded, KeeKee knew that whatever Kirill was after, they couldn't let him take it from the island. The revelations of betrayals within their own ranks added fuel to their fire, and she knew that the climax of this conflict was inevitable—soon, they would all face the largest confrontation that would determine the fate of Misfit Island and its inhabitants.

Chapter 26

The afternoon light broke through the fog clinging to Misfit Island, painting the scene with a surreal glow that made everything feel like a twisted dream. KeeKee could hardly believe the chaos unfolding before her eyes—the battle raged on, Kirill's forces pushing relentlessly, and Queen Mab's unexpected appearance rattled their already fragile defenses.

KeeKee stood back-to-back with Anastasia, now in her sleek leopard form, the young woman's shift a poignant reminder of the stakes they were fighting for. Each of the defenders—Marcus, Ree, Sofka, Maxim—moved with the precision of a well-honed team, but exhaustion loomed over them as the endless waves of attackers surged.

KeeKee's thoughts flitted to Christian and Aelita, their mission to infiltrate Kirill's ranks seeming like a dream from a different life. She was thankful they were far away, safe from this unfolding nightmare, but they needed them back. Her heart ached with worry, but there was no time to dwell on it as another group of Kirill's agents broke through their defenses.

"We need to push them back!" Marcus roared, his voice infused with a mismash of anger and desperation. "Split up but stay in pairs—"

Suddenly, a sharp cry tore through the air, a sound so wrenching that it stopped every heartbeat for a moment. "Ree!" Marcus's shout was filled with terror as he lunged forward.

KeeKee's heart plummeted as she saw Ree stumble, blood seeping from a wound on her side. Instinct took over, and KeeKee raced to her friend, her healing magic already pulsating beneath her skin. Anastasia, in her leopard form, stayed close, providing protective cover.

Ree's eyes were wide with shock and pain, but she was conscious. KeeKee knelt beside her, her hands hovering over the wound. "I've got you, Ree," she murmured, focusing her energy into healing her best friend chosen sister.

The magic flowed from KeeKee, warm and vibrant, wrapping around Ree's wound and stitching the torn flesh back together. The process was draining but swift, the island's magic imbuing KeeKee with renewed vigor. Within moments, Ree's wound was closed, though the draining effect left KeeKee light-headed.

"KeeKee, you shouldn't..." Ree's voice was weak, tinged with guilt. "You're giving too much—"

"It's fine, Ree," KeeKee assured her, pushing herself up with Marcus's help. "I have more in me."

Marcus's gaze locked onto KeeKee, a mixture of gratitude and fear. "We need to retreat. We've got to reorganize, gather ourselves—"

But before they could move, another surge of Kirill's forces swooped in, led by the alpha himself. Kirill, his eyes wild with bloodlust, snarled, "You won't escape this time! Your island's defenses are crumbling, your magic is weakening—"

KeeKee stood her ground, glaring at Kirill. "You're wrong. We won't fall. Not to you."

"Bold words from a little wolf," Kirill taunted. "You have no idea—"

His words were cut short as Anastasia lunged, her leopard form a blur of fierce, protective energy. She snarled, teeth bared as she swiped at Kirill, but the alpha sidestepped, his speed betraying a lifetime of practice in dodging such attacks.

Kirill laughed, "Nice try, kitty." Before anyone could react, he brought his own attack, a swift, brutal strike that sent Anastasia crashing to the ground.

KeeKee jumped to Anastasia's side as she instinctively shifted back to her human form. KeeKee's healing magic quickly knitting the wounds together. Anastasia's sturdy tactical gear had held, the knife and taser keeping her largely unscathed now that she was in her human form.

Sofka and Maxim drew nearer, their fierce protectiveness a comforting presence. "We need to gather everyone. We can't keep splitting up like this," Sofka urged, her voice thick with determination.

"Agreed," Maxim nodded, his eyes flicking to Kirill as the alpha circled them like a predator, his forces tightening the noose.

KeeKee knew that retreating to a single stronghold might be the only way to maintain their defenses. "Let's regroup at the main plaza. We need to strategize, figure out how to protect the weakest areas—"

Before they could strategize further, a sudden, booming noise shook the ground, sending tremors through the air like a shockwave. Kirill's forces scattered, his gaze locked onto a horizon where something ominous and threatening loomed.

In the distance, an immense shape began to materialize from the fog—a beast unlike anything they had seen. Scales glinted under the weak sunlight, and the air sizzled with a mix of electricity and fear. The dragon's wings spanned across the sky, blotting out the sun as it descended slowly, almost lazily, toward the island.

"Is that... a dragon?" Sofka's voice quavered, her usual steely confidence shaken by the sight.

Maxim's hand found Sofka's, squeezing it reassuringly. "We've faced worse together," he said, though the strain in his voice betrayed his own concern.

KeeKee's mind raced, sifting through possibilities. If Kirill had somehow secured more dragon eggs, could this be the creature he had managed to turn to his will? The implications were staggering, and the sight of the dragon brought a wave of dread washing over her.

"We need to focus!" KeeKee commanded, her voice steady despite the terror running through her veins. "Whatever that thing is, we can't let it destroy what we're fighting for. We regroup, establish a unified front—"

But their words faltered as the dragon's form crystallized further, its eyes burning with a malevolence that seared into their souls. Around them, Kirill's forces seemed to hesitate, a flicker of confusion and fear running through their ranks.

KeeKee's heart pounded with a razor-sharp clarity. To confront the dragon, they needed to combine every ounce of strength, every tactical edge they had. Their most powerful weapon—their unity—had to hold firm.

"Let's fall back to the central plaza," KeeKee ordered, her voice unwavering. "We'll gather everyone there. If this beast is under Kirill's control, we need a united defense."

The group began a tactical retreat, keeping a wary eye on the dragon as it continued its descent, its shadow growing darker and more menacing with each passing second. Kirill's forces, momentarily distracted by the dragon, scattered, some attempting to regroup while others seemed unsure of the new element in the battle.

Back at the central plaza, KeeKee rallied the residents, her determination burning like a beacon. "This is our home, our sanctuary," she declared, her voice carrying across the crowd. "We will not let it fall. No matter what comes at us, we stand together!"

The residents—from the elders to the youngest shifters—gathered closer, their resolve tightening as they watched the dragon approach. With KeeKee's words, a surge of unity flowed through them, the island itself vibrating with their combined strength.

As the dragon drew nearer, it became evident that whatever control Kirill thought he had over it was frail at best. Its actions were chaotic, its movements more driven by instinctual rage than any form of direct guidance. KeeKee wondered if this was due to an unstable alliance or a flawed command structure.

"It's coming in hot," Maxim observed, his vampiric senses keenly tuned to the energy radiating off the beast. "We need to deflect its attacks, dispense its energy—"

"But how?" Sofka questioned, her voice tense. "We've never faced anything like this—"

Ree, leaning heavily on Marcus, spoke up with surprising determination. "I might have an idea. Marcus and I can draw on his royal Fey ancestry. The power of our combined bloodlines might be enough to counteract the dragon's magic."

KeeKee looked at Marcus and Ree, her eyes widening with hope. "If that's true, it could give us the edge we need."

Marcus nodded, his hand tightening around Ree's. "We have to try. If the dragon's magic is derived from a dragon egg, our Fey magic stands a chance against it."

As the dragon descended further, the atmosphere around them sizzled with anticipation. KeeKee could feel the island's magic surging, combining with her own power. She looked around at her friends—at Marcus and Ree, ready to harness their ancient bloodlines; at Sofka and Maxim, standing in defiance with weapons drawn; at Anastasia, now in her human form fierce and unyielding.

"Ready yourselves," KeeKee called out, her voice steadfast. "On my signal—"

The dragon roared, its voice echoing through the island like a bellowing thunder. Its scales shimmered with a malevolent energy that seemed to draw darkness from the very air. But KeeKee knew that darkness was simply a byproduct of its enslaved state—beyond Kirill's control, it was a magnificent, powerful being.

"Now!" KeeKee yelled, breaking into a sprint toward the dragon, her hands already glowing with healing magic. As she reached its massive form, she redirected her energy, exploiting the gaps in the dragon's defenses created by Marcus and Ree's combined efforts.

Marcus and Ree moved with synchronous precision, their Fey and shifter magic interlacing with the dragon's energy, weaving through its defenses like a thread through a needle's eye. Their combined efforts disrupted the dragon's chaotic descent, causing it to waver and falter.

KeeKee, sensing a crucial opportunity, leaped up, using her shifter agility to latch onto the dragon's leg. With a grunt of determination, she channeled her magic, searing through the layers of malevolent influence that had been forced upon the beast. The dragon roared again, but this time with pain and release rather than rage.

Sofka and Maxim, quick to capitalize, launched their own offensive. Sofka hurled herself at the dragon's massive head, striking with all her might while Maxim's vampiric speed allowed him to dodge its thrashing tail, landing blows that weakened its control further.

Anastasia, despite her previous shift, joined the fray, her leopard form now graceful and fluid as she used her tactical belt to swing herself onto the dragon's back, slashing down with the embedded knife and shocking the beast with her taser. The dragon roared again, the sound a mix of defiance and surrender.

In the chaos, KeeKee could see the island's magic pulsating around them, responding to their combined will. With each strike, with each surge of unity, the dragon's dark energy was dispelled, its true nature slowly emerging from the shadows of Kirill's control.

Kirill himself, realizing the tide was turning, screamed in frustration, attempting to rally his forces. "Tear them apart!" he roared, his voice guttural. "They cannot win!"

But the dragon, now regaining its own will, turned its attention to Kirill and those who had enslaved it. With a bellowing roar, it unleashed a torrent of fire and fury upon Kirill's forces, turning the tide of the battle in a single, decisive move.

As Kirill's forces scattered, fleeing in terror, KeeKee looked around, her heart swelling with pride and relief. Despite the overwhelming odds, they had managed to stand against an unimaginable foe. Their victory today was a testament to their unity, their determination, and the magic of their island home. While they didn't catch Kirill or Queen Mab, they now knew who was bankrolling Kirill. That information alone would help them tremendously in getting more and more of Kirill's allies to defect.

Supes here on Earth weren't too keen on siding with Mab, or any Fae for that matter. The fae had a very long history of taking supes back to Faerie and using them as slaves. That is probably how Kirill got his idea for a supernatural black market where they trafficked in not only supernatural creatures, but also half-breeds, and humans.

"You know, I love a good barbecue just as much as the next supe, but this is taking it a bit too far." Aelita grinned and shrugged her eyebrows as she looked around at the team around her.

Groans and comments such as "gross" or "not now" permeated the atmosphere and almost killed the joy surrounding the team.

"Too soon?" Aelita winced and looked at KeeKee for affirmation.

Before she could say anything, a soft chuckle emanated from KeeKee. "Okay, it's too soon, but it is a little bit funny." She waved her hand back and forth weighing her decision.

KeeKee, watching the dragon soar away into the distance, now free from Kirill's grasping control, wondered if this was the dragon Aelita had told them about. The one who wanted to get away from Kirill. If he was, he just might have a chance of redemption with his dragon king.

Aelita turned to look at the last signs of the dragon and put her hands on her hips. Under her breath so as no one else could hear, Aelita pleaded with the retreating dragon to return. "You'll be safe here. They will accept you, I promise, my friend."

Chapter 27

The morning sun rose over Misfit Island, casting a warm, golden glow that seemed almost too peaceful given the chaos of the previous day's battle. KeeKee stood at the edge of the dock, coffee mug in hand, watching as the waves gently lapped against the pilings, the tranquil scene contrasting sharply with the turmoil within her heart. Around her, the island was a hive of activity as the residents worked tirelessly to restore the damage from the battle. No one had heard anything from the island yet, but that wasn't surprising, given how silent it was after the last big battle.

However, this time seemed different. KeeKee could sense how injured the island was. Whatever Kirill used in addition to the dragon egg caused more damage than anyone could see.

KeeKee turned to survey the scene off to the side of the pier, her eyes taking in the scattered debris and the remnants of the fight that had raged through the night. Sofka and Maxim were leading the cleanup effort, their stoic expressions belying the exhaustion that weighed on them all. KeeKee marveled at their resilience, knowing that despite the fatigue, their devotion remained unwavering.

Knowing that her moment of reflection was over, she pushed herself off the pier railing and guzzled the last of her cooling Pumpkin Spice Latte. Thankfully, the coffee shop hadn't been damaged this time. In fact, most of the stores had little damage to them. She wondered if Kirill had wanted it that way. It would have been easier for him to take control and get things moving again if there wasn't much in the way of reconstruction.

As she joined her friends in clearing away the rubble from the outbuilding that had been completely destroyed, KeeKee could feel the palpable tension in the air. The fight against Kirill had tested them all to their limits, and the impending choices they now faced seemed insurmountable. The best holiday of the year was approaching, a time when the magic of Christmas should bring hope and joy, but all she felt was the weight of responsibility.

Suddenly, a gentle hand rested on her shoulder, pulling her out of her reverie. KeeKee turned to find Anastasia standing beside her, a warm smile on her face. "You did amazingly yesterday," Anastasia said softly, her eyes filled with gratitude. "Without you, we would have been lost."

KeeKee returned the smile, her heart swelling with affection for the young woman who had become more than just a friend. Anastasia was quickly becoming a sister and packmate. "We all did what we had to do," she replied modestly. "And you, Anastasia, you were incredible. Your first shift—it was truly a testament to your strength."

Anastasia's eyes shimmered with pride, but also with a lingering fear. "I just hope I can control it next time," she admitted, her voice barely above a whisper.

Before KeeKee could respond, a sudden commotion caught their attention. The residents began to gather at the pier, their faces a mix of surprise and uncertainty. KeeKee and Anastasia exchanged a glance before making their way towards the gathering crowd.

As they reached the end of the pier, KeeKee's heart leaped into her throat at the sight before her. Standing in the middle of the pier, their faces lit with warm smiles, were Christian's parents—Paulo and Lizzy. Their presence was unexpected, yet somehow fitting in the wake of the recent battles. KeeKee felt a strange mixture of joy and trepidation wash over her.

"Well," KeeKee whispered to Anastasia, "if people didn't know before, they will now know."

Anastasia furrowed her brow and looked between the new couple on the pier and her new friend. "What does that mean?"

"Mom, Dad?" Christian's voice broke through the crowd, a mix of shock and happiness. He stepped forward, his arms wrapping around his mother in a tight embrace before turning to shake his father's hand.

Paulo's eyes sparkled with pride as he looked at his son. "Christian, we've heard about the remarkable work you've been doing here on Misfit Island. We're incredibly proud of you."

Christian's gaze flicked to KeeKee, his expression a silent plea for understanding. She nodded slightly, a signal that she was there for him, no matter what came next.

Lizzy stepped forward, her eyes warm as she took KeeKee's hands in her own. "And you must be KeeKee. We've heard so much about you from Christian. You've become quite the leader here, and we couldn't be more pleased."

KeeKee blushed slightly, feeling a rush of warmth at Lizzy's words. "Thank you," she murmured. "It's been a challenging time, but we've all stood together."

Paulo nodded, his gaze sweeping over the residents who had gathered around them. "And that sense of community is what has made Misfit Island such a stronghold. But we're here to discuss the future—both for the island and for Christian."

A tense silence fell over the crowd, the weight of Paulo's words settling heavily on their shoulders. KeeKee could see the worry in Sofka's eyes, the stoic resolve in Marcus's expression, the determination in Ree's gaze. They all understood the impending choices and the sacrifices that would have to be made.

Paulo turned to Christian; his voice steady but filled with an underlying tension. "Christian, your mother and I have decided that you should return to the North Pole after this crisis with Kirill is resolved. It's time for you to take up your rightful place in our family's legacy."

Christian's eyes widened, a mixture of shock and resistance flashing through them. "But...what about KeeKee? What about Misfit Island? I can't just leave them behind."

Lizzy interjected gently, her voice soothing yet firm. "We understand your attachment to this place and to KeeKee. But your destiny lies in continuing the work your father has dedicated his life to. You must reclaim your role as the future Santa Claus."

As the truth of who Christian really was began to sink in, murmuring started among those closest to the group. KeeKee knew that word would spread before they even made it back to the center of their little hamlet.

KeeKee felt a pang in her heart, a mix of understanding and desperation. She knew the weight of Christian's legacy, the importance of his role in the world. But the thought of losing him, of being apart from the one person who understood her so deeply, was almost unbearable.

Christian looked at KeeKee, his eyes filled with conflict and pain. "KeeKee, I can't just leave you. We've been through so much together..."

KeeKee took a deep breath, her voice steady despite the tumult within her. "I know, Christian. But we both have responsibilities. You have a duty to your family, to the legacy of Christmas. And I have a duty here, to Misfit Island and to the supes who need protection."

Sofka stepped forward, her voice firm and resolute. "KeeKee is right. We've all chosen our paths, and we must see them through. Christian, your role is vital to the world as a whole, and we understand that it comes with sacrifices. But know that you'll always have a place in our hearts."

Maxim nodded, his hand resting reassuringly on Sofka's shoulder. "We'll continue to guard Misfit Island, to protect those who need our help. And we'll always be here for you, even if our paths diverge."

Paulo and Lizzy exchanged a look, a silent communication passing between them. Paulo then turned to KeeKee, his voice filled with a profound warmth. "KeeKee, we would be honored if you would join us at the North Pole after this. Christian's future as Santa Claus is intertwined with yours. You are both destined for greatness, and together, you can bring hope and joy to the world."

Tears welled up in KeeKee's eyes as she looked at Christian, her heart aching with the weight of their choices. "Thank you, that is quite the honor. But first, we must see this through before we can make any final choices. We must defeat Kirill and ensure the safety of Misfit Island."

Christian nodded, his voice filled with a renewed determination. "Together, we'll face whatever comes next. And once we've secured the future of Misfit Island, we'll fulfill our destinies together."

A voice rang out, one KeeKee didn't immediately recognize, "are you the firstborn son of Santa?"

Christian nodded once. "I am. I'm sorry I kept my identity a secret, but it was important for my role that no one know I'm the son of Santa. It could have caused Kirill to attack sooner, before we were ready."

A voice KeeKee did recognize this time yelled out her question. Micky asked, "So, when everyone was questioning why Santa hadn't done anything about Kirill and the Supernatural black market, you just sat there and took it? You didn't think to speak up for your dad?"

KeeKee winced as she remembered one such event. Christian had told her that was why he was there on Misfit Island, looking for those who were working for Kirill. And that memory reminded her that they weren't sure they had found all of the moles. She still wondered about Aelita, especially since no one knew what type of shifter the female was. The only thing they knew for certain, was she was a fantastic fighter.

He nodded. "It was more important that my identity stay a secret."

Paulo put an arm around Christian's shoulders. "I agree. My son did the right thing. The safety of the shifter community, and the supernatural community as a whole, is more important than what anyone thinks about me." He held up a hand to stall any protests. "However, anyone, and I do mean anyone, is welcome to come to the North Pole and let me know what's going on if they think that I'm missing something. My goal isn't just to provide gifts to the children of the world, it's to share peace and joy with everyone, and that includes the Supernatural community."

The way Lizzie smiled at her mate caused KeeKee to sigh. The beautiful purebred Arctic Wolf Shifter still had a sparkle in her eyes for her mate, even after all of these years. KeeKee had never seen a couple so in love after what must be close to twenty-five years of marriage. Even Paulo's face softened every time he looked at his mate. No one could doubt their love and devotion for one another.

"Sometimes it might seem like Santa isn't doing something, but it could be he's playing the long game." Lizzie squeezed her mate's hand. "We have been watching Kirill for quite some time. The only reason we didn't move sooner was because we knew he was working for someone bigger." She looked around and paused when she noticed Aelita watching from behind Horatio, who helped to hide her - at least partially. Lizzie smiled and continued, "As most of you have already surmised, there is a mole here on Misfit Island. Probably more than one. But we are getting close to figuring out who it is."

KeeKee's eyes widened. The idea of sharing so much intel with everyone had never occurred to her. If the moles weren't here now, they would most certainly find out before the day was out about Santa and Lizzy visiting. And now, they would know that everyone was on to them. Or at least, getting close to figuring out who is working for Kirill on this island. Would that make them run, and therefore help to identify the traitors? Or would they do something else that might make their true intentions be known?

Horatio stepped forward and put a hand on Christian's shoulder when Paulo stepped back. "Christian, I trust that you and your family have only the best interests of the Supernatural community at heart. I do think you were right in keeping your true identity a secret. No hard feelings from me." He looked around and eyed the group that had only grown larger since the Clauses arrived. "What about all of you? Do you agree with me?"

Fists pumped the air all around and chants of "Down with Kirill," and "We support you," were soon taken over with everyone calling out, "Merry Christmas!"

The Claus family returned the sentiment and soon Santa and Mrs. Claus were ushered into the center of their little town on Misfit Island.

Chapter 28

Christmas Day dawned brightly over Misfit Island, the sun casting a golden glow that seemed to cleanse the air of the previous battles' scars. The island was abuzz with excitement and anticipation—a day to celebrate love and hope amidst the ongoing chaos that had become their reality. It had been three days since Christian's parents had departed, leaving behind words that echoed in KeeKee's mind: Christian had to come home. He couldn't stay on the island forever.

KeeKee stood by her window, recalling the warmth in Mr. and Mrs. Claus's eyes as they expressed their pride in Christian and their offer for her to join them. The thought of leaving Misfit Island for good filled her with a mixture of longing and regret. She couldn't imagine abandoning her friends, the community she had grown to love, and the place that had become her sanctuary. But today, she pushed those thoughts aside. Today was about celebrating togetherness, joy, and hope. The humans celebrated the birth of their savior on December

25th. She wondered if Jesus came to save supernaturals, too. But just as quickly she dismissed the idea. Then her thoughts turned to Kirill, of all days, the enemy had to enter her mind. She shook her head and thought about the baby who came to save instead.

However, she didn't dwell on the baby for long. KeeKee took a deep breath and stepped away from the window, determined to enjoy the special day with her family, friends, and the entire community. The village center was being prepared for a grand Christmas feast, a celebration of unity and strength. She couldn't let the weight of the future darken this precious moment.

As she made her way to the center of town, the sounds of laughter and festive music filled the air. The aroma of roasting meats, freshly baked bread, and sweet desserts wafted through the streets, drawing everyone together. She felt a warmth spread through her chest as she saw her friends and neighbors coming together, all set on celebrating despite the looming threats.

Sofka and Maxim were already there, helping to set up the long tables that would host the feast. Marcus and Ree stood nearby, Marcus with an arm around Ree, their faces reflecting the joy of everyone around. Anastasia, her eyes shining with excitement, waved at KeeKee from across the plaza.

KeeKee couldn't help the smile that spread across her face as she joined her friends. "Everything looks amazing," she marveled, taking in the decorations and the spread of food.

Sofka grinned. "We wanted to make sure today was special. After everything we've been through, we all need a moment to just appreciate each other."

KeeKee nodded in agreement. "Let's make the most of it."

Christian joined them, his face worn with the weight of his recent revelations but also shining with a determination to find joy in the moment. "Merry Christmas," he said softly, pulling KeeKee into a warm embrace.

"Merry Christmas," she whispered back, savoring the feeling of closeness.

As the day progressed, the plaza became a whirlwind of activity. Everyone pitched in to help, whether it was setting up more decorations, preparing food, or ensuring that everyone had a place to sit. The island residents had come together in a way that was both heartwarming and empowering. But still no sign from the sentient island itself. Something that bothered not only KeeKee, but Sofka as well.

"KeeKee, tomorrow we need to see if there is anything we can do to help the island recover quicker." Sofka bit her lower lip and winced. "I'm starting to get worried that the dome is still down, and we haven't heard anything from the island yet."

"So am I. But for today, let's not dwell on that. Let's enjoy the Christmas holiday. As Arctic Wolf Shifters, it's in our DNA to love this day. So for one day, let's just be who we are."

"Deal." Sofka hugged Keekee and they both smiled at everyone around them.

Late in the afternoon, as the feast was about to begin, a hush fell over the crowd. Suddenly, a heavenly chorus of Christmas carols filled the air, led by a group of angelic-sounding children. Their voices were so pure and soul-stirring that it brought tears to many eyes. The choir was followed by the arrival of several reindeer, each clad in festive garlands and bells that jingled with every step. Behind them appeared none other than Santa Claus himself, his jovial laugh echoing across the plaza.

"Ho, ho, ho!" Santa Claus called out, his eyes twinkling with genuine happiness. "Merry Christmas to all!"

Cheers and applause erupted from the crowd as everyone welcomed Santa with open arms. He was accompanied by Mrs. Claus, whose warm smile mirrored his own. Together, they moved through the crowd, exchanging greetings and well-wishes with everyone.

KeeKee, caught up in the moment, couldn't help but feel a sense of awe. The presence of Santa and Mrs. Claus, on Christmas Day, was a reminder of what they were fighting for—the magic and joy that embodied the spirit of Christmas.

Christian stood beside KeeKee, his hand intertwined with hers. "This is where I belong," he said softly, his voice filled with conviction. "My role as Santa Claus isn't just about gifts; it's about the joy and unity that comes with this season. I want to be part of this magic with you."

KeeKee looked up at him, her heart overflowing with love and admiration. "I understand," she replied softly. She wanted so badly to say she'd join him and leave the island behind, but she couldn't. At least, not yet. Instead, she leaned into him and took in his scent - a warm musk that also held hints of peppermint and wintergreen.

As the feast began, the plaza was filled with the sounds of laughter, conversation, and the clinking of glasses. Everyone came together, sharing stories, memories, and hopes for the future. The warmth and camaraderie were a stark contrast to the darkness that loomed over their heads.

Just as the meal wound down and the merriment reached its peak, an ominous atmosphere began to descend. The air grew heavy, and the sound of distant thunder rumbled in the sky, echoing with a foreboding sense of doom.

Marcus, standing with his arm around Ree, looked up, his eyes widening. "Something's not right," he murmured, a sense of unease creeping into his voice.

Sofka and Maxim, alert to the change in atmosphere, joined them. "We need to be ready," Sofka said, her eyes scanning the crowd. "Something's coming."

The joyous noise began to fade, replaced by a tense silence as everyone sensed the impending danger. KeeKee's heart raced as she realized what was happening—Kirill was making his next move.

"Stay calm," Christian commanded, his voice steady and authoritative. "We've faced worse and come out stronger. We'll face whatever comes next together."

Maxim motioned for parents to come close. "Take your children to the designated safe zone. Fighters come back here and help us once your family is settled. We are going to need everyone."

Suddenly, the sky began to darken, and a massive formation of clouds gathered overhead, blotting out the sun. Without the dome, they were sitting ducks. The clouds swirled and coalesced, forming a giant funnel that descended toward the ground. From within the funnel emerged figures—supes and other creatures, all bearing the insignia of Kirill and the dark forces he allied with.

"Everyone, stay back!" KeeKee shouted, her voice echoing across the plaza. "Santa, you and Mrs. Claus need to get to safety."

Santa Claus nodded, his jovial demeanor replaced by a resolute determination. "We won't leave our people," he declared, standing firm beside his wife. "We must protect you."

The darkness spread, and the funnel began to deposit a massive force of Kirill's allies onto the plaza. The scene was chaotic—warriors clad in black armor, powerful supes with glowing eyes, and mythical creatures that seemed to be straight out of a nightmare.

KeeKee's determination flared to life. She knew that this was the battle they had been preparing for, the other one was only a test. The community of Misfit Island had gathered to drive Kirill off, and now was their time to showcase their growth and attachments to one another, giving them all the incentive they needed to win the war.

"We need to defend the center of the city," KeeKee called out, her voice steady despite the tumult within her. "Everyone, work with a partner. Protect each other. Fight for each other, for our unity is our strength."

Christian, standing beside her, nodded, his stance resolute. "Let's show Kirill what we're made of."

The battle erupted with a ferocity that shook the very foundations of Misfit Island. KeeKee, fueled by her love for her friends and her determination to protect them, fought with every ounce of strength she possessed. Her healing powers flared to life, restoring those who fell around her, ensuring that the tide of the battle remained in their favor.

Sofka and Maxim moved with a precision born of their deep bond, their attacks coordinated and deadly. Marcus and Ree fought side by side, their love for each other evident in every strike and parry. Anastasia, now fully embracing her leopard form, pounced and clawed with a newfound ferocity, her new shifting ability proving to be a powerful asset.

As the battle raged on, KeeKee could feel the island's magic resonating through her, amplifying her abilities. Every time she reached out to heal a fallen comrade, her powers seemed to grow stronger, more potent, as if the island itself was imbuing her with what little power it had left.

But even with their combined strength, Kirill's forces seemed endless. His allies—the dark forces he had gathered from every corner of the supernatural world—converged on the small island, their numbers overwhelming. Even after all of this, there were still supes who came to her side and refused to allow her to kill anyone.

"Your gift is healing, don't ever forget that." Micky put a hand on KeeKee's shoulder and squeezed. "Let us get the blood on our hands, instead of yours."

KeeKee, her eyes blazing with determination nodded her thanks before searching the battlefield for Kirill. She knew that defeating him was key to stopping the chaos, and she was willing to do whatever it took to protect her loved ones.

Finally, she spotted him—Kirill stood tall amidst his forces, his eyes burning with malice. KeeKee locked gazes with him, her resolve unwavering. This was the moment they had been preparing for—the chance to let him know that he'd lost.

"Kirill, your reign ends here," she declared, her voice ringing out over the din of the battle.

Kirill laughed, a sound that sent shivers down KeeKee's spine. "You think you can defeat me? You're nothing but a misfit, a runt in a world of true power."

"We're more than misfits," KeeKee shot back, her voice steady and firm. "We stand united, stronger than any force you could bring against us. Your reign of terror ends today."

Sofka ran up next to KeeKee and locked her gaze on their former Alpha. "I stand with KeeKee. You should have let us go long ago and never come back to the island after your first defeat."

"Defeat?" Kirill scoffed. "That was just my forces testing the waters." He turned and watched as his own minions beat down the residents one after another. "I think you are the ones who should have run when you had the chance. That is all you know, isn't it?" He arched a brow and snorted.

"Think again." Maxim appeared out of thin air and stood next to the girls holding a long sword as though he was one of the knights of old, ready to defend the honor of the women he swore to protect.

"Don't count us out, either." Marcus materialized with Ree at his side.

Ree glared at their old alpha. "Why can't you just leave us all alone? We only want to live here on this island peacefully."

"This island?" Kirill motioned around them. "In case you haven't figured it out yet, but this island is the largest deposit of magic on Earth. You were never going to be allowed to keep this magic all to yourselves."

The three Arctic Wolf Shifters looked at each other and nodded, words not needed to convey to one another how much they loved each other. And how hard they were going to fight to save the island from Kirill and his silent master.

It was odd how calm and collected Marcus was. He stood there, arms crossed over his chest, head tilted as though he didn't have a care in the world. "I think you are going to be very surprised how much fight the island has left in it. And how dedicated the residents are to the protection of this place."

"Your mom was right, you aren't worth her notice or attention." Kirill sneered. "She gave me permission to kill you, you know that, right?"

Marcus shrugged. He'd known for ages that Queen Mab wouldn't shed a tear when he died. Once his brother had a kid, Marcus was no longer needed. The line of succession had already been guaranteed for at least the next two generations. "You aren't the first, and you certainly won't be the last who thinks he can kill me."

KeeKee'd had enough of Kirill's taunting. With renewed determination, she charged toward Kirill, her friends and allies rallying behind her. The battle wasn't just a fight for their survival—it was a testament to their unity, their growth, and their undying love for one another.

Chapter 29

KeeKee charged forward, her heart pounding with a mixture of determination and fear. Kirill stood before her, a sneer twisting his features as he anticipated the clash. The air around them sizzled with magic and tension, the weight of their impending confrontation hanging heavy in the air.

As KeeKee closed the distance, she suddenly felt a surge of power within her, a resonance that seemed to echo from the very core of Misfit Island itself. The island's magic was amplifying her own, bolstering her strength and resolve. She could feel it pulsating through her veins, ready to be unleashed against the embodiment of chaos and tyranny that was Kirill.

"You underestimate us at your peril," KeeKee declared, her voice steady despite the tremor beneath the surface. "Our unity is our strength, and it will be your downfall."

Kirill laughed, a sound that was both mocking and unnerving. "Unity? You're nothing but a ragtag band of misfits. You have no idea of the power I wield."

Around them, the residents of Misfit Island fought with steadfast determination, their combined efforts forming a unified front against Kirill's onslaught. Sofka and Maxim moved with uncanny synchronicity, their attacks precise and deadly. Marcus and Ree fought side by side, their love for each other evident in every strike and parry. Anastasia, in her leopard form, pounced and clawed with newfound ferocity, while Horatio, Bart, Micky, and countless others contributed their unique skills to the battle.

As she faced Kirill, KeeKee could feel the weight of responsibility settling on her shoulders. She was not just fighting for herself, but for all those who had placed their trust in her. Her rising status as a healer had become evident, and with each critical moment, her powers were tested and strengthened.

Kirill lunged at her, his speed and agility caught her off guard. She barely managed to dodge his attack, but as she moved, she could feel the magic within her reacting, healing the minor injuries she sustained from the near miss. She knew she couldn't afford any lapses in concentration—Kirill was relentless and cunning.

"KeeKee, watch out!" Christian's voice cut through the chaos, his eyes locked on Kirill with unwavering focus. He moved to engage Kirill, his blows precise and calculated, aiming to disrupt the alpha's relentless assault.

Together, they fought against Kirill, their coordinated efforts slowly gaining the upper hand. Almost in unison, KeeKee and Christian shifted on the fly to their Arctic Wolf form, and Kirill shifted as well.

KeeKee preferred battling in this form since she would no longer have to hear Kirill's grating voice. She wouldn't even hear him in her head since she was no longer part of his pack.

But what did surprise her, was the fact that she now heard Christian in her head. Only those who had chosen to be in the same pack could communicate telepathically while in wolf form. *"Are you here with me?"* Christian asked.

"I am," was all KeeKee could answer as she had to refocus on the enemy in front of her who was slashing in her direction. She moved in a perfectly choreographed move that Sofka would be proud of. They had practiced not only jumping out of the way, but also flipping side over side to quickly move away from an attacking claw. She had successfully made the move only a handful of times, but it seemed luck was on her side this time as she flipped to her right just in time to miss the lethal claw that screamed through the air toward her snout.

Christian slashed at Kirill's side, but he too knew the move Sofka taught them, and he flipped side over side and was practically on top of KeeKee. He growled and then reached out his claw once more.

Suddenly, KeeKee felt a searing pain in her side. Kirill had managed to land a blow, his claws tearing through her flesh. She stumbled, her breath catching in her throat as the pain threatened to overtake her. But before she could even think to heal herself, Christian jumped in, shielding her with his own body.

"I've got you," Christian whispered, his voice filled with unwavering support filtered through their new pack bond. He moved swiftly, his strikes precise and calculated, keeping Kirill at bay while KeeKee regained her composure.

Taking a deep breath, KeeKee summoned her healing magic, the warmth spreading through her body as her wounds closed and her strength returned. She knew that she couldn't afford any more mistakes—Kirill's relentlessness demanded constant vigilance.

"*We need to end this,*" KeeKee murmured through their bond, her eyes locked onto Kirill. "*We can't let him win.*"

Christian nodded, a fierce determination shining in his eyes. "*Together, we can do this.*"

With renewed resolve, KeeKee and Christian fought side by side, their movements synchronized and unyielding. Around them, their allies rallied, their combined strength forming an impenetrable front against Kirill's forces.

The battle raged on, the ground shaking beneath their feet as the forces of light and darkness clashed. KeeKee could feel the island's magic pulsating through her, amplifying her abilities and guiding her actions. She knew that their victory hinged on their unwavering love for their home.

With the dome down, the Arctic weather was coming through unfiltered. What had started out as a partially sunny sky, was turning out to be full of dark menacing clouds. KeeKee knew that a massive snowstorm was coming up on them quickly. It was difficult enough to fight in the extreme cold of Antarctica, but to add an enormous snowstorm on top of the Arctic freeze, they'd have a tough time all around. But, it also meant that Kirill and his army would have the same difficulties. Some of his fighters weren't used to the cold, but all of the residents had spent enough time on Misfit Island, even with the protective dome, to be accustomed to Arctic freezing temperatures and some form of the outside storms that seeped through the dome.

As the battle reached its peak, a sudden, blinding light erupted from the sky, casting a radiant glow over all that KeeKee could see. The light seemed to pierce through the darkness, illuminating every corner and crevice, and heating the cold atmosphere.

KeeKee's eyes widened as she saw the truth—a dragon was flying above them heating the atmosphere. Was he keeping the blizzard at bay? Or was it something else. She looked around at the battle and noticed several supes had stopped their fighting and were staring open-mouthed at the enormous red and gold dragon flying above them. At first, KeeKee thought it might be the dragon from the other day, then she realized it was a totally different dragon. The other one was black, this one was...beautiful.

Even Kirill looked up and for just a second he smirked. But then his face shifted and KeeKee could sense the anger roiling off his coat. In an instant, the man had shifted from his beast and yelled, "who is that?" He pointed to the majestic beast flying around the top of the battlefield.

Christian and KeeKee exchanged glances. "I don't know who it is, do you?" KeeKee had shifted back to her human form at the same time as Christian.

He looked around the field of battle and narrowed his eyes when one creature after another shifted back to their human form. The vampires, however, kept their fangs hanging out as their red eyes pierced the dragon in the air.

"Is it on our side?" Christian asked.

KeeKee shrugged. "I don't know if it has a side. So far, all it's doing is stalling the storm that is coming."

"Watch out!" Christian screamed.

KeeKee fell to the ground when she felt something hard and as strong as a tank shove her down. Then before anyone could react, she felt something biting her neck and then all went black.

"KeeKee!" Christian screamed again and dropped to his knees next to the female supe who meant the world to him. He put his hands around her neck to staunch the flow of blood, but it wasn't working. "Sweetheart, you have to heal yourself. I know you have it in you. Don't give up."

Kirill stood back, blood drooling down his smiling face. "I told you, I would get my revenge."

"I'll have mine," Maxim said as he grabbed Kirill from behind and chomped down on the evil shifter's neck. He pulled back and spit out the mouthful of blood and gore he'd torn from Kirill's neck. The body in his arms fell limp onto the snow which seemed to have blood pooling around him in a similar pattern to KeeKee.

Sofka ran to KeeKee's side and dropped to her knees. "KeeKee, you listen to me. You are going to heal yourself. I refuse to let you die. Do you hear me?"

Horatio pulled Sofka from her place next to her best friend and sister. "Let her do her work."

Christian looked up as tears ran down his cheeks unchecked. "What are you talking about? We have to help her."

Marcus pulled Christian up.

"Stop! We have to help her. Don't you see?" Christian looked at his friends, then down at the female he loved more than life itself. "She needs our help."

As everyone watched KeeKee dying in the snow, blood pooling all around her head, she began to sink into the island.

Christian struggled to release himself from Marcus' grip. "Let me go! I have to help her."

"Shut up!" The sheriff growled and stood in front of the spot where the island was swallowing KeeKee up. Then he roared so loud, that some stepped back afraid he would attack them. "Quiet down, all of you! The island is working with the Christmas magic that flows through KeeKee. Let it do its thing. KeeKee will be fine."

"How do you know?" asked Chris.

"Because I've been here a long time and I've seen more than you can ever imagine." The sheriff looked at Horatio who nodded once.

After rubbing the scruff on his face, the sheriff began to tell the small group what Horatio and a few of them had hidden from the girls since they arrived. "Just when the three of you," he pointed to Sofka and Ree, then back to the spot where KeeKee had been swallowed up, "first arrived, the island told Horatio and me that three wolf shifters were going to find their mates here and together they would all save the island." Roscoe stopped and looked at Sofka and Maxim, then turned his head to see Marcus holding Ree close to his side, and finally, his gaze landed on Christian. "The six of you have already done so much to help the island and its residents."

Horatio interjected, "Remember the first attack on the island when Christian showed up and saved Ree, then helped the rest of you investigate the moles?"

"But, who's the sixth supe?" Marcus asked. "I count only five of us."

Horatio and the sheriff shifted their eyes toward Christian

Flabbergasted, Marcus shook his head. "I can't believe it. He hasn't done anything, other than help Ree that one time."

"Yes, he has." Horatio walked toward Christian. "He has done so much more than save Ree in the beginning. He's been the one who helped KeeKee to find her gifts, not to mention all of the fighting he's done since arriving." He put a hand on the future Santa's shoulder and lightly squeezed. "You are more important than anyone realizes. Don't sell yourself short."

Maxim spoke up, "Ree would have died if you hadn't saved her from the Lion shifter. And if Ree had died, Marcus would have gone off the rails and who knows what he would have done to this island. So if you think about it, you saved the island and a lot of its inhabitants just from that one act alone."

Christian's face reddened. He scratched one eyebrow and looked down at the spot where KeeKee had been. "What about her?" He pointed to the spot that was now a sparkling patch of snow. To look at it one would never know that a supernatural fighter had just died there. "Wait, where's Kirill?"

Everyone looked around, but no one saw him. The spot where he had fallen was just a pristine as the spot where KeeKee had been.

Horatio looked to the Sheriff, who shrugged. "I think he might be in the same place as KeeKee right now."

"Wait a minute." Ree lifted a hand. "How could the island want to help Kirill?"

The sheriff took a deep breath, then scratched the scruff on his chin. "Remember the Bully Boys?"

"Ohh." Was all Ree could say.

Sofka chuckled. "I hope the island gets some good nourishment, but Kirill was most likely dead. I doubt he'll add much magic to the island."

Horatio rubbed his nose. "I guess we'll just have to wait and see."

For the first time since KeeKee had been injured, possibly killed, Christian registered that all of the fighting had stopped. Not a single supe was fighting another one. He looked around in amazement as some of the island residents he knew were helping the injured attackers to sit down. Mickey was bandaging a wolf shifter who seemed to be stuck in his wolf form while Carmen was kneeling next to one of Kirill's fighters who was lying prone on the snow-covered ground, eyes closed, barely breathing.

He marvelled as for the first time, he didn't see enemies flanking him, he saw supes who were injured and needed help. Kirill's forces were not just supes and dark creatures, but also shifters and vampires who had been coerced and manipulated into fighting against their will. With Kirill gone, true loyalties had finally been revealed, exposing the deception and manipulation that Kirill had used to fuel his reign of terror.

"Look!" Sofka exclaimed, her voice filled with both shock and understanding. "They're not our enemies...they're our allies!" She pointed to several Arctic Wolf Shifters who were trying to help Sienna get up. Her leg seemed to not work right, so they helped her back down and one of them ran his hands along her leg. When Sienna screamed, the two supes who had been on Kirill's side, shared grim looks. One took a small pouch out of his backpack, and they began to work together to help set what must have been a broken or dislocated knee.

The realization was a turning point in the battle. The coerced supes and shifters, now freed from Kirill's control, turned against their former oppressor, joining forces with the residents of Misfit Island and instead of trying to kill the island residents, they began to help those in need.

As everyone began to realize the fighting was over, a collective sigh of relief swept through the residents of Misfit Island. They had triumphed, their unity and determination proving stronger than any force Kirill could bring against them. The island stood tall and proud, with sparkling new snow softly falling around them and covering up the destruction of the fight.

Ree looked around, her eyes filling with tears of joy and gratitude. Then her gaze landed on the spot where KeeKee had last been seen. "Do you really think she'll be alright?"

Marcus pulled his mate even closer to his side. "I do. I've been here long enough to see things that you'd never believe outside of a fantasy novel. The island can do just about anything it wants."

As the realization of their victory sank in, the residents of Misfit Island began to gather, their voices rising in celebration. Laughter and cheers filled the air, the sound of joy and friendship echoing across the plaza. They had triumphed, and their future now lay open before them, filled with the promise of hope and peace.

Chapter 30

The mighty red and gold dragon flew circles around the leader-ship on the ground. As everyone waited to see what the enormous creature would do, and whose side it was really on, Maxim took Sofka's hand. Finally, after what felt like forever, the dragon landed gracefully on Misfit Island. With a surge of magic, she transformed back into her human form, her auburn hair shimmering in the evening light and her green eyes reflecting a mix of relief and exhaustion. She stood tall, her body shaking as she acclimated to the sudden change in form.

The residents of Misfit Island, who had been gathering to celebrate their victory, watched in awe as the dragon turned into a familiar face. Murmurs of surprise and recognition rippled through the crowd.

Sofka stepped forward, her eyes narrowed in suspicion yet filled with curiosity. "Aelita, what's going on? Why did you hide your true form from us?"

Aelita took a deep breath, her expression somber. "I had no choice. I had to fit in here on the island, and with my roommates, in order to gather information and protect the island. Shifters and supes with rare forms often become targets, and revealing my true identity would have endangered not only me but the entire community." She shrugged. "Plus, me being a dragon would have meant I couldn't get as close to those working on the island with Kirill. It's extremely rare that a dragon will go against his or her kind."

Ree raised her palm. "Uh, we just saw a black dragon not too long ago who was on Kirill's side."

"True." Aelita nodded. "However, I don't think Valyrian was a willing participant. You saw how he fought against the hold Kirill had on him until it shattered."

With hands raised, Ree asked, "I'm confused. You said your dragon contact was Callum, right? Who is this Valyrian dragon?"

Smoke escaped from Aelita's nostrils and those closest to her backed up. "I didn't know for sure whose side Valyrian was on, but I did know that Callum wanted out. So I didn't contact Valyrian."

"I take it Callum wasn't here to fight?" Maxim narrowed his eyes, not sure if he could trust Aelita, the dragon.

She shook her head. "No, he wasn't here. I'm not sure where he is right now, but I'd bet he's flying back to the dragon king to update him and beg for his life."

Sofka crossed her arms, her gaze unwavering. "And what about Nikolai Temuulen? He was one of your roommates and buddies. I saw him working with Kirill until it was obvious that Kirill was losing. He was the mole on the island all this time?"

Aelita nodded. "Yes, Nikolai was one of Kirill's most loyal followers. He, along with a handful of others, were deeply devoted to Kirill's cause, believing in the power and wealth he promised. They were never what everyone thought they were."

Marcus turned to Sheriff Roscoe, his voice firm. "We need to take Nikolai and the others into custody immediately."

Sheriff Roscoe nodded, his expression grave. "We'll ensure they receive a fair trial for their actions." He turned to Sofka. "Let's gather those we trust to help us secure any remaining moles."

Christian, who had been listening intently, approached Aelita with a mix of caution and gratitude. "Thank you for revealing the truth, Aelita. But why didn't you tell us who you were sooner? You knew exactly who I was." The idea that Aelita knew his secret but didn't share hers with him was beginning to grate on him. They would have never suspected her at all if they knew she was a dragon.

Aelita looked around, ensuring no one except the island leaders were within earshot. "You're right, I should have shared. So I will share something that I probably shouldn't. The dragons have been monitoring activities among the supernatural black market and gathering intel on Kirill's operations. My mission was to identify and neutralize any threats to the dragon community and to Misfit Island."

Ree's eyes widened. "So, the dragons were part of the plan all along? That's why you finally showed your true form during the battle?"

Aelita nodded. "Yes, it was time, and that storm would have killed or injured too many supes if I hadn't done what I could to slow it down." She looked up at the sky and noticed the thick clouds were still coming toward them, but they were holding back on the torrential snowstorm that was on the horizon. "We should get everyone inside, and soon. I'll explain as we head back to the center of town."

Sofka rallied the troops, so to speak, and moved everyone back to the center of town where they could hunker down during the snowstorm of the century, if what Aelita said was true.

Once everyone was settled, Sofka, Maxim, the sheriff, Marcus, Ree, Christian, Horatio, and Aelita walked over to the jail, which had more than tripled in size due to the influx of prisoners.

Christian paused outside the building. "I don't feel comfortable leaving KeeKee behind. What if the island finishes whatever it's doing to her and raises her back to the field of battle and none of us are there? Or worse, its the middle of the blizzard? Who will help her?"

Horatio put a hand on Christian's shoulder and nudged him inside. "First, the island is smarter than that. Second, it won't heal her only to insert her into a situation where she might die. I'm sure the island will have her at least overnight." He chuckled. "She's probably safer than we are."

Large fluffy snowflakes began to fall just as Christian closed the door to the Sheriff's office. "Just in time." He nodded back to the closed door.

"I expect we'll see several feet of snow if the dome doesn't come back up tonight," Horatio said as he took a seat.

The sheriff closed the door leading to the cells where the current prisoners were locked up tighter than a nutcracker the day before Christmas Eve. "Horatio is right, no need to worry about KeeKee, she is going to be just fine. But I want to hear more about Aelita and her...well." He scrubbed his chin. "Family."

Aelita took a seat against the back wall, then nodded. "Right. The dragons have been watching Kirill, trying to understand the true extent of his influence and his backing. They suspected someone more powerful was hiding behind Kirill's schemes. They wanted to ensure the threat was neutralized before revealing themselves."

"Do we know exactly what happened to Kirill? I mean, it seems as though he was taken by the island, like KeeKee was. But where is he?" Ree leaned against the wall and rubbed the back of her neck. The stress of everything going on was beginning to give her a tension headache.

"All we can do is trust the island has him." Horatio walked to the coffee maker and began a fresh pot of coffee.

As the conversation continued, the island seemed to respond to their collective thoughts. The ground beneath their feet rumbled slightly, drawing everyone's attention to a barely visible entrance to a hidden cave underground. Ree, who had been rubbing the back of her neck, gasped as she pointed to the cave.

"What is that place?" Ree asked, her eyes filled with a mix of curiosity and apprehension.

"That is the island's hidden cryo-jail," Sheriff Roscoe explained. "It's a unique place where the island imprisons and deals with those who pose a threat to our community. It seems the island is letting us know that Kirill has been taken there, held captive by the forces of the island itself."

Christian looked around at his friends in the room, his expression filled with a mixture of relief and concern. "Does that mean he's no longer a threat? Is he even still alive?"

Sheriff Roscoe nodded. "For now, yes. The island is powerful, and it has its own ways of dealing with enemies. Kirill will be unable to harm anyone as long as he remains within the cryo-jail."

Ree breathed a sigh of relief, her hands shaking slightly as she processed the information. "Good. That's one less enemy to worry about."

Maxim, always the practical one, turned to Aelita. "How will the Dragon King respond to Kirill's capture? Will this help in rooting out the larger force behind Kirill? It has to be Queen Mab, right? She was more than just an ally to him, right?"

Aelita's expression softened. "The Dragon King will be relieved that Kirill is captured. It means we can focus on uncovering the true mastermind behind these operations. We have a better chance at unraveling the bigger conspiracy now that Kirill is out of the picture. While it may look like it was Queen Mab who pulled Kirill's strings, I have a feeling she was only taking advantage of the situation to check on her son and ensure he stayed here, on Earth." She looked at Marcus and winced.

"Either way, my mother was involved, even if it was only at the end." Marcus' steely blue eyes pierced the door leading to the cells holding the supes they knew without a shadow of a doubt had worked for Kirill without extreme pressure, or magical influence. "Just like they were." He pointed to the door.

No one said a word, they just nodded and sighed. Sofka realized it had to be tough to discover that your own mother was working behind the scenes to ensure your death. She knew that Marcus always suspected his mother would come after him one day, or his brother, but suspicions weren't the same as knowing beyond a shadow of a doubt. While they didn't truly understand the extent to which Mab was involved, one thing was clear - she was involved somehow.

The group dispersed to take care of the remaining matters, ensuring that Nikolai and the other moles were kept under lock and key. The residents of Misfit Island would begin to clean up the battlefield once the storm passed, restoring a sense of normalcy amidst the chaos soon. It was important to ensure their safety while they were out and about working on the island.

Life must go on, after all.

Later that night, as Christian went to bed, all he could think of was KeeKee. He prayed she was safe and would return to him soon. A part of him wasn't sure if he could trust the island to care for KeeKee the way she needed. But another part of him had seen the island do so many fantastical things, healing one little wolf shifter who was full of Christmas Healing Magic shouldn't be difficult. He did something that night that he'd not done since he was a young pup, he prayed. He thanked the Creator of Heaven and Earth for helping them to win the battle. And he begged the Man Upstairs to look after KeeKee and bring her back to him.

The next afternoon, after a morning full of rebuilding and clean-up, Christian took a walk to the spot where KeeKee was sucked under the snow after the battle. Maxim had offered to join him, but Christian needed a few moments to himself, and with KeeKee. He knew she wasn't really there, but his last memory of her was there. And that was where he felt it in his gut that she'd return.

"KeeKee, are you here?" Christian looked around, hoping to see the island had released her. His patience was gone, totally ripped from his chest when he woke up, expecting to find her in the city center ready to work with the rest of the island. He dropped to his knees and hung his head. "If you can hear me, I need you. These last weeks with you have shown me who I am, and what I could be with you by my side." He waited a few moments, then sat down and drew his knees up, close to his chest.

A light breeze blew by him and ruffled his hair. His head popped up expecting to see the love of his life appear in the swirl of snow that the island was known for, but as he swiveled around looking, all he could see was light snowflakes falling from the cloudy sky. The protective dome still hadn't come back up. It was a good thing the island residents were accustomed to the cold. Although, without the dome, they were not nearly as protected as they had been. If Kirill's partners wanted, they could easily return with another army. Although, Christian didn't think that would happen. So many of the forced supes gave up and are now either looking for safe haven on the island or returning to their homes. The black markets are being raided all over the world now, if what Aelita told them this morning was true.

The fact that the poor souls who had been abducted or forced to work for evil monsters were being freed all over the world was the only thing that gave Christian something to smile about. If not for that good news, he'd be curled up in a ball on the floor of his house hoping and praying that KeeKee came back to him. At least here he wasn't lying in a ball, he was sitting on the ground - still praying she'd return to him.

As another, stronger wind kicked up behind him, he started to think it was time to head back to town. Everyone was needed to help restore the island. Maybe then the dome would return, too. Christian stood up, but felt warmth behind him. When he turned, he couldn't believe his eyes. There she was, as ethereal as a ghost. "KeeKee, was the island too late?" Before despair could take root in his heart, her image flickered, and then she smiled.

KeeKee felt herself moving back and forth between the bright light and the cold of the island. But, right in front of her, just out of her grasp, stood the one thing that had her praying she wasn't dead. "Christian, is this heaven?"

Before she was even fully corporeal, he ran to her and grabbed her up in his arms. "KeeKee, you're alive?" A part of his mind knew she was real, he was holding her after all. But another part of him couldn't believe what he had just seen. It was like something from a movie, where the love interest of the hero had died, but then out of nowhere was brought back down from Heaven to live again.

KeeKee shivered from the cold, even though Christian's warmth was beginning to surround her. "I must be. I don't think Heaven would be so cold. And hell certainly wouldn't be cold, we'd be burning alive in that heat." She chuckled as she thought back to her Bible Study lessons her parents used to share when she was but a wee pup.

Christian pulled back just enough to take her face in his hands. "Let me look at you." He stared deeply into her eyes for a few moments before tearing away his gaze to scan her up and down. "Are you healed? Did the island help you?"

She nodded. "Yes, it did. And it brought me back to you. How did you know I'd be coming back here? And that it would be now? You were here all night, were you?"

He chuckled. "No, my darling. Everyone told me you wouldn't be back for at least a day. But after lunch, a still small voice told me to come back out here. I had hoped to find you the moment I returned, but it seems I was a bit early." He pulled her close to his body again and kissed the top of her head. "I missed you. Words can't describe how worried I've been since the island swallowed you yesterday."

"I missed you, too. While I wasn't fully conscience, I did seem to be somewhat aware. Did I hear that Aelita was a dragon? Or was that just a strange dream I had?" KeeKee held tight to Christian as she waited for his response.

"I don't know how you heard that, the island had already taken you when we discovered the truth about her." Christian felt his heartbeat increase and all he wanted to do was kiss her and stop talking about anyone, or anything, else. She was the one for him, and he knew it. There was no doubt in his mind.

They stood there holding each other for a few moments. No words were needed as they enjoyed holding one another in their arms.

When they both felt they could talk again, it was KeeKee who started. "I think we need to go and see Sofka and Ree. I know they have to be worrying about me."

"You're right, they really are worried. I'm surprised they haven't come out here looking for you yet." Christian pulled back a little bit and stared down at KeeKee's lips. The urge to take her lips with his was strong. He knew what would happen if he didn't control himself, and he was more than ready to kiss her. But he wasn't sure she was, so he pulled back even further so as to keep himself in check.

A throat cleared behind them and they both jumped back.

"What?" KeeKee gulped.

"Sofka, I'm surprised you waited so long." Christian ran a hand down his face and chuckled. For a moment, he felt like a kid again when his mom caught him stealing candy cane cookies from the oven before they were even finished. He loved eating half-baked cookies as kid. In fact, he still did.

"KeeKee!" Sofka squealed and ran to her best friend.

"You're alive!" Ree screamed and was right on Sofka's tail.

Maxim and Marcus both chuckled as they watched the three girls hug and laugh.

"Thank you," Christian looked both of the male supes in the eyes. "I appreciate you letting me have some time with KeeKee before Sofka and Ree stole her away from me."

Maxim put a hand on Christian's shoulder. "We really did wait as long as the girls would allow, but you know how antsy Arctic Wolf Shifters can get when they want something so desperately."

Christian nodded. "Your timing was actually quite good." He debated on how much to share, then thought better of it. "You know, when she was..." he motioned with his hands in the air, "wherever she was. She had some sense of what was going on. She knows Aelita is a dragon, but I don't think she knows the whole story. We should probably go find her and get the rest of the story."

"I agree," Marcus stated. "She's still holding back. If my math is correct, and it always is, Aelita was born before the melding of the Claus house with the Dragon King's house."

"But, that would mean that she was hatched before the Claus magic restored their birth lines. I didn't think any female dragons had been hatched in decades." Christian thought for a moment. "She'd have to be royal in order for that to have happened."

"Who's royal?" KeeKee asked.

"Aelita," Maxim answered for Christian.

KeeKee put her hands up in the air. "Whoa, what all did I miss?"

Chapter 31

The Island Shack, a burger joint and a favorite gathering spot for the community, had sustained significant damage during the battle. Today, it was the focus of their collective efforts. All six of them had walked back into town to question Aelita, again.

"I believe Sofka said Aelita was going to manage the rebuilding of The Island Shack today." KeeKee frowned. "When I came out of the snow, everyone should have started out with telling me all about Aelita."

The three male supes looked at each other. Maxim raised his brows, Marcus leaned against the side of the Island Shack and crossed his arms over his chest - as cool as ever. Christian, on the other hand, scrunched his nose and ran a shaky hand through his hair. "Maybe I should have, but I was more focused on you, than I was another female."

KeeKee, her heart still racing from the joy of being reunited with her friends, grinned and felt her cheeks heat up. She too, had been much more interested in Christian than anyone else. "Okay, maybe you're right. But now it's time to find out what the Frosty is going on with Aelita. A dragon?" She shook her head and still couldn't believe it. Even after they all spoke about the situation on the way back into the tiny village.

"Trust me," Sofka raised her palm, "I was there and I'm still shocked. I think I would have believed her to be a nutcracker shifter easier than I could have believed she was a dragon. That is some serious magic going on there."

"But, when I think back," Ree screwed up her lips. "We should have guessed. I mean come on, she runs the best barbecue joint in the world. Aren't dragons known for their barbecue, just like Arctic Wolf Shifters are known to make the best peppermint anything in the world?"

Marcus stood up and dropped his arms. "You know, she's got us there. I think we were all so focused on other things that we missed the cues that were right in front of us."

A scuffled noise sounded around the corner and all six of them tensed and turned to see who was coming toward them.

"You know, if you wanted to know what type of Supe I was you could have just asked." Aelita tossed her hair over her shoulder, then froze in mid-motion. "KeeKee?" She ran to the newly healed shifter and wrapped her arms around the female and squeezed.

"Uh...need...to...breathe," KeeKee rasped out.

Aelita released her tight hold and pulled back. "Sorry." She shrugged and scrunched her pert nose. "I was just so excited to see you up and about. I mean, I knew the island was going to heal you, but...well," she rambled on until everyone started to chuckle.

"It's good to see you, too, Aelita. Now, explain to me how you're a dragon." KeeKee put her hands on her hips and tilted her head, waiting for a reply.

A half smile tugged at the corners of Aelita's mouth. "You see, when two dragons love each other they do something to make babies. Now, if you need the details of dragon sex, I think you're going to have to ask someone else. I have no desire to explain that to you." She waved a hand in the air. "But, once the deed is done, then the mommy dragon gets pregnant and after a short gestation period she lays a giant dragon egg, sometimes two."

"Haha," KeeKee interrupted. "I don't need those details." She felt her cheeks heat up when Aelita spoke about dragon sex, but put her cold hands on her face and she knew the redness was abating. "What I want to know is how a female dragon was hatched before the dragons had an influx of Claus DNA."

Aelita cleared her throat and drew a circle in the snow with the toe of her boot. "My connection to the Dragon King is a closely guarded secret."

"I think you know by now that we can be trusted with your secret." KeeKee crossed her arms over her chest and jutted her hip out. "Spil l...dragon."

"Yes, I'm a dragon." Aelita shrugged. "I'm one of the few females who were hatched before the Kringle bloodline was mixed with our royal family."

"Hold up." KeeKee raised a hand. "I had heard that a member of Santa's family had mated with a dragon, but don't know much about that." She also wanted to ask if the royal who mated with Christian's aunt had abducted her, or rescued her. The stories she'd heard growing up had her confused.

Aelita smiled. "Christian's Aunt Mandy was rescued by our Prince. They fell in love and mated. But before that happened, I was hatched to a noble family. The only ones who knew of my existence were the dragon King and Queen. Not even the prince knew about me. It was for my protection."

"Wow, so you lived in hiding, even though you are from a noble family? Like what? Is your father an Earl? Or a Count?" KeeKee didn't know anything about the dragon society. She knew about the English court and the different titles that those aristocrats held, mostly because of books, but she'd never read anything about aristocratic dragons.

Aelita's head bowed and she confessed, "My father is a Duke. He's a cousin of the Dragon King."

"Woa, so you're royalty, in a way." Christian whispered.

"Sort of. But distant. It would take a war to see me on the throne. There are too many dragons between me and the King." Aelita waved a hand as though it didn't matter that she was technically in line for the dragon throne.

"Where do you stand in the line of succession?" Horatio asked. The lines on his forehead had Aelita worried she'd kept this from him for too long.

"I've been away for a while, so can't be sure the royals haven't had more dragonlings, but last I checked I was twelfth in line for the throne." She rolled her eyes. "I've always known I wasn't ever going to be queen."

"Then why are you out here, risking your life, instead of back on a mountain top mated to some nobleman and giving him lots of baby dragons?" While KeeKee knew they were called dragonlings, she preferred using her term – baby dragons. It sounded cuter.

Her nostrils flared and smoke escaped. A shimmer surrounded her, like when an Arctic Wolf was about to shift. Then she closed her eyes and put her hands in front of her chest, as though she was praying. Aelita took a few deep breaths and slowly released them in tune with her heart beats. When she opened her eyes, everyone around her had taken several steps back. "Sorry. My mate is a sore subject." She gulped and her nostrils flared again, but no smoke, and no giant dragon in front of them. Instead, it was a calmer Aelita with downcast eyes and pursed lips. "I was promised to another noble house, but the dragon I was to mate disappeared last year. I've been searching for him ever since."

KeeKee blinked, then looked around at everyone present.

It was Horatio who asked the question on everyone's mind. "Have you found him?"

Aelita nodded once, then tilted her head from side to side. "In a way. I was able to track him to the supernatural black market, but I don't know how willing he was to be part of their circus. From what I've seen, he did go to Kirill of his own accord, but I doubt he stayed because he wanted to."

Horatio scratched his chin. "I can't imagine it would be easy to force a dragon to do anything they didn't want to. I've seen you fight, I don't know of any creature who could stand up to you."

Aelita's chuckle held no mirth. "I've been training to fight ever since I could control my fire. Not all dragons can fight like I can. Since my life was in jeopardy from the moment I was hatched, it was important to train me to be the best fighter possible, in both of my forms."

"So, you're betrothed?" Horatio's nose scrunched as though he smelled rotten fish guts.

Aelita put a hand on his arm, but Horatio backed away from her touch. "Horatio, it's not like that. Our betrothal was broken when he disappeared."

"Then why did you go after him?" KeeKee asked.

"Good question." She bit her lower lip. "It wasn't out of love, but more out of duty. Some weird things had been happening back home and I wondered if Valyrian had been involved. I thought either he left before anyone could figure out he was behind a string of dragon egg thefts, or he was taken. Since he had grown up safe, or as safe as a male dragon could, he wasn't the best fighter."

"But surely, most supes wouldn't stand a chance against a dragon's fire?" KeeKee, who didn't have much experience, or knowledge, with dragons scratched behind her ear.

"You'd think." Aelita rolled her eyes. "I felt I owed it to him to find out the truth."

"And have you?" Horatio asked.

Aelita took a moment to think about her answer. Then she shook her head. "The last time we saw Valeryian, he's the black dragon from the other day, he seemed to be in some sort of trance. I think he broke it. But I'm not really sure what's going on with him now."

KeeKee tilted her head and studied Aelita. "No matter how you feel about him, he did try to help us. I think you owe it to him to find out exactly what happened."

Aelita's nostrils flared, and she turned her back on the group. "Maybe, but not today. Today, we have to get this island back together.

It's important we do as much as we can while the island is working on healing itself and getting the dome back up."

Two hours later, KeeKee and Christian were both helping to finish cleaning up the debris from the Island Shack. Once it was all cleared away, they could see what parts of the building they could repair, and what should wait for the island. They had stopped to take a coffee break when Mickey brought over a large carafe of their standard brew and enough disposable cups to outfit a chain of coffee shops on the mainland. As KeeKee swept up debris and helped set right the toppled furniture, she couldn't help but think back to all they had been through together, the battles they had fought, and the bonds that had grown stronger with each passing day. This island was her home, but more than that it was her safe place. Would she still see it that way after almost losing her life to Kirill right here on her own home turf?

"KeeKee, grab the other end of this table," Sofka called out, gesturing towards a heavy wooden table that had been tossed aside. "Marcus, can you help Maxim with those chairs?"

Ree, her eyes gleaming with renewed energy, nodded as she picked up a pile of broken planks. "We'll have this place looking good as new in no time."

Christian, who had been working alongside KeeKee, paused to look at her with a mixture of relief and admiration. "We make a good team," he said, his voice steady despite the lingering tension.

KeeKee smiled, her heart swelling with affection. "We do. Together, we can face anything."

The residents worked tirelessly, the clatter of hammers and saws filled the air, accompanied by laughter and conversation. As the day wore on, the shack began to take shape once more, a symbol of their resilience and ability to come together when the island needed them. Even residents from the Black Hills could be seen working side by side with the townies.

As evening fell, the rebuilding was well underway, and the residents took a well-deserved break. They gathered around a large bonfire, sharing stories and laughter as they celebrated their achievements. KeeKee, sitting beside Christian, looked around at her friends—Sofka, Maxim, Marcus, Ree, and Anastasia—and felt a profound sense of gratitude.

A hush fell over the crowd as several supes from Chile, who had fought alongside them, joined the gathering. They brought with them gifts of food and drink, a token of their appreciation for the alliance that had formed. The Chilean supes had proven to be valuable allies during the battle, and their presence now was a testament to the bonds that had been forged.

"We are grateful for your friendship," one of the Chilean supes said, lifting a cup of mulled cider in a toast. "Together, we defeated a common enemy, and together, we celebrate our victory."

The residents of Misfit Island raised their glasses, cheering the sentiment. The night was filled with joy, laughter, and camaraderie as they shared a grand dinner, feasting on the delicacies that the Chilean supes had brought.

However, as the night wore on, the supes from Chile began to bid their farewells. They promised to be allies forever, ready to come to

Misfit Island's aid whenever needed, but their home beckoned, and it was time for them to return.

After the Chilean supes departed, the residents of Misfit Island remained by the fire, their conversation turning towards the future and the decisions that needed to be made. Christian sat beside KeeKee, his hand enveloping hers, their fingers intertwined as they gazed into the flames.

"This island has become more than just a refuge for me," Christian said, his voice low and thoughtful. "It's become a home."

KeeKee nodded, her heart fluttering with a mix of joy and apprehension. "It has for me too. But we both have responsibilities that go beyond this island."

Christian looked at her, his eyes reflecting the flickering light of the fire. "You're right. My role as the future Santa comes with its own set of responsibilities. But I don't want to leave you, KeeKee. I can't imagine my life without you by my side."

KeeKee squeezed his hand, a lump forming in her throat. "And I can't imagine leaving this place. The island needs us, and the supes who call it home need us. But you have a destiny to fulfill, Christian. The fate of future Christmases rests on your shoulders."

As they spoke, a powerful discussion about leadership and legacy arose among the gathered residents. They debated the importance of having strong leaders who were willing to make sacrifices for the greater good, and the responsibilities that came with those roles.

Suddenly, a soft glow enveloped KeeKee, drawing everyone's attention. The island itself seemed to be communicating with her, revealing its true nature and her role within it. Images flashed through her mind—visions of her as a healer, her magic intertwined with the very essence of Misfit Island. She saw herself as a beacon of hope and love, her powers growing stronger with each passing day.

As the glow subsided, KeeKee looked at Christian, her eyes filled with understanding and determination. "The island has shown me who I really am and what my future holds." She sighed and looked down at their joined hands before releasing him. "I am meant to carry on the legacy of healing and joy that the Christmas magic embodies. I am meant to stay here and protect this place, to nurture the current and future residents."

Christian's face fell and he felt the cold that had just separated their hands. "If this is what you want, then that is what we will do. I will return to the North Pole, fulfill my duty as the future Santa, and you will stay here, continuing the work that has become your legacy. Through all of this, I learned that I am supposed to be Santa, I can't ignore it." But it wasn't what he wanted.

Their decision was met with nods of approval and understanding from their friends. Sofka, who had been watching them closely, spoke up, her voice filled with conviction. "We will all support you, KeeKee. The island is our home, and we will do everything in our power to protect it and the supes who live here, but just know that if you change your mind, I will stand behind you one hundred percent." She smiled at Christian, and in that moment felt his pain.

"Why can't you stay here?" Maxim asked Christian. "You have brothers, couldn't one of them take the mantle of Santa while you stay here and help protect those from the Supernatural community who need this safe haven?"

Christian snorted and wiped his eyes. "I'm feeling so torn. I want nothing more than to be Santa, but," he looked at KeeKee, "I also want to stay here, with you. I can't do both."

Not ready to let go quite yet, KeeKee took Christian's hand in hers once more and squeezed it. The island had shown her what she was supposed to do, but much like Christian, she was torn between the two.

The conversations turned towards the future, assessing new opportunities for growth and adventure. The rest of the damaged buildings would be rebuilt, stronger and more vibrant than ever before. The residents of Misfit Island would continue to work together, forging new alliances and strengthening their community.

As the night drew to a close, Christian and KeeKee walked hand in hand along the shore, the wind whipping around them, and the moon casting a soft glow over the waves, that was in stark contrast to the recent events. They paused, their eyes locked together, their hearts filled with a love that transcended time and space.

"Christian," KeeKee said softly, her voice barely a whisper, "I think we need to talk more about our futures."

Christian looked at her, his eyes filled with a mixture of longing and indecision. "I know, KeeKee. I've been wrestling with this choice for a while now. Even after everything said tonight, I still don't have peace. My parents expect me to take my place by their side, but my heart is here, with you."

KeeKee took a deep breath, her eyes meeting his. "I love you, Christian. And I want to be with you, no matter where that takes us. But I also know the importance of your role as the future Santa Claus. The legacy your father has built is vital to the world."

Christian pulled her close to his side and wrapped an arm around her waist. "KeeKee, I can't imagine leaving you. But I also know that my duty to continue my father's work is something I can't ignore. It's not just about gifts and joy; it's about hope and unity for the entire human and supernatural world."

KeeKee leaned her head against his shoulder, a resolve settling within her. "Then we'll find a way to make it work. Maybe I can come with you to the North Pole for part of the year, and we can travel back here for the other part. The island will always be our home, but we can spread its magic of community and love beyond its shores."

Christian's eyes brightened with hope. "You'd do that? You'd come with me?"

KeeKee nodded, a soft smile playing on her lips. "Yes, I would. I believe that our love can find a way to blend your legacy with our life here on Misfit Island. We're stronger together, and together, we can bring hope to many."

Christian pulled her into a warm embrace, his voice filled with emotion. "Thank you, KeeKee. Together, we'll face whatever comes next. No matter where we are, no matter what challenges we face, we will always be together in spirit," Christian said, his voice filled with unwavering promise.

KeeKee nodded, her eyes shimmering with tears of both joy and sorrow. "Together, we will create a future filled with hope and love. Together, we will fulfill our destinies."

As they stood there, hand in hand, the island seemed to hum with approval, its magic resonating through them both. In that moment, they knew that their love would endure, united in their shared mission to bring joy, hope, and healing to the world.

Chapter 32

The next morning, KeeKee awoke to the sound of laughter and the scent of freshly brewed coffee. She opened her eyes to find herself in her cozy apartment. She stretched, feeling a sense of renewal wash over her. The island had healed her so well that she felt like a new creature, and she was ready to tackle the day ahead.

She joined the others at the Welcome Center just beneath her little apartment, where they were discussing the aftermath of the battle and the revelations from Aelita. The air was filled with a mix of determination and anticipation. The threat of Kirill might have been dealt with, but there were still many loose ends to tie up.

As they planned their next moves, KeeKee looked around at her friends—Christian, Sofka and Maxim, Marcus and Ree, Anastasia, and now Aelita. She felt a surge of gratitude for the bond they shared and the strength they brought to each other. Together, they had faced insurmountable odds and come out victorious.

Christian stood beside her, his hand intertwined with hers, a silent promise of their future together, no matter where life took them. With a sense of purpose and adventure, they prepared to face whatever challenges lay ahead, knowing that their love and the magic of Misfit Island would guide them through.

KeeKee flinched when the door to the Welcome Center crashed open. She turned, praying that everything was alright, and her mouth dropped at the sight in front of her.

Standing in the doorway, not caring that the entire room was staring at him, was a short gnome-looking creature. It was something out of a nightmare. He wore red trousers, a blue puffy jacket, and a red pointed cap. His eyes glowed a bright red, but that wasn't what sent shivers down her spine. It was the creature's teeth.

KeeKee knew exactly what this was – Redcap. A creature from the land of Faerie, but nothing like Tinkerbell or the other fairies people read about. No, this creature was something she'd seen living in the Dark Hills and prayed she'd never see again.

The teeth alone were enough to scare the villagers in any story. This particular one was grinning when he looked at KeeKee and his sharp pointy teeth – the ones used to rip out a person's neck, were dripping with his saliva. If she were alone, KeeKee knew that this evil creature would have already attacked her and tried to rip out her throat before devouring her completely. These nasty dark fae even ate the bones of their victims. She couldn't stop the shiver that started at her head and went all the way down to her feet.

Marcus lazily walked in front of the creature. "Blazewhisker, I see your master has let you out for a day. How nice."

The dark fae bowed, slightly. "Prince Marcus, I come with a message from the glorious and most beautiful Queen Mab."

"Of course, you do." Marcus put his hand out in front of the Redcap's face.

KeeKee never would have been so bold as to get close enough for the creature to try biting her, never mind offering up her hand for him to snack on. But, Marcus was from Faerie, and he seemed to know this creature.

The dark fae licked his lips and his head moved slightly closer to Marcus' hand than was necessary. "My Lord, the Most Benevolent Queen of all Faerie wishes to congratulate you on your victory against the evil Kirill." The Redcap moved back a few steps and wiped the drool from his mouth. "She also wishes me to convey her pleasure that you have survived to fight another day." And with that, the creature turned and practically disappeared before KeeKee could even think about what he'd said.

Rec wasn't so slow in her response. "Marcus, does this mean that Mab was involved with Kirill? Or not?"

Marcus rubbed his chin. "It's tough to say. Just because she sent her minion to give me a message, doesn't mean she wasn't involved."

Horatio stepped forward. "I think it's safe to say she wasn't directly involved in the battles, but she might have been pulling Kirill's strings. Or at least funding him. Maybe even giving him the magic he needed to attack the island, both times."

Everyone in the store agreed.

"I'd say we keep our eyes open and be ready for her to send someone else, if she was behind all of this." Marcus turned away from the front of the store and walked over to his mate. He took her in his arms and held her tight.

"If it wasn't Mab, who do you think was behind Kirill?" Maxim asked.

It took Marcus a moment to answer, and when he did, the crown of a Fae Prince hovered above his head and his eyes blazed with fire. "If I had to bet on it, I'd say my mother was behind Kirill's movements. But without proof, there isn't anything to be done. We just have to be vigilant from here on out. We beat her and her army. The supernatural black markets are all going to be dismantled. If, and that's a big if, she wants to attack again, it's going to take her a long time to rebuild. For now, I'd say we just focus on our own rebuilding and then begin to craft our own defense forces. Just in case anyone tries to attack again."

After moving back behind the counter, Horatio nodded. "I agree." He turned to Sofka. "I guess this means that you'll get your dream of building and training an Army."

KeeKee slapped a hand over her face and chuckled. "Please, anything but that."

Everyone else joined her in making fun of Sofka and her Drill Sergeant attitude.

Sofka smiled and took it all in, glad she had such good friends who knew her so well.

The residents of Misfit Island worked to restore their beloved island to its former glory. The Island Shack was almost fully repaired, its walls reinforced, and its interior furnishings replaced. The aroma of fresh paint and the sounds of hammering filled the air, interspersed with laughter and camaraderie. After everything they had been through, rebuilding their community was a source of both physical and emotional healing.

KeeKee and Christian were at the center of the restoration efforts, giving everything they had to the island. As they worked side by side, Christian couldn't help but feel a deep sense of contentment. This island had become a second home to him, and the residents, his family.

Suddenly, a murmur rippled through the crowd, drawing everyone's attention. A pair of familiar faces approached, smiling warmly. Santa Claus, with his bright blue eyes and a beard that sparkled slightly in the sunlight, stood tall and jolly. Beside him, Mrs. Claus, her eyes twinkling with warmth, wore a gentle smile. The sight of them brought a wave of comfort and joy to the residents.

"Santa! Mrs. Claus!" the crowd cheered in unison, their faces lighting up with excitement.

The Claus couple approached KeeKee and Christian, their eyes filled with a mixture of pride and understanding. "Hello, everyone," Santa said, his voice booming and filled with warmth. "We've come to see the marvelous work you're doing here on Misfit Island."

Christian stepped forward, his voice steady but filled with affection. "Mom, Dad, it's great to see you both again."

Santa put a hand on Christian's shoulder. "Son, we're incredibly proud of what you and KeeKee have accomplished here. Your commitment, strength, and love have truly touched us."

Mrs. Claus nodded, her gaze softening as she looked at KeeKee. "The island's influence can be felt in everything you do. Your magic,

KeeKee, has brought so much healing and hope to this place. We couldn't be prouder."

KeeKee felt her cheeks flush with gratitude and a sense of belonging. "Thank you, Mrs. Claus. Christian and I have realized that our connection is what makes us strong, and we've decided to find a way to balance our responsibilities and our future together."

Santa's eyes sparkled with approval. "And that's why we're here. We want to propose a solution that will allow you both to fulfill your destinies while also honoring the bond you share."

The residents gathered around, listening intently. Sofka, Maxim, Marcus, and Ree exchanged glances, their faces filled with anticipation.

Santa continued, "We propose that you, Christian, and KeeKee stay here on Misfit Island for another two years. During this time, you can continue your important work and assist with making the island a safe refuge for any and all supes who will choose to live peaceably here. But every year before Christmas, you will come to the North Pole to learn and prepare for your future roles as Santa and Mrs. Claus."

A gasp of surprise and joy swept through the crowd. KeeKee looked at Christian, her eyes shining with hope and excitement. "That sounds like a wonderful plan. We can continue our work here and slowly transition into our future roles." While she had thought of herself as a future Mrs. Claus, Christian hadn't exactly said he wanted to mate with her, it was just something that everyone expected. *Could it be true?*

Christian nodded, a sense of relief washing over him. "Yes, that sounds perfect. Thank you, Dad. Thank you, Mom."

Mrs. Claus smiled warmly. "We believe in you both and trust that your love and dedication will guide you through whatever challenges lie ahead."

The residents of Misfit Island erupted in cheers and applause, their morale high with the news and the promise of a brighter future. The sense of peace and togetherness was palpable, a testament to the strength they had found in each other.

As the excitement settled, the residents continued their restoration efforts with renewed vigor. The Island Shack was soon fully repaired, its new furnishings gleaming and inviting. The other damaged buildings were also quickly brought back to their former glory, with the help of the entire community.

Later that evening, as the sun began to set, the residents gathered at the heart of the island for a grand celebration. Aelita and her crew set out a barbecue feast that was fit for a king. The Chilean supes who had helped defeat Kirill's forces were honored guests, and their presence brought a sense of friendship and solidarity.

Some of those who had attacked the island, now free from Kirill's influence, approached members of the island community with humility and remorse. They expressed their desire to stay and help rebuild, to make amends for their past actions. Others spoke of their desire to help dismantle the supernatural black market and free those who had been sold into slavery.

Santa Claus, with his booming laughter and warm demeanor, offered his support and the help of his most trusted Arctic wolf shifters from around the world. "Together, we can put an end to this darkness and bring light and hope to those who need it most," he declared, his voice filled with conviction.

The celebration continued late into the night, filled with laughter, music, and dancing. As the stars twinkled overhead, Christian turned to KeeKee, his heart pounding with anticipation. "KeeKee, there's something I've wanted to do for a long time."

She looked up at him, her green eyes reflecting the starlight and the warmth of their shared bond. "And what's that?"

Christian leaned in, his lips nearly touching hers. "This," he whispered, before closing the gap.

As their lips met, a surge of magic flowed between them, a resonance of their love and friendship. Suddenly, fireworks erupted overhead, filling the night sky with a dazzling display of colors and light. The residents of Misfit Island cheered and applauded, their hearts filled with joy and a sense of belonging.

KeeKee and Christian pulled back, their faces glowing with love and happiness. They looked up at the fireworks, marveling at the sight. "It's beautiful," KeeKee whispered, her voice filled with awe.

Christian smiled, his eyes shining with love. "Just like you, KeeKee. You're the most beautiful thing I've ever seen."

Santa stuck his head in between the two lovebirds. "Did you know that when a future Santa kisses his one true mate, Christmas Magic explodes in a beautiful array of fireworks?"

"What? You mean those," KeeKee pointed to the large display worthy of any Independence Day celebration, "were created by us..." she knew her cheeks were flaming red and dipped her head.

"Yes, my love. We did that." Christian shoved his father back and held her closer to his side.

Santa chuckled his deepest HoHoHo he could muster. "This display is impressive. It tells me that your love is as true as mine with my

Lizzie." He wrapped an arm around his wife who leaned up and kissed his cheek.

KeeKee wanted to argue that they'd not discussed mating yet. Sure, she and Christian had discussed being together, but nothing as permanent as mating. She was a bit old-fashioned and didn't think she could just assume he would ask her to be his Mrs. Claus. With the ups and downs of their relationship over the past weeks, she wasn't sure he wanted that. She knew so little about the Clauses and their mating rituals.

Growing up, they were all taught that the Claus pack didn't have sex until they were officially mated. Something about waiting sealed their lifelong mating. Most Arctic Wolf Shifters waited, but she knew quite a few in her previous pack that didn't. So she was pretty certain Christian wouldn't be asking her to move in with him, but what did he want?

Tonight wasn't the night to ask those questions. They'd have the next two years to discuss what they wanted.

As the fireworks continued to light up the sky, the residents of Misfit Island welcomed the new era with open hearts and unwavering spirits. They knew that with KeeKee and Christian's love and leadership, their future was bright and filled with endless possibilities.

Across the celebration, Aelita stood with a small group of trusted friends, her eyes sparkling with determination. "I have something to share with you all," she announced, her voice carrying over the festive crowd.

The group turned to her, their faces filled with curiosity and support. "With the supernatural black market still active and countless lives in need of help, I plan to journey around the world, using my abilities to bring justice and freedom to those who need it."

KeeKee and Christian exchanged glances, their hearts swelling with admiration for their friend. "We support you, Aelita," KeeKee said, her voice filled with respect. "Your courage and dedication are an inspiration to us all."

Aelita smiled, a warmth spreading through her chest. "Thank you, KeeKee. Thank you, Christian. With your support and the help of the North Pole's most trusted wolf shifters, we can make a real difference."

As the celebration continued, the residents of Misfit Island basked in the warmth of their unity and the promise of a brighter future. They knew that new adventures lay on the horizon, and together, they would face whatever challenges came their way with strength, courage, and unwavering love.

And so, with hearts full of hope and spirits bound by love, the residents of Misfit Island embraced the new dawn, ready to embark on their next journey, guided by the light of their shared destinies.

Epilogue

On the Island of Misfits, the townies liked to celebrate the New Year with a giant bon fire and potluck.

"I can't believe how large that fire is." KeeKee grinned mischievously. "Do you think Aelita helped light it?"

Christian chuckled. "I wouldn't be surprised to learn she had."

For the special occasion, the island has erected a giant clock on top of a disco ball that stood almost fifty feet above the central square in town. It was their version of a ball drop in Times Square, New York.

KeeKee basked in the warmth of Christian's arms around her. She turned her head just enough to kiss his cheek. "Have you ever been to Times Square on New Year's Eve?"

"Nope. Have you?"

"Never."

"Then I guess we'll both be in for a treat." Christian kissed the tip of KeeKee's nose and she giggled.

With the glow of the bonfire lighting up the entire square, Christian and KeeKee looked around as all of their friends held hot drinks and smiled. They were only a few moments away from the new year. One KeeKee was anxiously awaiting.

A New Year always meant new beginnings, and this was one new beginning she couldn't help but welcome warmly. "Are you excited about our two years here?"

Christian squeezed her tighter. "I'm excited for all of our new adventures."

All of a sudden, the din of excitement quieted around and KeeKee looked up to see the clock had changed to a countdown.

Everybody who had crammed into their tiny version of Times Square counted down with the Island.

10

9

8

Christian interrupted the countdown and turned KeeKee to look at him. He got down on one knee and pulled something from his pocket. "My family has a tradition that is similar to the humans." He looked up at her, his eyes full of love and emotion. "KeeKee, if you'll let me, I'll work for the rest of our lives to make you as happy as I am with you. I love you and don't want to wait any longer to begin our lives together. Will you not only be my mate, but also marry me?"

After the count of eight, KeeKee couldn't hear anything but the words coming from Christian's lips. She felt herself smile from ear to ear and couldn't believe he was actually doing this now.

On New Year's Eve.

In front of the entire little town of Misfit Island.

She knew he held a ring, but she couldn't see it through the tears of joy that were just about ready to fall down her face.

"Yes! Christian. I would love to be your mate and your wife." She pulled him to his feet and before he could put the ring on her finger, she pulled him close to her.

With their faces only centimeters apart, KeeKee closed her eyes and tilted her head just enough to feel Christian's lips as he grazed her mouth with his. The warmth from Christian's hands pressed against her back, pulling her closer to him. Her arms snaked up around his neck pulling him even closer to her. She would have been surprised if there was even one single air molecule between their two bodies, they were so close.

And his kiss, oh my. It was enough to make a girl sigh until she passed out. The energy she felt passing between them was unlike anything she'd ever witnessed or felt before. Her mind went blank and she felt as though they were drifting in space for eternity.

Then all too soon, she felt a tug at her shoulder. Then Christian backed away from her. "What?"

"Congratulations!" Sofka and Maxim yelled in unison.

As soon as KeeKee could catch her breath, she glared at Sofka. How dare she interrupt a kiss that was so powerful, it felt like they were inside of a plasma globe.

Before either Christian or KeeKee could say anything, they were surrounded by their closest friends and family.

"Oh, let me see the ring!" Anastasia bounced up and down on her toes and clapped her gloved hands together.

"The ring!" Christian opened his left hand and sighed with relief; it was still there. He took her left hand and put the ring on her ring finger.

"Wow, that's a sparkler," Ree exclaimed.

It was the first time KeeKee could see it, and she was speechless. She never in a million years thought she'd get an engagement ring. And certainly not one worth more than a year's salary. "I can't accept this, it's too much."

Christian pulled her closer and whispered in her hear, "my love, it's a family heirloom. My great-grandmother wore this ring when she was Mrs. Claus. And my parents gave it to me to give to you."

"What if I lose it?" KeeKee wasn't used to wearing jewelry. So she prayed she'd not take it off to wash her hands and forget it somewhere.

Christian's hand lightly touched the side of her face. "Darling, it's just a ring. If you lose it, I won't be mad. But I want everyone to know that you are taken by someone who loves you so much, they are willing to put a huge ring on it."

KeeKee couldn't help the laugh that bubbled up. "Thank you. And I love you so much Christian. I know we are going to have a truly blessed life together."

"And when our time as Santa and Mrs. Claus is over, we can come back here and help run this Island," Christian said.

"As long as we can continue to come and visit each year, I'll go wherever you are." KeeKee pulled him close, not caring that all of the island was watching, and listening. She kissed him long and hard, ignoring all of the cat calls and pleas for them to stop. She didn't care that everyone could see them kissing. This was what she wanted to do for the rest of her life.

The End

Author's Notes

Unity, community, and forgiveness are all very powerful concepts.

I wrote a lot about unity and community, and it was quite obvious, but I did it for a reason. In today's world, everyone is so divided. Neighbors fight with neighbors, fathers and sons fight, brothers and sisters fight, and friends are no longer friends. We need to come together once again and forgive those who have hurt us, even if they don't ask for forgiveness. When we do this, we can work together towards a better world. But it won't happen unless we take up the banner and do it together. Which is the heart of unity.

It's strange, but when I first began writing this novel over a year ago, Unity and Community weren't foremost on my mind. But as this past year progressed, it really hit me how much we are all missing out on. Is a name coming to mind of someone you have a beef with? Maybe you should be the one who makes the first move toward reconciliation.

I hope you enjoyed my little island of misfits where family is a choice. Did you know that Aelita was a dragon before the big reveal? I wasn't necessarily trying to hide it from you, but I was trying to hide it from the characters in this novel. Would you like to see Aelita and her quest to help those in need? Or more of Misfit Island?

Please consider leaving a review on any site you prefer, reviews are the lifeblood of the Indie Author! Thank you so much for joining me on this strange journey of misfits. It really has been a blast. I still want to take a trip to Antarctica. How about you?

Be sure to join my newsletter so you can hear more about upcoming books.

Newsletter Sign-up

Do you love a cozy romantasy? Want more in the Misfit Island universe? Then sign-up for my newsletter and receive a free copy of the prequel to the Miss Claus series now, where you will get to meet the ever-allusive Santa Claus!

How does Santa find his Mrs. Claus? It's not like he can "Swipe Left" and meet the perfect girl!

Ever wonder why no one has seen Santa Claus? One of the reasons is that he's an Arctic Wolf Shifter!

Get your copy and find out these answers while you enjoy a bit of Christmas excitement as a rival pack makes a play for Santa's job!

If you enjoy a sweet romance with a paranormal flair, then this is the book for you! The romance is clean, but the action is fast! Come and join the new Santa Family!

By signing up for my newsletter, you'll not only receive this book, but a couple more free stories as well!

If you want to make sure you hear about the latest and greatest, sign up for my newsletter at: Subscribe to J.L. Hendricks newsletter. I will only send out a few e-mails a month. I'll do cover reveals, snippets of new books, and giveaways or promos in the newsletter, some of which will only be available to newsletter subscribers.

Contact Me

For those of you who love social media, here are the various ways to follow or contact me:

Newsletter: https://jlhendricksauthor.com/newsletter/
BookBub: https://www.bookbub.com/authors/j-l-hendricks
TikTok: https://www.tiktok.com/@jennacleanauthor
Instagram: https://www.instagram.com/j.l.hendricks/
Twitter: https://twitter.com/TinkFan25
Facebook: https://www.facebook.com/JLHendricksAuthor
Website: https://jlhendricksauthor.com/